M000299961

MAD SCIENTIST JOURNAL PRESENTS

SELFIES FROM THE END OF THE WORLD

HISTORICAL ACCOUNTS OF THE APOCALYPSE

EDITED BY
Jeremy Zimmerman
AND **Dawn Vogel**

SELFIES FROM THE END OF THE WORLD:
Historical Accounts of the Apocalypse
Edited by Jeremy Zimmerman and Dawn Vogel

All rights reserved. Any reproduction or distribution of this book, in part or in whole, or transmission in any form, or by any means, electronic, mechanical, photocopying, recording or otherwise, without the written permission of the publisher or author is theft. Any similarity to persons living or dead is purely coincidental.

Cover Illustration and Layout by Luke Spooner

"Untitled" is Copyright 2015 Shivangi Narain
"Elegy for a Mountain" is Copyright 2015 Brandon Nolta
"Sounds of Silence" is Copyright 2015 Nicole Tanquary
"Winter in My Bones" is Copyright 2015 Sylvia Heike
"Happy At the End" is Copyright 2015 Matthew R. Davis
"The Adventures of Zombiegirl" is Copyright 2015 Garrett Croker
"An Impromptu Guide to Finding Your Soulmate at a Party on the Last Night of the World" is Copyright 2015 Caroline M. Yoachim
"The Last Real Man" is Copyright 2015 Nathan Crowder
"The Silence and the Worm" is Copyright 2015 Samuel Marzioli
"The Men on Eldama Ravine" is Copyright 2015 B. T. Joy
"Not Even a Whimper" is Copyright 2015 Dusty Wallace
"Down There" is Copyright 2015 MJ Wesolowski
"Dog Years" is Copyright 2015 Kristopher Triana
"Streetcleaner" is Copyright 2015 Natalie Satakovski
"The Story of After" is Copyright 2015 Alexis J. Reed
"In a Manner of Speaking" is Copyright 2015 Charity Tahmaseb
"Apocalypse in an Armoire" is Copyright 2015 Herb N. Legend
"Soul Jam" is Copyright 2015 Nick Nafpliotis
"Last Stop: Hanover" is Copyright 2015 J. C. Stearns
"In Transit" is Copyright 2015 Kate Elizabeth
"Limbo" is Copyright 2015 Mary Mascari
"Our Blessed Commute" is Copyright 2015 Rhoads Brazos
"Smoke Scream" is Copyright 2015 Samantha Bryant
"Bridge To Nowhere, Train For The Forgotten" is Copyright 2015 Mathew Allan Garcia

ISBN-13: 978-0692514702
ISBN-10: 0692514708

TABLE OF CONTENTS

FOREWORD

The title for this book came to me long before we decided to make it an anthology. The phrase just popped into my head and for a while I wished it could become a *thing*. You know, like the young folk do. A meme. Selfies where you Photoshop mushroom clouds or zombies or whatever into the background. After *That Ain't Right*, this seemed like a good idea for a second anthology. There's something bittersweet about a last bit of self-reflection while facing the end.

The stories we received were beautiful. Picking the final roster was no easy task. Some of the stories we selected are heart breaking. Some of them are irreverent. Some defy easy classification. We loved them all.

This book would not be possible if not for the generosity of our Kickstarter and Patreon backers. In particular, we would like to recognize the contributions of Todd Ahlman, Adam Alexander, Argent, Megan Awesome!, Eric J. Boyd, Ian Chung, Pam Cobb, The Mac Daddy, Erik Scott de Bie, Michael Deneweth, BJ & Zedd Epstein, Dave Eytchison, Malcolm Heath, Jeremy Heitjan, Quek JiaJin, Keegan King, Rowena Knill, Nicholas Lapeyrouse, Cosette Newberry, John Nienart, Torrey Podmajersky, Simon Roake, Deb "Seattlejo" Schumacher, Josh Schumacher, Anthony Sison, Alexandra Summers, Joshua F. Surface, Charity Tahmaseb, Clive Tern, Wendy Wade, and Matt Youngmark.

Yours,
Jeremy Zimmerman
Co-Editor

"Your generation would probably 'livetweet' the apocalypse"
you say, and you laugh
You mean it as an insult, and I understand,
Or you don't
because the word lies awkwardly on your tongue, stumbles as it
leaves your lips, air quotes visible
You meant it as an insult, so you don't understand, when I look
into your eyes and say "Yes"
Because we would.
It would be our duty, as citizens on this earth
to document its end the best way we know
and if that means a second by second update
of the world going up in flames, or down in rain, or crushed
under the feet of invading monsters
so be it.
It would mean a second by second update of
"I love you"
"I'm scared"
"Are you all right?"
"Stay close"
"Be brave"
It would mean a second by second update of humanity's
connection with one another,
Proof of empathy, love, and friendship between people who
may have never met in the flesh.

So don't throw the word 'Livetweet' at me like a dagger, meant
    to tear at my 'teenage superiority'
Because if the citizens of Pompeii, before they were consumed
    by fire,
had a chance to tell their friends and family throughout Rome
"I love you"
"I'm scared"
"Don't forget me"
Don't you think they'd have taken the chance?

—*Shivangi Narain*

SHIVANGI NARAIN is a young adult running wild on the internet, with dreams of working in either AV production or journalism. She is a student by day, and a writer by night. Her first published works can be found in *So You Think You Can Write*, a collection of works by the OCE future author's program. She was raised in Florida, but currently lives in Bangalore, India, with her parents, brother, and dog.

ELEGY FOR A MOUNTAIN

An account by Abbot Galant,

AS PROVIDED BY BRANDON NOLTA

My name is Brother Galant… well, Abbot Galant, actually. Of course, "abbot" is only a title. I've held it for a decade or two, but I was a brother from the first day I donned the cassock and spoke my vows to the Mountain, and that's how I think of myself. I had a name before joining, I'm sure, but whatever it was is lost to wind and stone. Surely the Mountain knows, but as one can surely imagine, It has other things to think about just now. We have many, many things to do.

Moving an abbey is no small thing. How does one move the earth? Carved from the flesh of the Mountain itself, the abbey is one with the world, perched on the peak that Brother Quillus, with his fossils and radiocarbon charts, says once stood highest in the world. The Mountain has never mentioned this, never cared about highest or oldest. It simply is. I do not know if It would even understand if we asked about it, no matter how painstakingly we rendered our query on the Quincunx Organ.

In any case, the abbey. We cannot move the physical structures; only by Its grace did the Order dare to carve the original buildings, and what few additions have been made since. Would the Mountain allow it? By the time I became abbot and had to think of such things, there was little time to form the question. Even with the reduced character set developed over centuries and the automation built into the Quincunx, formal permission to open a conversation takes years to request.

Standing on the observation deck, the infrasonic tones of the fluted brass and steel shafts bored hundreds of feet into the rock humming in my bones, I imagine the resonance plates and strikers working in tandem, pistons and bound electrons winding the machine into one Voice. Millennia and more of effort and mechanics and craftsmanship, bound to generations of the humble in service to the Mountain. From where I stand, I see scores of my siblings, maintaining the hardware, fine-tuning and testing the instruction sets, recording data and harmonic patterns for indexing and translation. They work, unhurried but with great alacrity. Ever since the Mountain declared that the fire was on its way for our planet, third from the sun that will swell in its cradle and devour us whole—well, I think it safe to say alacrity has been the general state of working.

Of course, this isn't a new development. I have been with the Order for nearly a hundred years, and the news was many generations old when I joined, but generations for a monk are shorter than reflex for the Mountain. For this massive being of thought and stone, heat and consciousness, the fire approaches swiftly, and I believe It fears for us. As individuals, we are but dust motes, but the abbey has persevered for untold eons, and It seems to value that. We speak to the Mountain and thus keep It from loneliness, or so I've come to believe.

Sister Kliendi approaches quietly as I stand at the brass railing, looking into the Quincunx heart without seeing. She steps carefully, purposefully, without the odd shuffling the Thrianx can't seem to shake no matter how long any of them try. So unlike her people, who usually thrash about as they likely did in the ancient seas from which they arose. A hint of iridescence catches my eye, and I turn to face her.

The slash of scale above her eyes glitters in the light.

"Abbot," she says, bowing slightly, "we have the latest reports in from Fourthworld. The air-makers have been repaired, and the habitat should be fully reestablished well within evacuation schedules." She hands me a list of stations and other abbeys around the world, fellow seekers who have agreed to help with departing, or traded knowledge for knowledge. This world once held untold numbers and there are still many, even as twilight approaches. Our abbey will not be alone on Fourthworld.

"Fine news, Sister," I tell her, impressed by her efficiency. I remind myself to make a note in the Abbot's Journal that future project management should generally be done by those who spent at least a decade in the Archives on purpose. Those personalities are perfect for large-scale management, should the need to move a god arise again. "Has the Mountain signaled for us to begin the birthing?"

"We're receiving a signal now, Abbot. Should be complete in another decade; the Mountain seems to be in a hurry."

"Aren't we, Sister?" I ask, smiling to soften the rebuke I do not intend but she might hear. A run of chromatic notes, pinks and blues and a watery reddish-brown, plays across her face. Having seen it before, I know she's blushing. The effect is quite lovely, and strangely soothing. A moment goes by, and I allow myself to forget the magnitude of what the abbey, under the painstaking instructions the Mountain has given us over centuries, is about to do. Then it passes, and I take up my worries again.

"If Brothers Quillus and Tacton have finished their planning, tell them to be ready for signal's end. Once confirmed, they'll begin," I tell Sister Kliendi. "Fourthworld, and our siblings already there, await the Mountain."

"Yes, Abbot," she says, and turns away. She speaks to her tablet as she goes, passing the order and the double- and triple-checked instructions to Quillus and Tacton, in turn passing their orders along to the teams of monks training, learning, preparing the cutting tools and marking where to apply crystalline paste to the outlines of the great geode near the heart of the Mountain. Nearly ready now—grown on heat and pressure and all the Mountain's memories and knowledge—to be carefully excised from this world, carried by focused light and gravity to a new world, where an extinct volcano will awaken through the Mountain's beneficence. An infant deity, given new stone, while the progenitor faces the fire. Not many of the monks seem to think much about what that truly means.

I look into the Quincunx again as I ponder this, while my fellows in the Order practice to deliver a child god from the earth.

Work in the translator corps long enough, many monks claim, and one can learn to feel the changes in the tones before they happen, to anticipate the notes in the earth. Given that these tones are invariant and play for months or years on end, this claim is suspect, but every brother or sister who has worked long shifts in the bowels of the Quincunx, the translation matrices, or the receptor plates believes this. When I was a translator, I felt the same, and still do.

Thus, as I walk the long paths downward to the heart of the Quincunx, a long-unfelt sensation flits from the soles of my feet upward, passing through from stone to blood to bone: imminent change, a new tone from the Mountain. I stop for a moment, half-listening, half-searching with skin and nerve. Vibrations continue to rumble beneath me. Foolish thing, I think after a minute.

Now, the song of warning, the litany of geologic wisdom, stops. For the first time in decades—since before I became abbot—there is only silence from the Mountain. My legs tremble, as if I had stepped from a boat and not yet recovered my land legs. I shift to one side, regain my balance. Was this the scheduled end of communication?

Where was the Quincunx in full bellow, acknowledging transmission?

"Sister Kliendi," I say to the glowing icon on my wrist. A moment of silence, then her voice enters my ear, as clear as if she were there and not several levels down and north of here. "Yes, Abbot?"

"The Mountain has stopped speaking," I say. "Where is our response, our invitation to talk further?"

A poignant sigh. "We reached partial translation of this signal recently, Abbot, and the probability of this signal being a farewell was high. Given the brevity of this last tone," here, a muffled conversation with another voice, "the probability becomes certain. The Mountain has given us permission to deliver Its infant self, and has decided no further communication is needed."

"Until when?" I say. Surely she has reported this, but with the exodus to Fourthworld, I've pushed all non-critical matters off on other personnel. With a stab of irritation, I realize most of the day-to-day responsibilities have fallen on the shoulders of Sister Kliendi. No need to report to herself, I think, and regret my pique.

"Ever," she says. "The Mountain has nothing more to tell us."

"Then time is indeed brief," I tell her. "Quillus and Tacton have already started, I assume." Before she can answer, I feel a change in pitch running upward from the Mountain stone into my feet. I wonder if the Mountain feels the cutting, the severing of the links, even though it happens far too quickly for stone gods to perceive.

"Preparations are ongoing, Abbot," Sister Kliendi says. She almost sounds curt, which for her is a shout of rebellion. I suspect I have pushed her too hard, a fault I inherited with the position.

"Your work continues in excellence, Sister," I say. "Thank you, and please keep me apprised of Quillus and Tacton's progress." I sign off, and look at my hands. The weight of years rushes over me for a moment as I regard the faded grey of my skin, my narrow-spanned fingers: the only sign of my true age. I am old for my people, and yet, I'm a shadow in the corner of the eye to the Mountain; blink, and gone.

I expected the work center to be nearly full with brothers and sisters, planning the disassembly and transportation of the Quincunx, looking forward to the trip outward through the blackness to the red planet, safe while our home planet burns. While the Mountain burns. However, the rows of workstations, plans and coding terminals stand empty, their usual tenders working diligently elsewhere or not at all. Surely Kliendi knows of this. I bring up the digest of notes and memos on my tablet; indeed she does. Apparently I knew of this too, or she's learned to forge my approval sigil flawlessly. A memory stirs, and I sigh as a blizzard of administrative details in my head surface for examination.

I decide that, just for now, my advanced age is sufficient cause to rest for a moment and think of nothing, a task my earliest instructors in the Order thought suited to my nature. Old joints fold slowly, and I rest my weary back against a sparsely decorated slab cut from a species of tree extinct for more than five hundred years. Another change in pitch, followed by a steady rise in intensity; the cutting has begun in earnest.

My hand brushes against the cool surface of a cavern wall, a part of the Mountain long since adapted and molded for the Order's unending work. Beneath my hand, I can sense the texture just below a surface worn smooth by generations dead long before me, brothers and sisters whose names exist only in the oldest of the Archive volumes, if at all. What does the Mountain feel? Surely nothing. Surely we are like atoms, forming and flashing into particle decay far faster than perception. These are old thoughts, I know, and yet, like dear friends or mortal enemies, they persist. The Mountain is nearly as old as the planet, and an entity of stone, the most patient of fundamental qualities. Its perceptions must be vaster than ours, slow as worlds.

The cutting continues below. I think of the sustained effort culminating in these hectic days, of all the Order who worked their lives through to reach a goal they would never see. A sunburst of pride, warming and breath-catching, silently fills my chest, and I offer a quick prayer of thanks to the Mountain. To be a part of this endeavor, to allow the Mountain's wisdom to outpace world's end and take root in new soil: I know no other word for it than joy, though some of my contemporaries might feel purpose to be a better term. Either way, it is a gift.

Reaching out, I touch the cavern wall again. Though we are blessed by this mission, I cannot deny a touch of sadness in my thoughts. Moving the child Mountain seed to the red planet will keep Its wisdom, and the Order, alive for ages to come, but the original Mountain will die with our home world. Its memories are copied into the child, not moved and cleaned from their original physical form. In death, Its new life will be born, but the old will be destroyed. For some time, this has bothered me, though I haven't spoken of it to anyone, not even Brother Averoth. If thoughts like this have occurred to the Mountain, It hasn't seen fit to share them.

"Are you afraid?" I whisper to the stone, certain It cannot hear me. Though we have no prohibition against it, I feel I am breaking some ancient rule by speaking this thought aloud. Brother Averoth would tell me I'm being stupid; if we pray to the Mountain and expect It to hear us, It surely knows our thoughts, even those we don't say. His logic is, as always, impeccable, but my feelings are what they are. If I have any wisdom, it is only that I act on them slower now, and try to apply a measure of Averoth's good sense first.

"I would be afraid," I say to the Mountain.

The whine and pitch of my brethren's cutting tools rolls through the Mountain, a faint insistence against the papery skin on my fingers. It feels like nervous energy, a trembling before momentous things.

On the last night of cutting the child Mountain seed free, the Order celebrates. Why not? The actual operation took the better part of a year, and the cutting was the quickest part. Preparations that had unfolded over lifetimes had come to pass. The barbarians were finally at the gates, and as we prepared to flee, all we could register was relief. My predecessor would have probably waited until the Order's relocation to allow it, but my feeling was that the Mountain deserved to be there. Strange, but having had many weeks to meditate on the matter, I hadn't changed my mind.

"Serenity in the face of alcohol," Averoth says to me, a cup in his hand full almost to sloshing. Gentle black orbs regard me with keen kindness, a trick only Averoth seems to have mastered. "Since you're upright and apparently able to track movement, you must be sober."

"Perhaps I'm many cups ahead," I say, smiling.

"Have you learned to hold your wine?" Averoth asks. He knows better, but he cannot refuse to tease now; he would lose face among the initiates and junior Order. "Never mind; no point in spreading hot air now."

"Your promotion is assured, Averoth," I say. "No need to flatter me further."

I laugh alone. Averoth's smile is still there, but it slips a fraction. "Well, that answers my eventual question. Do you plan to announce it soon, or wait until it's too late to dissuade you?"

"Should I? This decision is mine."

"Others might wish to choose the same path," my friend of many decades says. "You haven't asked my thoughts, for example."

"One of the few delights of being abbot," I say, "is that one gets to decide who is invaluable, while not suffering under the delusion of being that way. Thus, my friend, you are irreplaceable, while I am not."

"Ah, the corruption of power," Averoth says, his mood darkening as quickly as his eyes.

"You'll see," I say. I hold out my hand to him, and after a pause, he enfolds my gray fingers in his solid grip. In the days to come, we'll have few chances to speak. This moment will have to do.

Eventually, he nods, releases me from his grasp and walks away, solid and sober. The celebration has run its course around us, and steps must be made. I wave my arms to catch attention, and soon enough, all eyes are on me. Except for a few specialized support personnel, the entirety of our Order is here, so what I tell them will be untouched by rumor.

"Siblings, we are nearly ready to journey to Fourthworld, the child Mountain in our arms. On the red dirt of our sister world, you will raise the Order anew, with this world's ancient wisdom to guide and nourish you.

"However, I will not be among you for this new chapter. After much reflection, I have decided to stay here with the Mountain, and tend to It as best I can until the end of this world's days. My reasons for this decision are many, but I feel my place is here with the Mountain, as It faces the fire. Your place is on another world, and I am grateful you will continue, protecting our accumulated knowledge for all our peoples.

"Once you have departed for the new world, Sister Kliendi will become the new abbot. Brother Averoth will become Senior Advisor to the office. Under their leadership, and the Mountain's continued grace, I expect a new era of intellect and compassion to begin. If it doesn't, Averoth is authorized to take drastic measures."

A few laughs here and there, but mostly silence. Well, I never was good at jokes.

"Thank you for your work and devotion. We will endure and thrive because of it. Now, our last preparations must begin. Please, to work."

Loyal and obedient, the brothers and sisters of the Order turn and file away, talk of tasks and checklists already beginning to fill the air. I believe Averoth was expecting different. Then again, Averoth is sometimes too iconoclastic for his own good. In times of change and uncertainty, routine and hard work does more to soothe hearts than any prayer, something my friend, for all of his logical prowess and clear thinking, never took to heart.

A beeping from my tablet draws me back from my thoughts. Without glancing, I know it's Sister—soon to be Abbot—Kliendi, wanting to discuss last-minute details, or perhaps ask me what I was thinking by naming her the next abbot. Not that she would be rude enough to come right out and question my sanity. No matter; her subtlety speaks volumes. I tap the icon to begin our latest conversation, walking out of the hall toward the observation deck.

Without the rumble of the Mountain or the multivoiced hum of the Quincunx to disguise them, the rumblings of the Order's departure flow down from the surface to pool around me, humming faintly through the railings as I stand at the deck. The Quincunx—now disassembled and stored in three cargo transports—is vast in its absence, only a cavern large enough for a city left behind to observe. I have already said all my goodbyes, stood at the rough-hewn landing space near the top of the now-abandoned abbey and waved farewell to the departing ships. After my siblings left, flying into the airless black, there was only cargo, none of which cared if I watched it depart.

Soon, even the ship songs fade and disappear, and I am alone with the Mountain. I walk along the hallways and the passages, only my footsteps and the Mountain's silence as company. Every few steps, it seems, I reach out and touch the stone, brush my fingers along walls worn smooth by millennia, tread floors hollowed by millions upon millions of footsteps. It feels warm to the touch, almost as if late summer had soaked through into the Mountain's heart.

I cannot prove this, but I believe the Mountain is aware of me.

On the fiftieth day after the Order's departure, as the light swells to crimson in the noon sky, the Mountain begins to sing. Without the translator matrices and the massive Quincunx to render it, I have no way to know for sure what the message is, or even if there is one. Perhaps Its voice is enough, seemingly endless runs of shifting pulses, subsonic trills, archipelagos of meaning lost in a sea of thunder. This close to the Mountain's core, where all its messages begin, my eardrums should be split and my bones liquefying without the protective measures built into the observation hall. The fact I am whole and unharmed is evidence enough to convince. The Mountain knows someone is here with It, in the last moments before the fire consumes It whole.

I place my hands against the cavern wall, the empty space that held the Quincunx to my right. Its power courses into my skin, shaking me down to the molecules. I know that my fragile shell and the Mountain's ancient solidity will soon be plasma and wisp between the shock wave and the heat. Even now, a flicker of fear tremors in me. Maybe the Mountain feels it, too, but I doubt it. The Mountain knows many things, perhaps all. What greater comfort can there be than in knowing?

As the thunder rises, and the air turns to flame, all I can feel—in my hands, my skin, my heart—is joy.

Part of the Order of the Mountain for more than a century, **ABBOT GALANT** has led the Order for longer than he cares to admit with any specificity. When he's not writing down his recollections for future generations or shaping various operational policies, Galant spearheads the largest single engineering/relocation project the Order has ever embarked upon. He enjoys a purposeful existence as abbot, and plans to continue his service to the Mountain as long as breath and strength allow.

BRANDON NOLTA is a writer, editor, and professional curmudgeon living in the transportation-challenged wilds of north Idaho. After earning an MFA, he went slightly mad. Nothing much happened with that, so he gave it up and started working for respectable companies again, which he still does when he wants to pay his bills. His fiction and poetry have appeared in *Stupefying Stories*, *The Pedestal Magazine*, *Every Day Fiction*, *Perihelion*, *Strong Verse*, and a cacophony of other publications. *Iron and Smoke*, his first novel, was published by Montag Press in January 2015; he has yet to admit to a second.

SOUNDS OF SILENCE

An account by Dylan Reynolds,
AS PROVIDED BY NICOLE TANQUARY

I had set my alarm for seven a.m., but Katherine's aunt called me at six-forty-five, sharp. Usually I would've let my parents' ancient land line ring on and on until it cut to the message machine. If I got a happy-go-lucky, we-want-to-offer-you-a-stellar-deal voice, I let it go and got on with my life. If I got a disgruntled, "Dylan, I know you're there, so pick up," I would touch the answer button, lean back in my chair (an antique, with beaten old cushions and little wheels on the feet that would get stuck in the carpet), and see what they had to say.

At the sound of Aunt Judy's voice, I threw back the sheets and jumped into my chair, feeling it squeak against the floor. I was exhausted; my calf muscles ached, and my head felt stuffed full of cotton balls dipped in acid. From where I sat, I could see six freshly emptied beer bottles in the plastic bag where I put my returnables. I couldn't remember drinking that many, but the bag never lies.

"I hope I didn't wake you up," said Judy when I got on the line. Some people sound different on the phone, but Judy always came through crystal clear. Hearing it, I could actually *see* her, hair pressed and molded into contours around her face, lipstick smile frozen on, tight at the corners, as if it'd fall off otherwise.

"No," I said. "I was awake; I didn't sleep much."

"I'm sorry to hear that," she said, and I knew she wasn't sorry. She didn't give a rat's ass about me. She didn't flat-out hate me, though, which was something of an achievement—she addressed most people with a thin, icy smile, beneath which anyone could see the rage burning in a red-black fire. She belonged to the class of millennial-generation, middle-aged adult who believed *my* generation was supposed to be the knight in shining armor, full of brilliant knowledge of science and mathematics and biology and fuck knows what else, able to figure out how to turn things around for everybody. When, surprise surprise, they found out we were just like them, they took it personally. We "let them down." Same old song that's been sung for years about the young.

Aunt Judy wasn't one for formalities, so with the obligatory four seconds of introduction fulfilled, the conversation turned to business. "Our flight is scheduled for next week, Tuesday afternoon. I talked to Katherine on the phone all last night, but she's still adamant about staying. Silly girl." Judy barked out a laugh that twisted my stomach to hear. It made me feel five years old and guilty about something—drawing on the walls with marker, maybe.

Then again, I'm used to being talked down to. People think I'm slow... something about the way I slouch my shoulders, the way I don't look them in the eye. In a way, talking to Aunt Judy was business as usual.

"I know your space flight is this evening, and you probably have plenty of preparations left to do... but would you try to talk some sense into her? I've done everything I can think of short of threatening nuclear war, and even that probably wouldn't convince her."

"Sounds like Katherine," I said. My bare feet were cold on the floor, beginning to numb at the toe tips. I flexed them and listened to the joints crackle. "I'm mostly ready anyways. Just one more suitcase to pack. My folks are taking care of things, so I have some free time."

"Thank you," said Judy. There was a sniff. I stared at the phone. Judy, actually showing a moment of weakness? Well, I thought, if that's not a sign of the apocalypse, nothing is. Then I bit my lip. I'm glad she couldn't hear that thought over the phone. Me and Katherine had been together for a while now, long enough for Judy to learn to tolerate me, so whenever we talked I always hoped that I wouldn't say anything stupid to fuck that up. "That girl is driving me insane. It would be so much easier if I could talk to her in person."

I sighed. "I can't tell you where she is, Judy. If she found out, she'd never speak to *either* of us again."

"Yes… you're probably right. Lord knows you've spent more time with her than I have." There was a moment of silence. I shifted around in my chair, suddenly very aware of the quiet in the house. My parents were still asleep. It's funny, but when you live with people for a long time, you can tell what they're doing just by the way the house feels.

Finally, Judy said, "Please call and tell me how it went," ended the conversation with a clipped goodbye, and hung up. I stared straight ahead for a moment, my eyes sore and itchy. I rubbed the crust out of them with the tips of my fingers. Then I stood and went downstairs to the kitchen. I was in boxers, but it was just my parents in the house, so I didn't bother pulling on pants.

I looked around, no leftover coffee from yesterday. I got out the pot, the filters, the grounds, and with the ease of well-practiced motions began assembling them together. My coffee cup had a Monet painting wrapped around the side, one of those gentle pond scenes. See, the slouched-over kid has class, after all.

After a pause, I got out a thermos for Katherine, and a carton of milk from the fridge. She didn't drink it black.

For a while I stood waiting for the water to boil. My parents' kitchen had a big window opening out onto the front lawn and its ring of garden. A sweep of mock orange framed the left pane, sagging under flowers with yellow centers and white petals, like fried eggs, but prettier. Beyond the mock orange were clumps of hydrangea whose buds were just starting to get the blue tints.

Katherine loved this house in summer. My dad was a gardener, see, and he was good at arranging things so when one thing's blooming period was over, another's began. The beds were constantly changing in color, texture, smell. If she came over and it was nice out, we'd sit on the porch and drink Coronas, watch Dad in his stupid straw gardening hat, working out the weeds and spreading mulch.

And with the memory, a question: Would the flowers still grow once we were gone?

The water was ready to strain. My eyes moved from the garden to the task at hand, and I worked in comfortable silence. If Katherine was still mad at me, the coffee would make a good peace offering.

The thermos jiggled in the cup holder as I pressed the brake, watching as the car ahead of me swerved into place in the traffic jam. Summer in the Cape was always miserable. All the rich Bostonians flocked over and brought their road aggression with them, them and their fucking SUVs and convertibles. I rubbed my thumb along the wheel grip, seeing things pass in increments as I headed for the exit that would take me to the highway. There was a cranberry bog; a walking path winding down to the harbor, where you could see the foundations of old flooded homes, if you looked hard enough; sidewalks full of golden retrievers and labs and the other well-groomed breeds owned by summer residents; houses with crushed white shells covering the driveways; the Stop-'n-Shop; the seafood buffets; the sweeps of neighborhood on artificially raised grounds.

It was all familiar and steady. Hard to imagine that by tomorrow morning I'd be gone, bunked with my parents in a tiny shithole room in deep space. No roads. No ocean. No fresh air.

But at least we wouldn't have to watch each other rot to death.

I turned on the classic radio station from Hyannis, which was playing Simon and Garfunkel, followed by cheery reports of the weather and how it would be excellent for those of us leaving today, may they have a safe journey. Just make sure to pack for all contingencies, folks. Extra water bottles are especially important, and remember, always read the safety cards...

Off the radio went.

The highway was narrow, two lanes full of cars, their hoods colorful and glistening beetle shells in the sunlight. The trees flanking either side weren't tall, not with the sandy soil. Weeds covered the ground and squeezed up against the trunks, gnarled and old.

Then the tree cover broke, and the Port appeared, all metal and black walls designed to suck in sunlight and generate solar energy. Weaves of neon streamers were strung on the exit leading there, shaping the line of traffic going in. Cars were being unloaded and then driven by autopilot to the junk yard, where they were compacted to make room for the new. Otherwise there'd be no way to fit them all, what with their owners leaving by the thousands. I thought of my parent's old Honda driving mutely to its death, its carcass left to rust in the unmarked graves where the cars were being dumped. My teeth clenched, so I rotated my jaw to the side, relishing the crack.

In normal times, the Port would've made no sense; here in this hard-to-reach place full of civilians, why would anyone build a launch station? But Ports were springing up any place where money flowed freely. The plan was to get as many people off planet as possible, and the more Ports were built, the faster it could happen. This one was set up to evacuate the well-to-do of the Cape population, a lot of eastern Mass, too.

I lowered my eyes and drove on. I'd have enough time to look at the place later. Besides, now that the Port was passed, the way ahead was blank and clean, not another car in sight.

Katherine never got her drivers' license—just a permit, and that was only to keep up the pretense of actual intent to learn. You had to protect yourself with a lot of unspoken pretenses when living with someone like Aunt Judy, and for the years Katherine stayed with her, I saw a lot of them rise up on rickety foundations, only to crash down when Katherine finally got sick of play-acting.

Katherine couldn't drive, so she had taken the bus to Provincetown instead. Not that I would've told her Aunt Judy she was so close to home. That'd make about as much sense as pressing a loaded gun to my head and pulling the trigger.

I drove carefully in; the streets in P-town were old and narrow, built back when the only vehicles around were horse-drawn carriages. Strings hung with rainbow flags criss-crossed the street and flipped around in the wind. Gay pride, and all that—marriage for them might be legal, but discrimination doesn't die off easy, so everyone said.

I turned into a parking lot next to the harbor, since the streets couldn't be parked on without blocking traffic. It had been a few months since the Port was built and people in the area began leaving en masse, but even so, the emptiness of the lot was disconcerting. Summertime in P-town used to be so fucking packed. It used to make you feel like part of a sardine swarm.

I eased up to the ticket machine and waited for it to scan my car in, the window open and my elbow resting on the edge. The breeze from the ocean was salty sweet. Fresh, but with a real-ness to it... that undertone of fish and seaweed. I breathed in through my nose and held the air in my lungs for a moment before letting it out again. No way the stuff circulating on the ship was going to be this good.

A spindly tree offered a bit of shade, and I parked beneath it with my window open a crack. Across from me was the Dolphin Fleet Whale-Watching ticket office. I only went whale-watching once, when Katherine got me to do it on her birthday. We had burned in the sun, clinging to the railing in the spray and wind as we watched spouts of water appear, followed by sleek dark shapes that were impossibly massive, impossibly fast.

The whales ignored us, which bothered me more than it should've. We were only going to be on the planet for so much longer... couldn't they just give us a glance? Just a bit of silent acknowledgement—so long, you itty-bitty motherfuckers—before diving down deep where we'd never see them again?

I didn't say any of that out loud, but Katherine had known anyways. She hadn't made me go again.

I shut the door, checked my watch, and ran a hand through my hair. Let the Katherine-hunt begin, I thought to myself. There was a feeling of irritation; why did she have to make everything so fucking difficult? I mean, I was her *boyfriend*, wasn't I? Why did she always have to hide?

Well, I knew the answer to that, but I kept myself from thinking about it. It had been two years, but the pain was still there. Still fresh, like a long-infected wound.

My first stop was the Red Shack, a little shanty set up next to the parking lot. It was about lunchtime, so I planned to check the food places Katherine liked. And if that didn't work, there were always the art galleries she hung out in.

A girl my age with a red apron was manning the window. I ordered a Bula-Bula... banana, mango, green tea icy stuff... and paid my dues before asking about Katherine. "I'm looking for a friend of mine. Tall, long curly hair, always wears Birkenstocks. Orders a medium Java-licious coffee with her food when she comes here. Seen her around?" The girl looked me up and down for a moment, her gaze lingering on my face. Deciding if I was a crazy ex-boyfriend of Katherine's, I guess.

Call it sad, but I was used to that look. Katherine was a pretty girl, and her drifting made people suspicious. They *say* the romantic period is over, but I swear, people have secret thoughts inside them that insist she *must* be trying to escape a heartbroken, homicidal boyfriend.

Apparently I wasn't intimidating enough for crazy ex material, because the girl answered, "She was here this morning, but has not been back." She was an exchange student from Eastern Europe, judging by the precision of her English. P-town got a lot of them during the summer, and plenty of the local businesses ran on their labor. At least that hadn't changed yet.

"Thanks anyways." I dropped my change into the tip jar, which had a modest pile accumulating at the bottom. I added, "If she comes by, tell her that Dylan's looking for her."

I moved down Main Street, blinking in the sun, already feeling the itchy warmth of sunburn on my nose and forehead. A few couples dressed in shorts, flip-flops, and sunglasses walked around looking at shops. Killing time before their flight off planet, I guess. P-town used to have all kinds of couples—man-woman, man-man, woman-woman, everything in between. Occasionally, there were single guys wearing tight shorts who eyed me up and down, and I never knew whether to be flattered or embarrassed. At least when Katherine was there, I could wrap an arm around her waist, and they'd know I was taken.

I peeked into The Lobster Pot, which had a dark hallway that went back, back, back to the main dining room, perched on the edge of the water front. There was a seater behind the counter, next to a tank where gray-shelled lobsters moved in slow scuttles, waiting to be eaten. Me and Katherine could eat plate after plate of the stuff...

put us in front of good seafood, and we went from an average couple of college-aged kids to a pair of savage, shell-cracking, meat-slurping animals.

The seater was an old man who knew me from before. "Sorry, kiddo, Katherine hasn't been around." Smells of food blew across my face, and I had to clench my gut so it wouldn't grumble. The Lobster Pot wasn't outrageously expensive or anything... though trust me, the food would've been worth it... but it was out of my price range. The only times I ate there was when I was with Katherine. Since the accident and the settlement two years ago, she's always had money.

The light in P-town had this brightness, this golden sheen that made it heavy, like water; it pooled around buildings and over street corners, lingering in gutters and cracks in the road. That day, it was like I was wading through it as I worked my way through town, poking my head into everywhere I could think of. A South African place, a couple Thai places, a French place, more seafood joints, some grills... no luck. Eventually I went back to the Red Shack and ordered a sausage so I could eat as I walked.

I eventually struck gold when I found the trumpet player. She was sprawled out on one of those cheap foldable chairs, blowing a sad song through the brass. Some of the couples had stopped to stand around her. A black trumpet case was open on the sidewalk in front of her, with paper money tossed inside. A cardboard sign propped up against the case read in black Sharpie, NEED CASH FOR PORT TICKET.

I rummaged around in a pocket and came up with a five. When I bent over and let it drop, she winked at me, and started playing in my direction. Eventually the other people drifted on—funny how much tourists loved those prissy souvenir shops. Soon it was just me and her.

She set down the trumpet and took a deep gulp from a water bottle, drips of it running down her shirt. She wasn't wearing a bra, and the sweat from her neck and armpits made her nipples pop out. I squinted my eyes up to keep from staring. "Looking for Katherine?" she asked, as she wiped the side of her hand across her mouth.

"Uh huh." I never did learn the trumpet player's name, but over my many Katherine hunts I'd come to learn that she was a mutual friend. She was on the street most of the time, so if Katherine had wandered by, she'd know.

"I saw her an hour back. Headed towards Dune Beach. Had her sketchbook with her. Stopped and said hello." The trumpet player gave me a curious, narrow-eyed look. "She said you were leaving today. Evening time."

"That's right," I said. I tried to keep my smile on, but I could feel it falter. The trumpet player took another gulp of water, her eyes never leaving my face.

Finally she said, "I'll have enough to leave soon. Maybe I'll see you up there." She leaned back and closed her eyes, resting in the sunlight. "You know, I wanted to be an astronaut when I was a kid. Not sure I wanted it like this, though. This way, you have no home to return to, after you go see the stars." Another pause. I wanted to get moving again, but she wasn't quite done, so I stood in place, shifting my weight from foot to foot. One of the things I learned from Katherine was, you don't leave if a girl's not finished talking. Even if *you* forget about it afterward, *she* won't.

Finally the trumpet player went on, half to me, half to herself. "Strange, isn't it? All that stuff about all classes of people deserving equal rights, gone up in smoke. Everyone who can afford it is leaving the planet to avoid getting the rot, leaving the others behind. Damn shame." She let out a sigh.

After a while, a clump of couples turned the corner and began window shopping their way toward us. Up came the trumpet, and the music started again, eddying between soft and loud, high and low. The people drew closer, and I turned and left before the trumpet player was surrounded again.

I went back to my car long enough to get the thermos of coffee, then headed off on a road that went out of P-town, toward the more secluded dunes.

Long scrubby grass sprouted between the sand crests, sometimes with a spray of color that meant wildflowers. The road was dry and gritty, obscured by sand films brushed around by the wind. You couldn't avoid the sand, no matter how hard you tried. Pretty soon I felt grains crunching in the bottoms of my sneakers.

There were no signs for Dune Beach. No paths either. It hadn't even been a beach until a few decades ago, when the water sloshed its way higher and higher, sucking against the edges of land and pulling it under.

After about thirty minutes of walking, I veered to my left and kept my eyes to the ground. Finally I found a bit of flattened grass where someone had stepped recently. I ventured in, navigating over roots and avoiding patches of mud when I could.

At the edge of the trees, I stopped and stared past the sandy-soil dunes to the water. Katherine sat on an overhang, her feet settled on the sand bed, water cupping around her knees. Her hair was pulled into a water-clogged ponytail, to keep out of her eyes while she was swimming.

My feet followed the footprints she had left through the earth, until I was standing next to her. I took off my sneakers and socks, then sat, dipping my legs into the water.

Katherine turned to look at me. "You found me," she said. Her face wasn't disappointed, not happy either. Just kind of blank and far away.

Ten feet out in the water was a beach house that had been flooded. The salt water had worn away most of the wood, and now just the skeleton was left behind. A seagull was perched up there, turning its head back and forth to survey the land. Streaks of black stood out on its white shoulders.

From where I sat, I could see Katherine's sketchbook and a clutch of pencils. She had been drawing what was left of the house—and more. Inside the house stood a figure the color of shadows. Her arms dripped into the water. She was staring at us with hollow eyes.

I turned away and looked out with Katherine. It's not that she's a bad artist. Fuck no. It's just that her pictures are hard to look at; something inside you cringes away from them. I knew for a fact that Aunt Judy hated them, would've burned them all, if she could've—maybe that was a reason Katherine had moved away, so she could draw in peace.

I pulled the thermos out and offered it to Katherine. She took it readily and twisted off the cap, then threw her head back and drank half of it down in one go. "You're such a gentleman, Dylan. Taking time out of your busy schedule just to bring me coffee." There was a jab to her tone, but I ignored it. It was too late in the game for arguments.

"What's been going on with you?" I said, instead.

Katherine shrugged. "The usual. Problems sleeping, but nothing some melatonin couldn't fix."

"I hope that shit isn't addictive."

"No, *Mom*. It was even doctor recommended. Though the weed wasn't."

"You had weed?"

"Yeah, still got some. It's back at my place if you want a hit."

I shook my head. I had tried some sophomore year of high school, and yeah, it was fun at first, but it had given me some serious paranoia problems. I didn't need any of that again. Not with the Port waiting for me at sundown.

Katherine took hold of her ponytail and began wringing out the water. She flicked the droplets off her hands, across my face. I wiped them off, not minding it, smiling a little. She smiled back. But it was a strange look. Right beneath the surface, I could see something blue and sad welling up. It lasted only a moment, after which she moved her gaze to the water and kept it there. "They make you drink recycled piss on the ships to save on water," she said. "You know that? Even salty ocean stuff like this is better than piss. Isn't it?"

I dug my fingers into the sand and moved them around, feeling the solidness in the clumps, the grit, the texture that defined this place... and Katherine, too, if I thought about it. "I'd rather drink piss than be eaten alive by bacteria," I said.

She shrugged. "You're dying right now. Everyone is—a little bit every day. We just don't like to think of life like that."

"There's no life here anymore. Not for us."

"So maybe I'll find a way to turn into an ape. Not too different genetically, shouldn't be a problem. And they're immune to the rot."

I rolled my eyes. "If the scientists couldn't figure out a way to protect us and still remain on planet, what makes you think *you* can?"

"I don't. That was never the point." She was still wringing her ponytail, twisting it one way and then the other. She used to have such thick hair... you could stick a pencil in it and it would stay there for hours. After the accident, though, it thinned out, the curls going limp to match everything else about her.

I leaned forward and snatched her into a hug, before I knew that that had been the plan all along. Her eyes drifted from the water to my leg, and she rested her warm cheek on my shoulder. Her breasts pressed against my abdomen; her skin was hot to the touch.

Fevers were the earliest symptom of the rot.

I tensed all over, pulling her even closer, as if I could merge her body with mine and in that way carry her with me when I left the planet.

"I know Judy sent you," she said. Her voice wasn't accusatory. In fact, a little warmth had come back into it.

"I would've come anyways. No way I'm leaving you here."

I felt the softness of her lips on my neck. "Yes you are."

And that was the fucking Hell of it. We both knew I was going to leave in the end. I had to.

We sat there for an age. Neither of us pulled away, even when we both started getting sweaty in each other's hands. I don't know what was going through her head. Maybe the nights we had shared, at her place. We'd never made it official, didn't go around declaring it to all our friends, but it was all the same anyways.

What broke the trance was my phone ringing. It was Mom. She wasn't hysterical or anything—she knew where I was, she always knew when I was with Katherine—but she told me in no uncertain terms that it was time to come home, to make sure I had packed everything before leaving.

I ignored the summons long enough to try to convince Katherine to come with me. I told her that the temperature rise and the water rise, what had bred the rot disease in the first place, were only going to get worse. I told her she didn't have to go with her Aunt Judy. She could switch her departure to today and stay with me and my folks. They'd love to have her, I knew they would, she was like a daughter to them anyways.

I told her everyone was leaving, even those who couldn't afford the whole ticket price and instead had to go into indentured servitude to pay off the loans. I told her the only people staying were the crazy ones.

"And the insane shall inherit the Earth," she replied.

Finally I couldn't wait anymore. The light was going orange; my parents would be getting worried.

I kissed her on the temple, got up and tugged my shoes back on, sand grains working their way down between my toes.

Fuck, I thought, keeping my eyes on the ground. Katherine wasn't looking at me anymore, didn't want to see the way my face was twisted up. She was back to her sketchbook, filling in the shadows in the water.

We didn't end with any crap about seeing each other again one day. Up until this point our relationship had been crap-free, and why would we spoil such a good thing?

There were a lot of protests when they first showed the video of the *Hermes* on the news, as shot from the International Space Station. The announcers went all stiff right before they ran the vid, said that if there were young children in the room, that their parents might be advised to send them away. Even so, there was still talk that it wasn't decent to show something like that on public television, live deaths like that. People compared it to old news reels of the Vietnam War—not the fighting part, but the dying.

I remember seeing the hulking shape of the *Hermes* against a flat black screen, disfigured by the energy cells strapped to its back. Then the explosions, silent. Fireballs colored by ions I couldn't name, supplemented by fission-based generators. The hull cracked open after that. You could see the civilians on the ship had been caught unaware, when the camera focused on the people who were sucked out of the crack. They were still in their pajamas. It had been designated "night time" on the ship, since, you know, things like time are kinda ambiguous in space.

A lot of them were young children. There had been plenty of test runs before the *Hermes*, and the program had been deemed safe and family friendly. I expected stuff like clutching at their throats, mouths coming open to scream, but it wasn't like that. There was barely any thrashing at all.

I remember seeing it through a fog. Everything was a dull sheen, over my one thought: Katherine.

I could hear my dad gasping, my mom scrambling for a phone and ringing up Aunt Judy's number, trying to find out if she knew anything. We weren't related to them by blood, but they were like our second family.

I didn't do anything. I just stood there. It sounds stupid, thinking about it now, but I was waiting to wake up.

My parents didn't say anything while we strapped ourselves into the seating area, where we would be kept until we were safely out of Earth's gravitational pull. They could tell I wanted to be left alone. They knew about Katherine—when I came home, they must've seen the numbness on my face and guessed what had happened.

Katherine had been one of the very few survivors of the *Hermes* disaster. She had gotten up while everyone else was asleep—she had left her tablet in the seating area on the ship, and that's where she'd been, rummaging around in the net attached to the seat, when the explosion happened. They played the whole moment on the news— there'd been cameras in the seating area, and the film was salvaged later by clean-up crews. Katherine's head jerked up as everything rattled. A crew member scooped her up in his arms as he raced past, toward the flight deck. You could see her struggling and screaming, even as they strapped her into the emergency detachment, which was then sealed off from the rest of the ship. She couldn't even move, the harness was so tight.

Later on, when the *Hermes* was big news on the networks, the announcers had tried to get interviews from the civilian survivors,

Katherine included. I remember telling some asshole with a camera to go fuck himself; he'd come up to our table in the Lobster Pot and started asking dumb-fuck questions like, "How did you feel when you learned your family didn't survive?" Hoping to get an emotional story out of her, I guess.

Oh, her face right then. It was so broken I could have shot the guy in the balls and watch him bleed to death.

By some stroke of luck (or misfortune, I couldn't decide which), I had gotten a window seat. I leaned my forehead against the layers of clear plastic, thinking to myself how flimsy it looked. Beyond us were trees rooted in sandy soil, their shapes dim, since the sun was setting. For a moment I swear I could see Katherine there, leaning against a withered trunk, searching the windows for my face.

My mom took my hand and squeezed it. I didn't look at her.

The way the disease works, it rots your body first, leaving you a pile of stinking meat and bones. But your brain still works perfectly, right up until the end.

I tell myself I won't think about Katherine that way. I won't. I can't.

Instead, I'll think of her relaxed on the beach, sketchbook handy, the paper chewed up from the touch of sand and dampness. Walking around Provincetown, even if she was the only one left. She'd get to see the disintegration of everything we couldn't take with us on the ships. Be totally chill as the waterline crept higher, gnawing at the edges of buildings before finally pulling them under, roiling with the larvae of insects that were *supposed* to be tropical, damn it, we didn't *want* tropical shit at the Cape, the Cape was the Cape and we didn't want it to change...

I wondered if she'd skinny dip because no one was looking. Or steal from Provincetown's restaurants to eat, even as the disease began to eat *her*. I wondered if she'd make friends with the other people staying behind. Maybe they'd do weird shit like sniff glue and make bonfires on clear nights, dance around naked, fuck each other as their bodies fell apart.

I wondered if the radio would keep playing. If she'd put it on when she lay down for the last time, let it be the thing she listened to as she drifted toward death. Or if it would be quiet when she finally went.

Or if it even mattered at all.

I felt a buzz at my side. I flicked on my phone and saw a message, simple text, in the short blocks of words Katherine uses when she's being serious about something: Call after you land.

I stared down at the screen for a moment. Then the picture in my head began to change. Katherine wasn't wallowing in all that silence by herself, or even with the crazies. She was still rotting, the message didn't change that, but now she lay curled in the grass with the phone by her head. And even though her eyes were crusted shut in pain, even as mold grew on the edges of her lips, she was still smiling.

She could talk to me as she was going. We wouldn't do a vid chat, she wouldn't put me through that, but we could be together in our minds for a while, at least. When she could no longer speak, I could talk in her place, talk and talk and wonder what she was thinking about.

You are such a tease, I wrote back. There was a little jingle as the message sent. The person in front of me turned around to glare; we weren't supposed to be using our phones until we had reached the correct level of orbit. I wanted to give him the middle finger, but seeing as we were spending the rest of our lives on this ship, I figured I didn't want to make enemies I'd have to see again and again until the day I died.

I wiped a hand across my eyes, then set the phone down and

stared out the window. The walls began to hum. I suppose we lifted off at some point, but I didn't feel it happen. I was too deep inside my own head. Beyond the window, blue changed to black, not the ink-black of the bottom of the ocean, a place of fullness and crushing gravity, but a charcoal black, like an old hearth. An empty hearth.

A silent hearth.

DYLAN REYNOLDS lives with his family aboard the Massachusetts III, having been evacuated from the Cape area in which he was raised. He is currently employed as an engineer-in-training in the ship's Upkeep Division, and on his hours off, writes pieces for the many memoir-based journals that have cropped up within the ship network publications. Dylan wishes to dedicate this essay to girlfriend Katherine Soffietti, and to the others who chose to remain on Earth, despite the medical risks.

NICOLE TANQUARY is a student in Upstate New York working on a degree toward Writing and Rhetoric, Geoscience, and Studio Art, respectively. As a writer, she enjoys working with the 'speculative' genres; she has been known, however, to venture into unknown territories for the sake of a good story. She has had pieces published by a menagerie of venues, including *Something Wicked*, *The Colored Lens*, *Isotropic Fiction*, *The Again*, *Kzine*, Alban Lake Publishing, *Wicked Words Quarterly*, and, most recently, *Plasma Frequency Magazine*. She is employed as both a writing tutor and a research assistant within the Geoscience department at her institution, and in her spare time, likes to stay inside her head (which, fortunately, is an interesting place to be).

ART BY **Errow Collins**

ERROW is a comic artist and illustrator currently near Seattle. She focuses on narrative work themed around worlds not quite like our own. She spends her time working with her partner on *The Kinsey House* webcomic and developing her solo webcomic when she's not playing tag with her bear of a cat. More of her work can be found at errow.cardbonmade.com.

WINTER IN MY BONES

Handwritten message discovered in a bottle signed by Frank Hope,

AS PROVIDED BY SYLVIA HEIKE

When you get old, you know things. I know what the gnawing cold in my bones is telling me. I know the white on my fishing boots on the patio will melt upon touch. I know winter doesn't come in July.

I turn on my TV and discover that finally, they know it too.

The meteorologist of World News wears a padded jacket and a smile that never reaches his eyes. Behind him looms Niagara Falls, frozen over since yesterday.

When the car horn blares outside, I already know what it's about. That's the kind of people the Weavers, who have a cabin five miles east, are, although I half-wish they hadn't wasted their petrol or their time.

My dog, Sammy, jumps against the front door and whines. We don't get many visitors, and it's never good news when we do. Sammy doesn't remember bad news.

I pull on a thick jacket, grab Sammy's leash, and step outside. The trees are green, but I can smell the change of season.

"Frank!" Paul Weaver slams the door of his van, leaving the

engine running. "You seen the news? We're heading to the city. You should come with us."

I shake my head at Paul.

His jaw drops, then tightens. "You can't stay out here on your own. We have to go. Now."

"I'm not leaving my home."

His wife, Mary, rolls down a window on the passenger's side. She tells us to hurry. Paul flails his padded arms in the air, arguing with my decision.

Let him think I'm a stubborn old fool. Truth is, I know better than to fight the end of the world. I'd rather someone younger got my place. Few are going to make it.

Sammy whimpers at my feet. My eyes shift from Sammy to Paul. I must convince Paul to take him. I offer the leash to Paul. "He'll protect you."

After a short, one-sided argument about who should go in the car, Paul agrees.

Sammy doesn't want to go, but I order him to jump into the back of the van. The door shuts behind him. I wave after the van as it pulls off.

I should be grateful. Sammy deserves a chance.

I go back inside. On TV, people are ice skating along the Thames. People who don't have a clue. On other channels, it's all about estimates: how long and how bad. The thermometer on the wall tells me they are all guilty of optimism or simply lying. I turn off the TV.

Good. I won't have to miss Sammy for long. But I hope the Weavers make it to the city in time.

I sit in the darkness, the silence broken by the ticking of my great-great-grandfather's clock. I pick up my wedding photo. Eight years. That's how long ago I lost her, but somehow I'm still here. Someone had to look after Sammy.

I swallow, but the lump in my throat won't go. I need fresh air.

I walk down the path from my house to the seaside. I start a fire and sit in my fishing chair. The sea looks peaceful and as blue as I have ever seen it. It's not really the end of the *world*, is it? The sea, the skies, the mountains—all the great things will persevere. It's only us small things that struggle with letting go.

Large snowflakes land on my cheeks. They melt, drizzle down my face like tears. I refuse to give them company. I close my eyes, for just a minute.

When I wake up, a wet nose nuzzles against my neck.

"Sammy!" My breath hangs white in the air. The fire has died.

Sammy's tail is wagging like crazy. The leash hangs down on the snowy ground, trailing after him.

"You silly fool. How did you make it back here?" I wrap my arms around him, hot tears stinging my eyes.

With him back, this is going to be harder. I feel a panic rise inside me. Should I return indoors, start boarding up windows, build a fire in my living room?

Stop. That's the old me talking. The one who wouldn't accept things.

There's hardly any food left, no petrol. With the Weavers gone, no one will come for us.

While I slept, the sea has frozen over. Waves stand at their highest peak, sculpted, never to fall back into the sea again. The temperature keeps dropping.

Soon.

I stand up and grab Sammy's leash. He looks up at me, eyes full of trust. *A lot harder.*

The snow keeps falling. Everything is turning white, all becoming one.

"Let's go for a walk." I climb over the barrier of frozen waves. Sammy follows me, eager but shivering. Our walks always were where he was his happiest.

Out here, I have nothing, the least of all hope. But I have Sammy, and that is everything.

We tread through the white with snow on our shoulders; we walk until we too will reach our peak.

When you get old, you know things. I know what I left behind is not winter, just as I know beyond the sea it won't be summer.

A figure waves at me. Her dress flutters in the warm breeze, waves crashing softly and obediently at her feet.

I emerge from the ocean with Sammy, leaving behind the snowy shackles around my ankles, leaving behind the winter in my bones.

Little is known about the sender of the mysterious note that was discovered in a bottle in the ocean after the world thawed. **FRANK HOPE** was a retired school teacher who is believed to have died during the early onset of the Great Winter. It is unclear how he managed to recount the events of his last day in such detail if it all happened as he claims. The fine beach sand accompanying his message is perplexing historians, as is the stick-figure drawing scribbled on the other side: a man, woman, and a dog smiling on a sunny beach.

SYLVIA HEIKE lives in Finland. She writes short fiction, poetry, and is working on her first novel. Her work has been published in *Flash Fiction Magazine, Mad Scientist Journal, SpeckLit*, and other publications. When not writing, she enjoys hare spotting in her garden and long walks in the forest. Find out more at www.sylviaheike.com or follow her on Twitter @sylviaheike.

HAPPY AT THE END
An account by Happy El-Bayoumi,
AS PROVIDED BY MATTHEW R. DAVIS

We had a list of places we could go and things we could do for the last night, but ultimately my best friend Stephen and I decided to go to Bellamy Park to watch the end of the world. To be accurate, it was my decision, but as always, he was happy to follow me wherever I went. We crossed the grass and made our way through the playground until we reached a wooden fort that dangled knotted ropes from one side and poked a slippery dip out from the other like a smooth steel tongue. I climbed up first, holding Stephen's cane and helping him to follow, and then we sat on the edge and let our legs dangle over the woodchips two metres below as we stared up at the Object burning ever larger in the night sky. He was maudlin and I, as ever, was Happy.

"What a bitch, huh?" Stephen said eventually. "I was going to ace my final exams, go to uni, be the hot new brain on campus."

"I was going to finish my novel and be the literary sensation of the decade. I was going to visit Egypt and see where my parents grew up. I was going to learn the theremin!"

"I was going to get laid."

"You really weren't."

He nudged me with an elbow. "Shut up, girl. It could have happened."

"I, on the other hand, was going to get *so* laid. I was going to have actors and rock stars and models... I was even going to have a bisexual phase."

Stephen stared at me, and I could almost see the images he was conjuring up reflected in his eyes. We'd been best mates for five years, and I think he'd been a little bit in love with me the whole time—and since we'd happened to meet during the throes of puberty, there'd always been a hint of frustrated lust that he tended to express through jokes that weren't really jokes at all.

"You and other women? That's it, Happy. We are *cancelling the apocalypse*! If I save the world, will you let me watch?"

I laughed and gave his arm a playful slap. "Men! Even at the end of the world, that's all you can think about."

"What do you expect? I've got less than seventeen hours to lose my virginity before an object twenty kilometres across hits me in the face."

An object just didn't do its scale justice. *The* Object was what they were calling it, or the Doombringer, or the Morningstar, or Big Scary. Some people thought it was Jesus returning to Earth, some people thought it was the furious judgement of Allah, and here Stephen seemed to think it was the Cockblocker From Outer Space, sent by the universe itself to stop him ever getting his end wet. I just thought of it as The End.

"You know what really gets me?" he asked. "It's out there in the vacuum of space, hours from entering our atmosphere, but it's *burning*. How is that even possible?"

I shrugged and pulled my handbag onto my lap, fished out a pack of Peter Stuyvesants. "Speaking of burning. You want one?"

Stephen threw his hands up in acquiescence. "Sure. I mean, it's not going to kill me."

I pulled my eyes down from The End and stared out at Bellamy Park as I smoked, running one hand through my short mop of black hair. I could remember how it felt to have a river of the stuff flowing down my back, so long I could sit on it. Being here, I was remembering a lot of things.

"So what *is* going to kill us, exactly?" I asked.

"Hard to say. They reckon it's going to hit here in Australia, so if we're lucky, we'll be instantly killed on impact. If not, we'll be burned to death by radiation when ejecta re-enters the atmosphere, or choked on displaced earth, or, if we last long enough, we might freeze when the sunlight's blocked out."

I tried to put on a brave face. "You're such a Gloomy Gus. No wonder you're not getting any."

"The closest comparison we have is the K-T extinction event that wiped out the dinosaurs. That asteroid was half the size of the Doombringer, and it made a crater one hundred and eighty kilometres across. Its impact was equivalent to over a billion atomic bombs. A *billion*, Happy. Yeah, I *am* a little gloomy, because we are totally *fucked*."

We smoked in silence for a while after that. I pulled my legs up and hugged them to my chest, thinking, *in case of atomic blast, duck and cover!* The thought made me smile, but I wouldn't want to have seen what that smile looked like. I couldn't let the darkness swallow me, not when it was due soon enough. There were too many people out tonight who had let the desperation of our plight crush them; I could hear them off in the distance, screaming, sobbing, blaring music bitterly up at the night. Grudges would be settled tonight, desires gratified against another's will, one last outpouring of bile and resentment and outrage before fate rendered all actions null and void. But we had a quiet place here, a silent trust, and what little time was left should be used to speak of better things.

"You know why I wanted to come to this place, instead of all the other ideas we had?"

Stephen turned to his head to watch me, shook it gently from side to side.

"Ten years ago, I had a party here. We used to go to the beach a lot for birthdays and stuff, because Dad's always been keen on the water—our last name means "of the sea"—but I wanted to come here, because I wanted to have this playground to run around in. Heaps of my school friends came, and folks my parents knew from the diaspora, and we had basbousa and baklava, and I ate so many sweets I must have been running around on a sugar high all afternoon. I'll always remember pausing late in the day, as the sun was starting to fade, standing right here on this fort and looking out over *my* party— my friends laughing and chasing each other, Mum and Dad having a great time together, lifting me up into their arms every time I came near to kiss me in joy—and I remember feeling like a princess, like a queen. Like my namesake. Like the whole world was mine, all of its wonders laid out before me, and my life was going to go on forever and it was going to be *amazing*."

Stephen flicked his cigarette into the woodchips below and regarded me with a solemn sympathy that aged him. For a moment I could see him as a grown man, stronger and more handsome than he would ever realise—enough so to make a cane-assisted limp look distinguished and not awkward—and a pang of regret bit at my heart.

"I'm so sorry. It's been a big day, what with it being the last one we'll see and all, and I totally forgot." Stephen surprised me by leaning over and planting a soft kiss on my cheek, just an inch from my lips. "Happy birthday, Hatshepsut El-Bayoumi."

My proper name sounded weird coming from his mouth, as he almost never used it, and neither did I. My sister got lucky with Hypatia, but despite the inspirational origin of my name, I always felt uncomfortable with its awkward clutch of tongue-twisting syllables. I'd been called Hattie for short as a child, but when I started school a few people misheard, and I'd been Happy ever since. I parted my lips to say thanks, but then Stephen kissed me again, and this time it was right on the mouth, and it lingered. Startled, I stared at him with no idea what I might say.

"Maybe your life isn't going to go on forever, but it *is* amazing. *You* are amazing. And I didn't want the world to end without telling you that."

Stephen pulled his face away and returned to his earlier position, staring at the ground below his dangling feet. He looked like he was expecting to catch a bollocking for his presumptuousness. It was kind of sweet. So like him, really.

"Thanks," I said, my voice soft. "That won't stop Armageddon, but it does actually make me feel a little better."

He looked at me, smiled. "You're very welcome."

I took his hand. Though the night was cool, his fingers were warm and a little moist to the touch, and I was flattered to think that the heat in him might be because of me. I shuffled closer until our hips were touching, then reached into my handbag and pulled out my phone.

"Say cheesy," I said as I held the glowing screen out as far as I could, and Stephen complied as I thumbed the red button. There was just enough illumination from the park's light posts and the moon above that the photo turned out okay. A little gloomy, which was appropriate, but it caught us looking very much like ourselves.

"I'm going to send this to everyone I know," I declared, and set about doing just that.

"This is something I won't miss," Stephen grumbled. "Everywhere you look, people pointing phones at themselves, Snapchatting every instant as if it's going down in the history books as a momentous occasion."

"But that's exactly why I'm sending this," I told him. "This *is* a momentous occasion. You and me, together on the last night of our lives. I want everyone to see this, to know us, to remember."

"For all of sixteen hours, anyway."

"But you don't get it. The world is saturated with information, right, shitloads of it all bouncing around the globe and off satellites up *there*. A lot of those signals are travelling out through space. Eventually, perhaps, they'll be received by something. And perhaps this picture will be one of them, and we'll be seen, and we'll be *remembered*—light years away, on worlds we've never even dreamed of."

Stephen blinked, gave a quizzical smile. "You're group-messaging a selfie just in case aliens see it. You're mental."

"Pretty frickin' cool idea, though, isn't it?"

"Oh, yeah." He grinned, squeezed my hand. "That's one thing I… like about you, Happy. You think big. The other thing is that you're completely insane."

I pulled a bonkers face, poking my tongue out at him, and for a moment I thought he was going to touch it with his own. Instead, he gave me a smile with a hint of sadness to it and stared up at the Object. I found that I missed his eyes when they weren't on me. They were as warm and welcome as his hands. Now… *there* was an interesting thought.

"So… it's my birthday. I'm eighteen. No longer a girl, but a woman."

"Technically."

"Shut up. So how should a woman celebrate her coming of age?"

Stephen thought about it for a moment. "Ah! By getting drunk."

"Yes, that too," I said, wondering if he was really as smart as he seemed. "Actually, now that you mention it…"

I'd brought my big handbag out tonight, the coffee-coloured one that didn't go well with my tight black jeans and baggy grunge sweater, and it was only so I could carry what I now produced with a flourish: a bottle of Auld Stag Scotch from my father's rarely-touched liquor cabinet.

"Ah!" Stephen sighed. "Happy, you totally rock."

"I know, but it's always nice to hear someone else say it. So, we've got booze. How else can we celebrate my birthday, our last night on Earth?"

He shrugged, all out of ideas—at least, ones he felt confident saying aloud. On this of all nights, he was the same old sweet loser.

"Oh, you're hopeless, Stephen Swanton! You're going to die a virgin if you keep this up."

I twisted off the cap and poured a small measure into it, excited by the way his wide eyes stayed on me the whole time, the way his jaw dropped in speechless awe. Then I handed him the shot, pleased to see that his hand was less than steady.

"Okay then, a toast." I hefted the bottle in one hand, flipped a middle finger at the sky with the other. "Happy birthday to me, and *fuck you!*"

Stephen repeated the toast with a defiant grin that turned to a grimace as he tried to keep the Scotch down. I patted him on the back and wiped tears from my own eyes, unused to the heavy stuff. But already I could feel a welcome warmth spreading through my gullet, and thoughts of what the night was bound to bring began sparking blazes elsewhere in my body. I'd never really thought it would come to this, but we were living in abruptly curtailed times, and we needed to make the most of what treasures we had.

We nailed another couple of shots before pausing for a cigarette break. The Scotch must have loosened Stephen up a little, because his eyes rarely left my face—and when they did, it was only to wander downward over various curves and junctures of my body. I smiled, encouraged him, and I guess he finally managed to get past his own insecurity, because as soon as our smokes were finished he was on me, laying me gently down on the fort's wooden platform with his lips on mine and one hand inside my baggy sweater.

His kisses strayed down to my neck, and as I stroked his hair I stared up over his shoulder at the night sky. The moon watched over us like a discreet and knowing eye, ever a woman's friend, while The End stood close enough to pair it like a squinting twin, glowing red like a case of galactic conjunctivitis. It was visibly larger than when we'd arrived in Bellamy Park, half an hour closer to devastating the planet, and I wondered what it would look like in broad daylight as it screamed through the lower atmosphere toward me like a falling country. I closed my eyes and imagined what might be going the other way, invisible streams of information shooting off into space like fleas leaving a dying dog, broken bits of crappy TV shows and snatches of iPhone conversations and clutches of emails offering penis enlargements or Nigerian wealth, and just maybe there was a single image amongst all that digital noise that had more to say than any of the detritus around it, and maybe one day that message would be received and understood: once there was a world, and on it was a girl, and that girl was Happy.

HAPPY EL-BAYOUMI is an aspiring young writer born in Cairo who now lives in South Australia. Her favourite things include Passion Pit, Margaret Atwood, Peter Stuyvesant cigarettes, trashy TV shows, and sweets. She won a statewide short story competition at the age of fifteen and is currently at work on her first novel, a Millennial murder mystery with elements of fantasy. She lives with her parents, a sister whose name she wishes she had instead, and a spaniel called The Dog With No Name (or Tidwin for short).

MATTHEW R. DAVIS is an author and musician based in Adelaide, South Australia. He's had two dozen stories and poems of a dark persuasion picked up for publication around the world, is preparing a novel manuscript for submission whilst writing another one, and is the bassist and backing vocalist for alt/prog/metal band icecocoon (amongst other projects). Find out more at matthewrdavisfiction. wordpress.com.

THE ADVENTURES OF ZOMBIEGIRL

An account by Latisha James,

AS PROVIDED BY GARRETT CROKER

With my earbuds in, I could only just hear the knocking sound outside my room, slow and experimental. I did not register the knocks at first, focused on an old video of the President's Address. But when they started coming faster, I couldn't help it. My eyes darted to the shuttered window. I paused the video and pulled my buds out. Without the recording in my ears, I realized my mistake, sighed, and turned to the door. I would just have to finish watching later. I had memorized the whole thing years ago, anyway, all about the length of the battle ahead and triumph in our history's bleakest hours and the need for hope to survive against the corpses, about all the good people of the world living together. I still wore my "Living Together" T-shirt, those words emblazoned across the front with a cheap and badly peeled iron-on. It was silly, but all of it still gave me hope. The speeches, the T-shirts, the slogans and jingles. However misguided. All of it.

Cassie and Paul rushed into my room before I even had a chance to let them in.

"Auntie Tisha! Auntie Tisha! Is it time yet?" I don't think anyone ever explained how twins learn to say the exact same thing at the exact same time so often. It rankled Paul whenever it happened.

"I told you to stop copying me," he spat, pushing his sister. She pushed him back harder and stuck her tongue out.

I reached for my buds and yawned, finger poised to switch them into SI mode. Sound Integration is a music composition app that uses the surrounding noise to create music. It's noise cancellation's rebellious twin sister. I don't do noise cancellation because the silence creeps me out. With SI on, I can ignore anything just as effectively. With the tap of my finger, the kids' voices would be broken down into their composite notes and rhythms and rearranged into what was hopefully a listenable composition. Most of the time, amazingly, it would be; I had a whole backup filled with saved music. The twins snapped to attention as soon as it was obvious I was actually prepared to do this. They stared at me, united again, a question in their eyes. It was supermarket day. They'd been stuck inside for most of the week and were willing to do just about anything—even cooperate! even grocery shop!—just to get out of the house.

I put the buds back down slowly and looked over to the outdoor thermometer. 44 degrees at 8:30 p.m. It had been an unseasonably warm summer, and it was not cold enough yet to go outside. The corpses out there wouldn't be proper popsicles yet. But it was getting close.

"Not yet, but I think it'll be okay in a half hour. Go help your mom with the dishes, and I'll start getting the travel packs ready." They practically skipped away.

The twins belonged to Rhea, the other American in the house. She'd been a stay-at-home mom before all of this, and that had not changed after. I don't know how she made it through those early years carting around two toddlers from zone to zone, never knowing what had happened to their father when he stopped coming home from his new job as an aid worker. It was Rhea who got me into the house, already full between Hitomi, Maxi, Themba, herself, and the kids. With a biologist, a novelist, and a chemist all together under one roof, leave it up to the stay-at-home mom to figure out how to make the food fit into one more mouth without anybody going hungry.

I would do anything for Rhea and her kids. I never wanted kids of my own. I used to be a firefighter. I loved that job, and I told myself it wouldn't be fair to have kids as long as my work could mean my life. There weren't that many fires to fight once I landed on my feet in the cold zone, but it turned out I still didn't want kids. Having a six-year-old "niece" and a "nephew" was nice, though.

It wasn't a minute after the door closed behind them that I heard another knock. I swung around my desk and grabbed for the door. "Give me a break, you brats. I said a half-hour. Now go—" The twins weren't at the door. Of course. I heard the knock again, clearly coming from behind me. I closed and locked the door, walked over to the window, and pushed the button to open the shutters. They slid open with a light electric sound. They can make shutters that don't make those sounds, but studies have found people don't it like when things don't make any noise. The clammy dead fist came down against the reinforced glass again.

Sometimes you see corpses that used to be people you knew. It seems improbable. A whole world of corpses. Seven continents. Pretty much the whole living population migrated to the hot and cold zones. But there they are. The former prom queen from your Hollywood high school who happened to be visiting family in Alaska when she died, preserved in her youth by the cold. Watching her stumble around, you chuckle that she's no less dim-witted than before. But that's just a prom queen joke. Stacy was salutatorian of your class. Then one day you see the old co-worker who took two weeks off every summer, right when work was busiest, right when he was needed most, barely recognizable beneath the heat-rot. How he made it so many miles after dying just to find you, you'll never know. But you'll always recognize his douchebag yin yang neck tattoo, even with bits of neck falling off around it. You look at where his nose used to be and call it an improvement. He doesn't respond. They never speak or grunt or anything. They don't make any noise that they don't have to. You drive the point of a shattered baseball bat through his skull and walk away.

After the third or fourth time it happened, I learned how to think of them as corpses. I've heard it called the Funeral Effect. If you've ever been to an open-casket service, you know the feeling. The disbelief that a person from your life is really gone. The feeling that at any minute they're going to pop out of that casket and have a laugh over what a great prank that whole pretending to be dead thing was. How did you make it seem like your heart really stopped for all that time? How did you fake that gunshot wound? They would have a perfectly reasonable answer for every question. But then you see the body, and all of your uncertainty is lost. There's just not a living person in that body. That is a bona fide corpse.

Only, it takes a little longer for that reality to click when the bodies actually do pop up out of their caskets and walk around.

There's a lot that we don't understand about them. They don't make any kind of scientific sense. I looked at the one in the window. When he looked at me, his whole head moved, like a raptor, because they never move their eyes. I had a theory once that fine muscle function was lost in the dead, that controlling the eyes or speaking took too much motor control for their decaying nervous systems. But I've also seen their fingers dancing in the chest cavities of their victims, like Mozart on a good day. I've watched them take the careful, precise steps they need to navigate complex obstacles without making a sound. Hell, I've seen a corpse's arm, elbow stripped to the bone, bend with the speed, assurance, and strength of an athlete. They can do the most remarkable things with their frayed bodies, yet they don't move their eyes when they want to look at you.

This one was a textbook popsicle. It was probably made here in the cold, had never decayed badly. Its skin was burned a little bit blue, every feature sunken in a little bit too far. It couldn't have been more than 25 years old. Handsome. Black. Not particularly athletic. It had small depressions on the ridge of its nose where it might have worn glasses for most of its life. It could have been my little brother, once. He wanted to be a firefighter, too. He liked to play the drums. Its fist connected with the glass again.

I flipped the shutters closed, enjoying that light electric sound, turned my buds to SI and threw them in my ears, and started putting myself together. The buds began to weave the slow pounding into an elegiac percussive masterpiece. I imagined Tommy with his drumsticks, playing along.

I grabbed a couple of layers, a thermal, a heat jacket, gloves, and snow pants, and switched out of my T-shirt and shorts. I opened up my travel pack and double-checked the contents. A flashlight, a whistle, a set of emergency buds and rations, a hot water bottle, a first aid kit, and a long hunting knife. I glanced over at the thermometer, which showed 39 degrees, and got the kids' packs ready. "Save composition," I said, and switched my buds off.

"Cassie!" I called out. "Where are your buds?" Hitomi walked by on the way to the bathroom and smiled at me, a polite, pleasant smile. She was wearing a T-shirt covered in Japanese characters, but she would never tell me what they meant. "It is like your shirt," she would say in her precise English. "Only not as clever."

I could hear the jangle of Rhea's oversized purse followed by the rush of small feet attached to small legs. The twins were at the door in seconds, grinning, each with one hand in a pocket clutching the cash I knew Rhea had given them.

"Auntie Tisha, Mommy says we can get candy at the store," Paul said. "I'm going to get two chocolate bars!"

"No you are not," Cassie said, literally putting her foot down.

"Mommy said we could each get one candy."

"And she gave us each enough for two. I can get two candies and give one to Auntie Tisha."

"Then I'm going to get two candies and give one to Mommy."

"Copycat."

"Am not."

"Are too."

"Neither one of you are going to get anything unless we find Cassie's buds," I cut in, and they stopped fighting immediately. I'd like to say the kids were obnoxious when they started fighting, but it was always so easy to get them working together again. I thought about how much had to be lost to get the world working together like that, and I loved those kids for stepping in line over a pair of earbuds we could replace for $20 if we had to.

I went about overturning couch cushions and thought about what it meant, "Living Together." It's not that the world did not come together. We did. It's not even that we did it too late. Here we are, surviving. But coming together isn't what saved us. The hot and cold zones saved us, because of what they do to corpse bodies. A digital network that was too strong and well-integrated for something as small as a global apocalypse to knock it out saved us. Coming together was only a consequence.

What's strange is how little that fact seems to bother any of us. I spent two years worrying about worst-case scenarios. How bad would it have to get before my uterus become salable for the state, belonging not to me but the "species"? How fractured would our loyalties have to become before I had to hitch up with the strongest crew and shoot the heads off of other living, struggling people just to protect the little we had left? I never had to find out. I became a member of a new community, a sister in the new state. It didn't matter that unity had so little to do with our survival. It only mattered that we were united. I don't know if anybody actually saw that coming.

The President gave a speech about that, too. We all feared, he said, that in the face of true horror we would only become the monsters ourselves. But those fears were unfounded. For once in our history, he said, we could see the true monsters, and there was no mistaking them for ourselves. They made T-shirts with that line, too, but I always thought it was too many words to wear around the house.

Reaching under a recliner, I felt the familiar form of a bud. I lifted it to my ear experimentally.

"... nicht interessiert zu sein. Du solltest sie einfach vergessen und hoffen, dass jemand anders…"

I listened a few seconds longer than I should have, trying not to laugh. Maxi can never seem to keep his buds together, and every now and then everyone in the house has had the privilege of finding one of them and getting to listen in on his calls home. I knew enough German to know that this conversation wasn't for me. If Maxi wanted to pine over Rhea and his unrequited love all night, that was none of my business.

"Maxi!" I marched into his room, making sure he could hear me. "If you don't want me to hear you phoning your mom about your love life, stop mixing your buds up with other people's." He looked bewildered underneath his "Ziel für den Kopf" cap, his face bright red and puffed up like a balloon, his responses flip-flopping between English and German, like he always did when he was embarrassed.

Maxi's the only one of us who really uses his buds for phoning, because he's the only one of us who really knows where any of his surviving family is. When it happened, his parents were already at the equator, checking out retirement spots in South America. That, and a lot of good luck, got them through. I envy that good luck. That said, I don't envy hot-zoners in general. I'll take popsicles over flesh soup any day.

I held the bud I found out to him and explained. "One of the buds you're wearing is Cassie's. I'm taking the kids out, so I need you to figure out which one it is and give it to me."

He fumbled with his ears and gave me the bud, mumbling some more Germlish behind me as I called out to the twins. We would have to find her other bud later.

We did our final check before leaving the house, making sure the kids had their whistles around their necks and their buds in one of their security pockets, and then calling the market to check traffic along the routes. Jim let me know routes 3 and 4 had some minor clogs, but route 1 looked clear. We should have a fast trip. I just had one last check to make before we left. I hit the control to open the door, which clicked and creaked artificially, and stepped outside, taking the defense club we kept by the door. I made a quick check close to the house. If one of them was hiding out close to a building, sitting in a warm spot, it could surprise the hell out of you.

The one from my window was limping around the back of the house, but it obviously had cold feet, the slow crunch of its footsteps actually reassuring in the otherwise quiet night. Corpses with cold feet were nothing to worry about. They were too slow and too easy to hear. The coast was clear.

"Let's go," I said, stepping back inside as I hooked the defense club to my belt. "Rhea, it might be cold enough for Themba to get back from the community center tonight. If he gets back while we're out, let him know he can call, and we'll pick up whatever he needs."

Rhea nodded and watched us out.

It was a ten-minute walk to the store on my own, and a few minutes longer with the kids only because they can't walk as fast as I can. There was a mist coming down that stung at my nose and my eyes, not quite snow yet. No matter how long I spent in the cold, no matter how accustomed I got to the snow and the wind, rain always makes me feel coldest. We didn't get snow back in LA, so a cold night for my brother and me always meant rain. When it rained, we wrapped ourselves in blankets in front of the fireplace and bickered about things. Those kinds of memories don't leave a body easily.

I told the kids to be quiet and watch out for any corpses that were hiding in the warm spots outside of houses. A few with cold feet straggled along the side of the path, their heads turning in our direction, their feet crunching along the path as we passed them. We would have to take a different route home. Over my shoulder, I could see the one from my window following us.

"Auntie Tisha," Cassie said, walking close to me. "Were you watching cartoons online before?"

I reached down and patted her head. "I was watching the President's old speeches."

"Why?"

"Because they're important, and I like them."

"Bo-ring," Paul chimed in. "He's not even alive anymore."

"Can we watch cartoons on your computer when we get back?" Cassie asked, ignoring her brother for once.

"Is the TV broken again?"

"No, I just want to watch on your computer."

I looked down at Cassie and followed her little eyes from corpse to corpse. It wasn't fair. All she wants to do all the time is get out of the house, and when she does the world is so frightening she wants to get back inside as soon as possible. I talked to her once about them. I'd never talked to a child about them before. Adults all have theories about how they work or how to get rid of them or why God let this happen to us, and I realized a long time ago that that's just what adults do when we're afraid. We rationalize. When I was a kid, all the monsters under my bed were in my imagination. When I got older, I could rationalize them away. For Cassie and Paul, the monsters were real. She told me that every corpse she sees looks like her daddy, even the girl ones. I don't talk to kids about them anymore.

"Okay," I said, still patting her head. "We'll watch cartoons when we get back."

There were a lot of them out, crunching around. I knew the clean-up teams would be out in a few hours to bludgeon and dispose of as many as they could before sunrise, but it never seemed to matter. There were always more. I'd tried to do the math once, but I screwed something up. I ended up figuring that there were more than twice as many corpses as there had even been people alive when it started. It wasn't possible, but when I saw nights like tonight, I thought that maybe it wasn't so far off after all. Where did they all come from? There were too many out here with us.

"Last one to the store is a rotten egg," I said, and the kids were off.

I was breathless with the cold air when we got there, Cassie celebrating. "I won! I won! Paul's a stinky egg! Paul's a stinky egg." I smiled and winked at Paul before taking off my glove. Paul was a much better runner than Cassie was. The crunching sound was persistent behind us.

I pressed my hand against the heat-reactive pad, the door slid open with a hiss, and we rushed inside. The warmth of the room bloomed over us, a pleasure we all shared. After a moment, I shooed the kids away to the candy aisle and went about my business.

"Jim," I said to the clerk, "Can you hold a standard essentials kit at the register for me? I'm going to browse for non-esses. Oh, and route 1's practically flooded. Who told you it was clear? You've never sent me through so many."

"I didn't say they weren't out there," Jim said defensively. "I said the route was clear. It's like that everywhere tonight. Can't be helped. Got here safe, didn't you?"

"Just get the ess-kit together, will you?"

I was in a weird mood after getting to the store. I try not to linger too much on the past, because it doesn't do any good, but I was really missing the way things used to be. In the old world, Cassie would be afraid of the dark, not the warmth of the sun. In the old world, Tommy was preparing for his firefighter's exam, and I was making breakfast at the firehouse every morning while talking to the guys about his chances. I only made pancakes until the Chief got up early one morning to teach me to make crepes. Walking around the warm store, I found enough flour, eggs, milk, and butter to manage an old firehouse breakfast for the house. Just looking at the basket filled with ingredients made me happy. The real trick was going to be the fillings. I needed fruits for the adults and chocolate for the kids. The chocolate would be easy. The fruit would also be easy if I wasn't too picky about it. I was.

The twins found me in produce, sorting through boxes of strawberries.

"Auntie Tisha," Paul said, his hands behind his back. "Can Cassie and I get something extra please?" He was being extra polite and practically hopped when I didn't even wait before saying yes. He whipped out the comic book he had been holding behind his back and waved it around. I had to hold his arm in place just to see what it was, though I should have guessed. Paul loved the Zombieman comics. He'd dressed up as Zombieman for Halloween two years in a row.

"And what do you want, Cass?" I asked.

Cassie dug her toe into the ground and looked down, away from my eyes. "I don't want anything extra today," she said quietly.

I squatted down to her level before speaking in my warmest tones. "Now, I just don't believe that for a second, so why don't you tell me?"

She pouted. "Paul said it was stupid."

I shot Paul the kind of look I'd seen Rhea perfect years ago, and he cracked.

"She's such a copycat! She only wants a Zombiegirl comic because I'm getting a Zombieman comic. She can never just do anything on her own."

"Well, I don't think it's stupid," I said, and then conspiratorially: "And Zombiegirl is better than Zombieman, anyway. Let's go get that comic." She ran top speed to the aisle and back to shove the comic in my basket.

The twins paid for their candy at the register and then hopped around at the back exit to wait until I was ready to leave. I handed the basket over to Jim and he checked through it.

"Alright, Tish. That'll be $35.12 for the non-essentials. Want to know what routes are clear for the trip back?" As he finished speaking, I heard the back door slide open and the wind cascade in. A storm had started up while we were shopping, and the temp had dropped far enough for snow to land without melting. The cold cut into the heat of the store like a machete. I was about to respond to Jim when I heard the whistle.

"Shit." I snapped my attention to the door. The corpse that had been following us from the house was filling the doorway and I couldn't see Cassie. Paul was backing away, blowing his whistle like a madman. I was across the store in four steps, defense club unhooked from my side. The corpse was slow, but they were always dangerous in close quarters. I pushed Paul out of the way and shoved the club into its body like a battering ram. I hit it again. And again. And again. Each time pushing it back outside a little more. It grabbed at the club. I knocked it in the face to disorient it. It screamed.

I almost couldn't move. I had never heard one scream before, had assumed they couldn't. It was awful. It sounded like all the agony of death itself. I hit it again just to stop the noise, and it was out of the doorway. I slammed my hand on the door controls and shut it outside. I was shaking. I couldn't think clearly.

I spun around, screaming. "What the hell happened? Paul, did you open the door?" He was sobbing. "Did you open it? Did you? Did Cassie open it? What happened? Tell me!"

"We didn't," he choked out. "We know better. We didn't. It wasn't us. The door opened. It was there. Cassie got pushed outside."

I spun again. I wasn't thinking. I was all adrenaline. I was angry.

"How the fuck could a popsicle open your door, Jim? I'm going to have the cops look at your inspection records when this is over. If your heat pad is on the fritz, you won't have to worry about corpses. *I'm going to eat you alive.* How the fuck does this happ—" I stopped, and spun back to Paul. "Cassie's outside?"

He nodded.

"Shit." I fitted a bud into my ears. "Cass, do you hear me?" No response. "Cass? Cass, if you can hear me, stay by the store. I'm coming."

I'd been running on instinct and energy since I heard the first whistle. Now my emergency training really kicked in. I broke the glass on the e-kit on the wall with my elbow and grabbed the axe, then turned back to the register. "Jim, I'm sorry. I need you to call the cops. Let them know what happened. Report a little girl missing in the storm. Six years old. Brown hair. Four-feet tall. Responds to Cassie and Cass. Now. Paul, stay here. Try to get your sister on the buds. If she answers, tell her to stay close to the store and wait for me. Tell her she needs to whistle so I can find her. You can do that. She's going to be okay. I'm going out there."

I slammed my hand back on the door control and was face to face with the corpse. I don't know how I could have thought it looked like Tommy. It took a step toward me and I buried the point of the axe in his forehead. I pulled it out and stepped outside. That wouldn't be the only one.

I couldn't call for Cassie in that wind, so I blew my whistle, listening for five seconds between blows for the response. None came. If Cassie could hear it, she should have responded. The corpses would hear it, too. I could see them taking their first lumbering steps in my direction. She was nowhere to be seen. I told my buds to call up Maxi.

"Hallo, Tish," he said after half a ring.

"Maxi, grab the e-kits and get the house outside. There was an accident. Cassie's in the storm alone. We can't find her. We called the police. We're out on route 3 from the back of the store. Hurry." It didn't take any more explanation than that.

As soon as Maxi hung up, my bud clicked and Paul's voice came through.

"Auntie Tisha, she won't answer. I tried and I tried and she won't answer. What should I do?"

"Keep trying, Paul. We'll find her. Stay with Jim and keep trying."

I turned in circles, looking at each of the lumbering shadows in the snowstorm. One of them had to be Cassie. One of them had to be shorter than the rest. I turned and I turned, and some of them got closer, one step at a time, and some of them stayed where they were, but none of them looked like a child. If it had just been freezing for a little bit longer, another hour, they would have been stuck, frozen in place. But the true freeze had only just begun, and they kept moving. None of the shadows were small enough to be her.

Well, if I couldn't find her, I could give her a chance.

I blew my whistle until I was coughing in the cold air just to fill my lungs. Then I blew it again. I blew it until every shadow I could see was paying attention. I blew it until every one of them was walking in my direction. Then, I waited. I didn't bother to count them. The hordes from the old newscasts were a thing of the past, but these were more than enough. The cold was the only reason I stood a chance. It would take them minutes to reach me. If I was lucky and smart, I could pick them off one by one. I examined them carefully as they descended. They were all different sizes. Stocky. Lanky. Short. Fat. Pear shaped. Long-legged. Long-waisted. The one nearest me even had fake breasts. They stood up straighter in the cold than she did. I was going to kill her first.

The axe-point sank into her skull to the handle, and she dropped to the ground. Bits of darkened brain matter oozed out of the remaining hole, but no blood. I saw it then, their death rattle. Her eyes moved back and forth in their sockets so fast it was like they were vibrating.

And then she was gone. When I looked up, the others were almost on me. They shouldn't have been. It was too cold. They were too slow. How did they get to me so fast? It shouldn't be possible.

I careened the axe into the left temple of the first one I saw, the fat one. I waited for it to slide out, but it didn't, and his body weight pulled me down with him. I should have let go of the handle. I should have reached for my defensive club. But I wanted the axe. I wrenched the head to the side and pulled hard, the axe coming free, but one of them had a hold of my arm. I could feel the tightness of the grip, painful even through the layers of cold gear I had on. I lost my grip on the axe. There was a sudden pressure on my shin. One of them was trying to eat through my snow pants. I knew it couldn't get through the fabric, but it could easily break the bone if I let it keep biting.

I reached for my club with my free left hand and found it missing. I panicked, patting at my body, searching for my travel pack. I flipped it open and heard the contents spill out and, somehow, found the hunting knife in the snow. My swings with the knife were wild, desperate. I think most of them missed, but the ones that hit were hard. I sliced against skin and skull and after a few seconds, the pressure against my shin released. At the same time, I heard a terrible crunching sound where my right arm was and then I couldn't see anything. Everything was red. Everything was pain. The short one had broken my right arm. I screamed. I couldn't move. I couldn't see. There was another pair of hands on me. And another. And another. I could feel them squeezing. There was nothing I could do.

I screamed so loudly that I almost didn't even hear the gunshots. One. Two. Three. Four. Five. Six. Reload. Seven. Eight. Nine. Every hand released its grip on me.

He was at my side before I realized who it was, and I only figured out who it was because who else would be asking me over and over again if I were alright in German? Maxi had become a very good shot. He put his hands on my face and wiped away tears I didn't realize I'd shed.

There were other footsteps. I still couldn't open my eyes from the pain. I heard whistles, and the sounds of cops organizing around the perimeter. I hugged my arm to my chest and curled up.

"Did you find her?" I said at the same time another voice said, "Is she safe?" That was Rhea's voice. We'd answered each other's questions. I opened my eyes, and we looked at each other in horror, just making eye contact before she ran inside the store and pulled Paul to her. Maxi stayed with me, thumbs on my cheeks, hands warm from gunfire, wiping tears away.

When we got back home, I saw Jim had special delivered the ess-kit, the comics tucked inside with the rest of the groceries. In the moment, I'd left everything on the counter. The police were still out looking for Cassie. We'd all given statements. Jim was under official investigation for the door malfunction. And a half hour later, we'd done all we could do and were sent away. The authorities would handle it from there. We would just be in the way if we stayed. They set my arm into a cast on-site and then Maxi took me to get some painkillers for the night ahead. I hadn't spoken to Rhea since they found me.

I picked the comics up limply and walked them over to Paul. I didn't know if it was a good idea. I wasn't thinking clearly anymore. He took them from my hand.

"You're just like her," he said, opening the Zombiegirl comic to the first page. Right in the middle of the page there was a panel, bigger than the rest, of Zombiegirl outlined by a doorway, her trademark axe buried in the skull of some faceless corpse. "I wish I was like Zombieman." The comics hung from his hands, and he started shaking without crying. Zombieman doesn't cry.

I lost it. I cried until it felt like my eyes were dry heaving and it hurt to breathe. I couldn't stop. I stood outside Rhea's door and I cried, but I couldn't go in. I lay down in my bed, and I cried until all of my emotions were gone and the only thing left was the husk of my body.

I fell in and out of sleep. I opened my eyes to see Maxi in my doorway. He turned and looked embarrassed when he saw I was awake and walked away like he had something else to do.

I closed my eyes again.

Hitomi woke me up long enough to wash my face and change my pillow. "They still have not found her," she told me. "But they will keep looking." She paused before leaving. "You know that Rhea does not blame you. Not really. You did everything you could."

It was true, and I knew that. Rhea would tell me herself when time had passed. That's how things were in this new world. But it never helped knowing. I fell back asleep.

I woke again when the painkillers started to wear off, and I could not get back to sleep again. There was a small sound coming from somewhere on the bed. I groped around under my pillow and found a bud. Somebody was talking on it. I put it in my ear and heard Paul's voice: "If you come back, I'll share my chocolate with you. I was going to share it with you anyway." I pulled it out of my ear and threw it across the room.

In a fog, I got up and moved over to my desk, opening the computer. The tabs were unchanged. I pressed play on the President's speech and watched, right where I left it.

"We know the battle ahead will be long," his deep, self-assured voice rang out, its cadence perfect. "But always remember that no matter what obstacles stand in our way, nothing can stop the force of millions of good people working together. As our current tragedy has spread, we have all thought that we cannot survive this, and that cynical voice will only grow stronger as time goes on. We have been cynical, and have called it realistic. We have warned each other against being hopeful. But we will not survive without hope. We will not survive against these impossible odds if we tell ourselves that we are not ready, or that we should not try, or that we can't. But the world can survive against these monsters. Generations can put their problems aside, as we have done before during our history's bleakest hours, responding with a simple solution to problems that are no longer local, problems that are shared across the globe. We can prevail, as a world, living together."

As the speech came to an end, I heard another sound. A knocking at the window. Small. Persistent. I didn't look. I put my buds in my ears. I said, "Play last composition," and pressed my forehead hard against the desk.

LATISHA JAMES grew up in Los Angeles with her mother and younger brother. She went to college in San Diego because it was the furthest she could get away without feeling like she'd abandoned them both. Before the world ended, she stayed in San Diego and fought fires. When the world ended, she drove north until there was no north left to drive and started fighting zombies. After the world ended, she found Rhea, Cassie, Paul, Maxi, Hitomi, Themba, and home.

GARRETT CROKER studied writing at UC Berkeley and received his MFA in creative writing from Mills College. He lives and writes in the beautiful, temperate San Francisco Bay Area, which is only a little less beautiful now with all the zombies. Living in a temperate zone is more dangerous for him than is strictly necessary, but, well, it's home. Find out more at www.garrettcroker.com or on twitter at @ garrettcroker.

AN IMPROMPTU GUIDE TO FINDING YOUR SOULMATE AT A PARTY ON THE LAST NIGHT OF THE WORLD

An account by Logan Osborne Lewis,
AS PROVIDED BY CAROLINE M. YOACHIM

The world ends at midnight, seven hours from now. You might wonder why I'd bother writing a guidebook at this point. It's a good question. Basically, I'm lonely. I've run out of avocados, so I can't sit at home drowning my sorrows in a gourmet smoothie. Besides, I like making numbered lists.

This guide is for people who believe that some portion of themselves will continue beyond the cataclysmic destruction of the planet. Could be a soul, a digital copy, sentient mitochondrial DNA—whatever you want to believe, it's all good. The guide is also for people with nothing better to do. Guess which category I fall into? Hint: I like making numbered lists.

1. Create a list of yes-or-no questions.

"Do you like pumpernickel bagels?" (Yes.)

"Do you have any avocados?" (No.)

Don't use those exact questions. Those are my questions. Pick things that are meaningful to you. The important thing is that they must be yes-or-no questions. You don't want to waste four precious minutes listening to someone rambling on and on about the time they squeezed every avocado in the grocery store and none of them were ripe. I mean, who does that? Don't they know they're destroying the produce?

You can't waste time when there are only seven hours left to find your soulmate. Well, six and a half. This guide is taking longer to write than I expected. I probably should have started working on it earlier, like when the aliens first announced our time of death last week.

2. Food questions might not be such a good idea, because in the afterlife, we may not eat. Also, there are a lot of aliens at the parties, and talking about food makes them release weird pheromones. Ask deeper questions:

"Have you ever traveled back in time?" (No.)

"Do you like hats with birds on them?" (No! The hats would fly into the sun!)

"Can I melt your purple snow?" (Duck, duck, tentacles.)

Did I mention that alien pheromones cause confusion and hallucinations? If this happens, step outside to clear your head. Next time come up with questions that make sense.

3. Shouting questions at the whole room will make you sound

desperate and/or crazy, even if the questions are not about food and totally make sense. People will give you strange looks, and they won't respond favorably. Don't ask how I know.

4. If you don't find your soulmate at the first party, and people seem angry about the shouting, find a new party. There are lots of parties on the last night of the world. Your soulmate is at one of them, waiting for you.

5. Don't be shy. Your soulmate might be with someone else at the party, possibly having sex. Sex is a surprisingly popular activity at end of the world parties. Well, maybe it's not all that surprising. Wait for a pause in the action, and then ask your potential soulmate one of your yes-or-no questions.

"Do you —" (Hey! Get out of here!)

6. If you don't find your soulmate at the second party, and people are angry about being interrupted while they attempt to have sex, find a new party. Your soulmate is at one of them. Maybe.

7. Not everyone will appreciate your urgent search for someone with whom to share your last moments on Earth and/or the eternal bliss of the afterlife.

"Do you have any avocados?" (I'll tell you where you can put your avocados.)

"Does your dentist have a robot on his shelf?" (Metal monkeys will eat your brain.)

"Have you ever occupied the body of a reticulated squirrel?" (You're an evil tree!)

8. Remember not to ask about food. Even avocados. At least try to notice when the questions stop making sense.

9. This is a terrible guide. There are only four hours left and I haven't found my soulmate.

10. I don't believe in souls, but I do believe you are out there, at a party somewhere. The aliens will almost certainly kill us all before I find you, and we will never get to share our love of avocados.

The party is swarming with aliens now, fluffy pink quadrupeds that look mostly harmless. They look so silly that it gives me hope that maybe we won't all die after all, and I post my guide, such as it is, on all my social network sites. It gets a surprising amount of attention, given how little time we all have left.

The guide passes from my friends to yours, and you read it.

Across the room, I hear you ask, "Do you have any avocados?"

"Yes!" I run across the room to you. "I lied about running out. I just really wanted to find you. There is still enough time for us to make smoothies! We can jump across the stars and our sentient mitochondrial DNA will swim in the fire of the sun! Wait. Does it smell like pheromones in here to you? We should probably step outside."

Before the aliens invaded, **LOGAN OSBORNE LEWIS** worked as an ecologist for the Climate Action Team. Logan had a backyard avocado tree and enjoyed putting avocados in (1) smoothies, (2) burgers, and (3) numbered lists. If the aliens hadn't invaded, Logan would have made you an avocado smoothie, even if you don't believe in soulmates.

CAROLINE M. YOACHIM lives in Seattle and loves cold, cloudy weather. She is the author of dozens of short stories, appearing in *Lightspeed, Asimov's, Clarkesworld,* and *Daily Science Fiction,* among other places. She likes avocados in burgers or sandwiches, but not in smoothies. For more about Caroline, check out her website at http://carolineyoachim.com.

ART BY Luke Spooner

LUKE SPOONER a.k.a. 'Carrion House' currently lives and works in the South of England. Having recently graduated from the University of Portsmouth with a first class degree, he is now a full time illustrator for just about any project that piques his interest. Despite regular forays into children's books and fairy tales, his true love lies in anything macabre, melancholy, or dark in nature and essence. He believes that the job of putting someone else's words into a visual form, to accompany and support their text, is a massive responsibility as well as being something he truly treasures. You can visit his web site at www.carrionhouse.com.

THE LAST REAL MAN
An account by Dennis Shawn,
AS PROVIDED BY NATHAN CROWDER

I used to look forward to trips down off the mountain and into Kettle Hollow, but things had gotten bad in the past year. Used to enjoy sipping on dewy cans of Olympia with the boys at the Beaver, watching girls going in and out of Maybelle's Salon across the street. But the Beaver had been boarded up since the incident. The boys were all gone, too.

But I had to get supplies somewhere, and Kettle Hollow was just as bad as anywhere else. I could feel the locals keeping an eye on me as I rolled through town. Watching me. Always watching me, like they didn't know what a real man looked like anymore.

It took a while to build up my resolve as I sat in the parking lot of the Shop 'n Sav, puffing away on a Camel filter. Blue Turkish tobacco smoke burned the back of my throat. A worn out Eddie Money cassette whirred away in the truck's tape deck, keeping me company. There were a lot of cars in the lot, mostly hybrids with a handful of white Subaru Outbacks only distinguishable by the bumper-stickers. World Peace. My Kid is an Honor Student. Eat Local. I shuddered at the suggestion. Is that what this world has come to?

Eddie wound down singing about paradise, and I shut off the

engine. I was on a schedule. No point putting this off if I wanted to get home before dark. I flicked what was left of my cigarette out the window of the truck then got out. I tucked my keys down into my jeans pocket, took a deep breath of air scrubbed clean from the recent rain. I missed the diesel haze of the logging trucks, but just like the Beaver, those days were gone.

With a sigh, I sloshed through the Oregon puddles in my eleven-eyelet logging boots, stiff-legging it into the grocery.

I tried to snag one of the baskets off the stack smoothly on the way in, but grabbed two handles by accident. It threw off my gait, tugged me around awkwardly. By the time I laid claim to my basket, I could hear them whispering about me. There were two of them looking at me over the edge of their soy chai lattes at the coffee stand just inside the door. A few more stood over near the peaches mounded at the front of the produce aisle, open stares and sly smiles. The girl with the buzz cut wearing the Decemberists t-shirt stifled a giggle and turned away. My neck and cheeks blazed red.

Eyes down, I took my basket and made a bee line for the canned food. Figured I wouldn't have to deal with as many of them there. Damnation, this used to be a good town. Then they started burrowing their way in. Before I knew what was happening, it was too late and the town had been overrun with the wrong kind of folks. Didn't hardly seem right that I was being made to feel that I didn't belong. Me, who grew up in Kettle Hollow, whose dad taught him how to shoot a rifle at age 14 just over the ridge, who lost his virginity two years later to that slow, yellow-eyed girl behind the gas station just down the street. My parents were buried in these hills. My brothers, too.

When my time came, wouldn't be anyone around to lay my bones to rest.

Damn sure no one who was left in Kettle Hollow was going to do it.

I got to the canned food and realized they had stopped stocking my brand of chili. Reluctantly, I caught the eye of the stock boy, this muscular blonde kid with long eyelashes and broody eyes. I cleared my throat until he was paying attention. My voice caught a bit under his full attention and I hated myself for it, but I had a mission. "Where did you move the Colonel Josh Chili to?"

"We don't carry Colonel Josh Chili anymore. Or hash. Or frozen dinners."

My stomach cinched up. I was afraid it would come to this eventually. "Why?"

"No one was buying it. It wasn't organic. Just full of chemicals. We even got some complaints, so it's gone now."

I swear the son of a bitch was smiling at me. I mumbled an "Oh," and moved on down the aisle. It wasn't the end of the world. I told myself that but wasn't sure if I believed it. I grabbed several cans of beans instead, glad they had those at least. Few tins of beans, a few tins of corn, some tomatoes, hell, I could make my own chili. I could make this work. I was almost feeling cocky until I got back to the meat case to get ground chuck or something.

That was where they all congregated. Must have been a dozen or so of the bastards. Narrow jeans, tight, V-neck tees, scarfs, bright colors and floral prints. They turned toward me all at once, sniffed the air at my approach. Their separate conversations ground to a halt.

I avoided eye contact and shouldered my way through to the case. I felt them pressing in around me, musk heavy in the refrigerated air. Nothing was labeled. Chops, loin, roasts, ground, I couldn't tell at a glance if I was looking at pork or beef or lamb. It was just a field of red meat in little Styrofoam and cling wrap coffins to my left and right. Sweat beaded in my hairline as I was overwhelmed by the choices. I could sense a pack of them massed behind and around me, judging my lack of decisiveness.

"What you looking for, mountain man?" one of them asked. I didn't like how he said it. I didn't like how he put the emphasis on "man." But I swallowed my pride and ignored him, despite the fact that others had taken up the call. "How about some chuck, mountain man!" or "Oh, you're a manly man. Bet you want a whole roast, don't you! A whole roast all for yourself up in that lonely cabin."

I pushed away from them, saw the standing case across the aisle full of chickens and grabbed a whole roaster instead.

"What's the matter?" one of them called after me as I fled toward the checkout. "Big man like you is afraid of us?"

I could hear them howl after me as I escaped, heart racing. I snagged two random boxes of crackers off the shelf on the way past. I didn't care what they were. Anything at this point. Just get me the hell out.

I got to the register and was relieved to find there was no line. The checkout girl didn't look up as she rang me out. Her brown eyes stayed focused on her job through the thick lenses of her fake-vintage horn-rimmed glasses. I swear she was smiling a bit, the too-red lipstick shocking against her pale Northwest skin. What could I do about it? Let her smile. I didn't care. She was one of them, anyway.

I threw my bag of groceries onto the passenger side of my bench seat, fired up the truck, and hit up my last errand. Larry's was still open for a few hours when I pulled up out front. The streets were usually pretty empty around this part of town ever since the incident. I could almost see the Beaver from here, boarded up and silent. It was only a matter of time before Larry's was gone, no matter how much he changed his stock to suit his new customers.

He looked up at me from behind the counter when I came in and I could tell there was bad news. "You know what I'm here for," I told him.

The old man nodded, sadly. "I'm afraid I don't have any to sell you, Dennis."

My heart sank. "You're sold out? Of everything?"

"No thirty cal," he said. "No twenty-two. No thirty-eight. No nine mil, buckshot, or birdshot. Hell. I don't even have empty twelve gauge shells or black powder so you can pack your own."

I was damn near ready to choke on my own tears. "Damnation, Larry. It's my constitutional right."

"I know, Dennis. I know. I'm still selling guns," he motioned to the glass case in front of him like it made a damn bit of difference. "Hell, I'll sell you all the guns you want. But there's no demand for ammunition anymore. No one's buying, so I stopped selling."

"I'm buying," I pleaded. "Please, let me buy."

"I don't have it," he said. His face was hard, impervious to argument. "It's a new world, Dennis. I suggest you get used to it."

"I DON'T WANT TO GET USED TO IT, LARRY!"

Spittle hung from my chin and my face was blazing red with rage. The air was silent but charged between us. Larry, to his credit, hadn't even blinked during my outburst. But the back door from the office opened and one of his salesmen came out, short with a soft face hiding behind a mustache that belonged on a walrus more than a twenty-something hardware store employee.

"Is there a problem, Larry?" he asked, his voice like quiet steel.

"There's no problem," Larry said. "Dennis was just leaving, weren't you, Dennis?"

"No problem," I muttered. I backed toward the door. "No problem at all."

The bell over the door jingled as I left.

There were two of them on the sidewalk, waiting for me. They were making a big show of trying to determine the contents of my grocery bag by looking through the truck's window. I ignored them and stepped quickly to the driver's side of the truck. I started it up and cracked the window down a few inches.

"This used to be a nice town before you got here," I shouted.

"It will be nicer without you, old man," one of them laughed. "Your time is done. You're a walking fossil."

I put the pedal down, ignoring the posted limits as I blasted out to CR 204. Sinister, sprawling ferns crowded the road while mossy pines towered overhead, blocking the too-soon setting sun. Here and there, patches of clear-cut stretched up the hills, nothing but acres of stumps and seedlings. I'd worked the lumber until they closed the mill, just like my dad and uncles had before me. The hills around here used to be filled with lumber men in lined flannel shirts and vests for when it got cold, steel toed boots laced halfway up the calf. Burly men with booming voices that shared crude jokes and stories of conquest. Men with appetites that could devastate a plate piled high with flapjacks, slabs of ham, black coffee by the pot.

Those days were gone.

Those men were gone, too. Buried in the same hills where they had worked, or changed so much they were unrecognizable.

That would be me, eventually. I'd made it this far, but how much longer could I hold out with dwindling access to supplies? Another month? Two?

I fishtailed making the turn onto the dirt road that led up to my cabin. There was a time I liked the idea of living in town, close to civilization. But I gave up that idea when things got bad. I'd been heavily involved for two solid weeks fixing the porch when things went bad. I missed the worst of it. The boys from the Beaver, they all lived in Kettle Hollow and look what good it did them! The cabin was safer. More remote. More defensible.

I pulled up to my property, left the truck idling long enough to unlock the steel pop-up building I'd been using as a garage. Groceries balanced on my hip, I locked it up good and tight, telling myself that the heavy chain and padlock would be enough to deter trouble. The sun was riding tight to the horizon through the cut in the trees. I'd checked the almanac earlier. The moon would be coming up right about now on the other side of the trees. The thought put some haste in my step.

Careful to avoid the nests of razor wire on either side of me that sat between the porch rail and the heavily boarded windows, I unlocked the four deadbolts on the reinforced door. As I slipped in, I heard the first of the howls. Two of them, not too far away, answered by a chorus of howls deeper in the woods. Goddamn, they were close. Was hunting that bad that they had to crowd up on my cabin so soon?

I slipped into the dim interior of my cabin, slammed the four padlocks home and dropped the two crossbars. The air was close and stale, heavy with the scent of pine and sweat. I set the groceries on my small counter and stared a bit too long at the calendar on the wall above the counter. Full moon tonight. Maybe my last. I sighed then started putting away cans and the chicken, leaving one of the boxes of crackers on the counter. Sundried tomatoes and basil crackers. Son of a bitch. Maybe it wouldn't be so bad if this was my last full moon after all.

I wondered how it had been for the others, for the ones who hadn't turned, who had just been meat for the beasts. I knew that most of Kettle Hollow had fallen in one massive culling, a moonlit night of fangs, claws, and blood. Apparently, a handful had managed to escape that first night of slaughter. And several awoke the next morning, the savage bite marks they had somehow survived already healed, strange, new hungers burning in their bellies.

Did it hurt? Would it be so bad to give in? But that was crazy talk and I knew it. Then I would be one of them. I might be the last real man alive, but by god, I was going to go out fighting. I gathered up the crackers, my shotgun, and my last, half-empty box of shells. I'd packed the ten shells with scraps of the last silver I could find. It wouldn't win the war, but it would at least make a few of them pay.

The chair was where I had left it by the front door. I slid it into place and opened up the waist-high murder holes: one for lookin', one for the barrel of the gun. I settled into position and opened the crackers with one hand.

The howls were getting closer. I wondered if these were some of the ones from Kettle Hollow who had menaced me earlier, or if they had already been out here, waiting for the change the moon brought about. But did it matter? They were coming. The age of man was over. And either I held them off for one more night or I didn't.

And next full moon, I go through it all again. I put one of those horrible crackers in my mouth and I waited for them to come.

DENNIS SHAWN is a former logger and life-long resident of Kettle Hollow, Oregon. He enjoys hunting, the poetry of John Keats, and Eddie Money's earlier albums.

NATHAN CROWDER is child of the deserts of the American Southwest, currently exiled to the city of Seattle where he lives on coffee, karaoke, and teriyaki. He is the author of short horror and longer fantasy & super-hero fiction and the urban fantasy novel *Ink Calls to Ink* from CHBB Publishing. He exists online at nathancrowder.com and on Twitter @NateCrowder.

THE SILENCE AND THE WORM

An account by Joshua,

AS PROVIDED BY SAMUEL MARZIOLI

We continued north, because I remembered my dad once said, "You know, Joshua, the north is nice this time of year." I'm pretty sure he meant Wisconsin in the summer, but I digress. There were other good reasons to head in that direction, if only to keep moving. To get away from the life I used to know in a town no longer there. To forget family and friends who had died. But mostly, to stay ahead of the Silence.

A month had gone by since my last pick, and my supplies were growing scarce. The abandoned cities we'd passed through on the border between California and Oregon had been reduced to ruins, making scavenging impossible. Others had been too steeped in Quiet Folk—human servants of the Silence—ambling through the streets, tearing down buildings brick by brick and board by board to prepare for the coming of the Wilderness. Eventually, we came across a battered and muddy sign on the side of Route 99 that lifted our spirits. It read, "Welcome to Preston," and above the town name someone had spray painted, "New." An indication of enduring civilization? An honest-to-God remnant? I could only hope. It'd been far too long since I met my own kind, and my insides ached for their company.

"What do you think, Betty?" I said.

Betty's moist, pink body squirmed on my shoulder, in that way worms do, as if to say, "Might as well check it out. Can't be worse than starving."

I could already feel the presence of the Silence bearing down on me, and I wondered if this would turn out to be another trap. Even so, it was only a matter of time before we met again. One place was as good as any other.

In the span of four years, the world had changed. Grass, trees, and flowers had swallowed up whole cities; forests of conifers had smothered deserts; and kelp had choked the oceans. Bugs and animals seemed to do just fine, even thrived, speaking with our Silence-stolen voices and thinking with our Silence-stolen minds. But us humans? Not so much. We were a species on the brink of extinction, scattered embers in the dying fire of civilization.

Even in New Preston, the Quiet Folk had left their mark. Demolished houses sandwiched the streets, with trees reduced to fire-scarred trunks lining each sidewalk. Occasionally, we came upon rusted cars parked slapdash in driveways or on lawns. Inside one burnt out heap, a skeleton reclined, its lower jaw hanging wide as if caught in a scream.

The damage made it hard for me to remain optimistic that anyone was still alive; even Betty wiggled with unease. But once we took a right on Market Street, our patience rewarded us with a welcome sight: a row of unscathed houses, painted in happy shades of blues, greens, and oranges, with each yard effusing the sweet scent of freshly cut grass.

The building closest to us had a glass front, as if it used to be a store or a restaurant. When the three men inside turned and saw me, their jaws dropped and they jolted back. From my reflection, I could understand why. If I hadn't recognized my face behind the clutter of battle scars and a bristly beard, I might have jolted back as well.

They headed outside, settling under the shade of the eaves. Despite their harmless appearance, I slid a hand to rest on the heel of my hatchet, just in case.

"Stranger in town!" the youngest of the three men announced.

Eyes began to peek out through the cracks of curtains from nearby houses. Front doors opened. Those that came outside to investigate seemed curious, yet only a distant sort, as if my presence were a visual oddity and nothing more.

"Afternoon," I said.

"A talker, eh?" said the eldest of the three. He didn't look at me when he said it.

"Not infected," said the third.

"Is he alone? Looks like he's alone," said a woman plodding up the sidewalk.

And with every new voice that joined in, the same thing. They talked about me, but never to me, as if I were oblivious to the meaning of their words, a tourist with a foreign tongue. A little girl standing on the porch three houses down seemed to be the only one interested in interacting. She let out a noisy humph and mumbled, "Goddamn strangers" to the old woman by her side.

"So's your daddy," I called out.

I meant it to be playful, but it was obviously the wrong thing to say. For a second, she looked furious, fists clenched at her sides like little red hammers. The next moment, her face flooded with tears, and she scurried inside, slamming her front door with a wood-shivering bang.

"That was uncalled for," said the old woman.

I made my way over, stopping at the base of her porch. A throng of men and women trailed after me, like cats chasing a roving beam of light.

"You're unusually conversational. I was beginning to fear this town was Silence-touched," I said.

"Come again?"

"You know, on the way to being Quiet Folk." No reaction. "Mutes."

"Oh! You mean the dumb-sickness. We don't let dumb-sickies live with us; we learned that lesson quick. Anyone who gets it, we burn. Better that than the alternative," she said, motioning to the devastation all around.

She had deep-etched lines on the sides of her mouth that extended down below her jawline, giving her the appearance of a ventriloquist dummy. I half felt the urge to peer behind her, fully expecting to find a crazy old man with his hand up her skirt.

"That little girl's daddy got burned last week," she continued. "That's why what you said was uncalled for."

"If I see her again, I'll apologize."

"See that you do. In any case, I suppose you're looking for a place to stay?"

"That's right."

"All we got to offer is an empty closet."

"Thanks. That'll do just fine."

She leaned in close and narrowed one eye. "Just remember. You even blink at me or my family wrong, and I'll cut you ear to ear." To prove the point, she whipped out a knife from some unseen pocket. The razor edge glinted in the sunlight before she stowed it away just as fast. "Lord knows I can't turn away someone in need, but I don't tolerate murderers, thieves, or rapists. Understood?"

I shrugged. "Never had the urge and I don't plan on starting now."

I huddled in the old lady's closet with my hatchet, dressed down to my long johns. The old lady had offered to wash my clothes and hung them from mantel hooks to dry beside the fire. Soon, that familiar shudder at the base of my spine snaked its way up my neck, and I knew the Silence had entered town. Rushing into a populated place seemed too eager by far. But the years and road had taught me long ago never to second-guess such an inscrutable character. As a precaution, I mumbled any word that came to mind.

Eventually, I must have nodded off because, when I opened my eyes again, the dining room table had been set. The little girl and a wide-eyed old man stood around it, dressed respectively in a sun dress and a two-piece suit. The old woman entered from the kitchen—also in her Sunday best—and placed a few glass bowls on the table. She came to the closet's doorway.

"Haven't heard such restless sleep in all my days," she said.

"Hope I didn't startle you."

"Only startling part was how anyone could sleep and talk so much."

"Comes with practice. Keeps the Silence away."

"Kept me away too. How about some dinner?"

"Yes, please."

I stepped into the dining area. The little girl and the dog resting beside the fireplace turned and looked at me with the same lethargic wariness. The old man began to twiddle his thumbs, feigning disinterest, yet watching me out of the corner of his eyes. When the old woman came back from the kitchen, she carried four glasses filled with yellow-tinted water. We all sat at the same time.

Before I ate, I placed Betty on the table. Then I plucked an apple from a bowl and dropped it by her side. It was a Fuji, the same variety I'd found her in several months ago, back at that orchard in Tehachapi, California. I'd taken one big bite and there she lay, wrapped around the rotted core, just beyond the severed halves of worm babies writhing against the pull of death. Guilt made me coax her out and we'd been together ever since.

"What the hell is wrong with you?" said the old woman, watching me like I'd just sprouted a second head.

"Don't worry. She's not the talking type or else I would have smashed her myself."

"I meant why on my dining table?"

"A worm's got to eat too."

The little girl's eyes glinted in the firelight. A leer on her face, she turned to the old woman and covered her mouth with a hand. "He's got the dumb-sickness," she whispered.

"Trust me, I'm fine. The Silence and I have an understanding." As an afterthought, I said, "Sorry about your daddy."

The girl stood up, her eyes big wet saucers, and stormed out of the room. The old woman cackled and shook her head.

"You may not be dumb-sick, but you sure are dumb."

I shrugged and ate my fill. The road had shaved off the brunt of my social etiquette, and I wasn't about to feel sorry for it now. Once Betty finished, looking almost fit to burst, I placed her on my shoulder.

"What's there to do around here?" I said.

"You're doing it," said the old woman, with a twisted, toothy grin.

Once dressed, Betty and I stepped outside just as it began to drizzle. I spotted a man sitting on the porch bench of the adjacent house. When he saw me, he tipped his hat. Though I wasn't wearing one, I tipped mine too.

"Clouds are full. Looks like a heavy rain is coming soon," I said.

A sound like passing gas squeezed from his lips as he glanced into the sky. "No shit. It's Oregon."

Without another word, I tipped my absent hat again, and Betty and I set off toward the heart of that all-but ghost town. The destruction we saw before pretty much summed up all the rest. Along the perimeter of the city, scattered trees pressed in, their branches reaching out like old prospectors staking out their claim. It wouldn't be much longer before the whole town was overrun, just like all the rest.

At the thought, I shuddered. But it wasn't sadness, or even a sudden chilled wind. It had to be the Silence.

Before my dad had become one of the Quiet Folk himself, he said to me, "Joshua, we're done for. Mother Nature's grown weary of our disregard, and now she's got a servant boy to do her bidding." I chalked it up to a case of the crazies, like the many neighbors who had turned before him. Like my mom, all stuffed up in her bed and staring out at nothing. That was before she and the rest of them got up and did things too gruesome to repeat. They always took the normal people out before they tore into the cities, but some time had passed before I saw the pattern and understood the truth.

I turned at a crossroads, to face another row of desolation, when a voice crawled in from behind me.

"Hands where I can see them, stranger."

The voice sounded calm but gruff, the words stilted and uncertain, with just enough confidence that I couldn't take the implied threat lightly. I put my hands behind my head.

"Did I do something wrong? My worm and I were just looking around," I said.

"Nothing like that. And nothing personal. Head into Mrs. Danver's house—that wreckage to your right."

I did.

"Now close your eyes and spread yourself face-down upon the ground," the voice said, a growl pinned along the edges.

Whatever he had planned for me, I didn't like my chances if I complied. I made as if to drop to my knees, but instead of spreading out, I spun around and slid my hand across my stomach. Just as my fingertips enclosed the handle of my hatchet, I saw my attacker for the first time. Before, when lying down in a fluffed-up circle by the fireplace in the old woman's house, it looked like a harmless animal. But now, hair bristled, fangs bared, the dog was anything but that.

It pounced, moving so fast I could barely draw the hatchet an inch before it rammed me in the legs, sending me sprawling to the dirt and ashes. It caught my palm in its ample jaws and bit down hard, teeth sinking deep into my flesh. Something popped and, for a second, electric bolts seared a path into my brain.

Just like that, the fight was over. But to my surprise, instead of lunging and tearing my throat out, it lapped at my blood on its lips, uttering a deep, contented moan. That distraction was all I needed. With my good hand, I yanked the hatchet from my belt and sent it crashing deep into the center of the dog's head. Its skull splintered, and a yelp leaped out of its throat, vibrating my guts like a resonant frequency on brittle glass.

Betty wiggled from a puddle by my side, as if to say, "You got it! You saved us!"

I hid the dog's body under a heap of charcoaled wood in the middle of Mrs. Danver's place. Then we headed back to the old woman's house. By the time we arrived, I felt exhausted. The fight had turned my muscles into mush, and lurching from the doorway to the closet was all I could do to keep on moving.

Before I fell asleep, I heard the little girl cry out, "Grandma, I can't find Patches anywhere!"

A sharp pain in my skull woke me from my slumber. It had the distinct feel of a hammered nail, with the permeating ache of a migraine. It made me nauseous.

As my sleep-blurred vision came into focus, I found myself staring into the face of an unknown man leaning over me. He was an average height, with light—almost translucent—skin, a mane of shining black hair, and a long, bushy beard that curled over his belly. His eyes shone like a host of stars, cutting through light years of space just to settle on me.

"You've been sound asleep for so long I was beginning to think you'd sleep the whole day away," he said.

"Who are you?"

"Don't you recognize me?"

I didn't, and yet I had the distinct impression I'd met him some-place before. Not because of his face, but his presence, like a palpable absence of warmth—the same kind that had tracked me through countless miles, all across the country.

"The Silence?" I said.

"Correct."

"But—"

"You wonder how I'm talking to you? How I can withstand your voice enough to stand beside you now?"

"Something like that."

"I won't tell."

I grunted and struggled to my feet. "It's no mystery. You steal voices and minds from humans and give them to bugs and animals. You're magic, that's how you did it."

A condescending chuckle rolled from his throat. "If it were that easy, I would have had you already."

"Then you're not really here. You can't be! Which means you're an illusion of some sort, a figment of my mind. And that can only mean…"

But I had nowhere else to go with that train of thought, and he knew it. His smile spread wider, until he had the same self-satisfied grin he'd worn when we first locked eyes.

"My hand?" I said.

With the way the old woman and the little girl spoke about the Silence like he was some kind of disease, I wondered if that talking-dog bite was the cause. And yet a queer sensation was tapping at my brain, like I had missed something. Something obvious.

I looked around the old woman's living room, searching for a clue. The fire in the hearth had been reduced to burning embers. The food on the table sat exactly where we'd left it. I heard and saw no sign of the old woman, her husband, or the little girl, and nothing from their neighbors. Perhaps the Silence had attacked the others in their sleep and I was the only one left, mind and voice intact. Could he be stronger now because New Preston had fallen?

And then it dawned on me at last. Betty never left my side, not once since we first met. But now, I couldn't feel her wiggling anywhere on my body.

"Where's Betty?" I said.

The Silence shrugged; his smile shifted into a mask of indifference. Immediately, a voice called out from within my brain. Not the still, small voice of God, or my own thoughts, not unless both had taken on a particular feminine quality.

"Sorry, but the opportunity was too hard to pass up, what with you weak and unconscious so long," said Betty.

"What did he offer you? That voice?" I said.

"A brain feast and a voice. A real voice and not your asinine speculations."

"So it's like that, is it?" I threw the Silence a helpless look, putting extra effort into the appearance of malaise. "Is this because I ate your worm babies?"

"To start with, but let's not forget—"

Her words drifted into babble as I turned my attention to my skull. Starting at the base, I searched the surface of my scalp with my fingertips, making it look like I was massaging out an ache. Just in case, I moaned in pain, doing my best impression of a hopeless, helpless soul. I found the burrow above the middle of my frontal lobe. No bigger than a BB pellet and far too small to try rooting her out. That didn't leave many options.

I stumbled to the table, making a show of it, but ensuring my head came to rest in the right place. For a second, I contemplated my next step. As last resorts went, this wouldn't just be scraping the barrel bottom, it was tossing the barrel aside and mucking through the dirt. And yet, if I did nothing, I'd be as good as gone. Whether brain dead, dead-dead, or silenced, it all amounted to the same thing.

"Seriously, I don't know why I haven't tried human meat before. It's like apples on steroids," said Betty, with whatever passed for lips smacking appreciatively.

The Silence chuckled and a snarl tugged at my lips. I tried to think of something to quip, but could only imagine her taking great, big mouthfuls of gray matter. Instead, I let my actions do the talking. Grabbing my hatchet, using both hands to steady my aim, I slammed the bit into my skull.

There came a hollow "thunk." I screamed. The pain was so fierce I could taste it on my tongue, hear its vibrations coursing in my veins, and I screamed again for good measure. By the time I pried the hatchet loose, my body shivered and shook so hard I could barely stand.

Betty screamed and even the Silence gaped like a fish out of water. Taking aim, I let the hatchet sail again, catching the first crack at an angle, leaving a triangular wound in its wake. I shoved the edge of the hatchet bit inside the gap. Using the butt for leverage, the skull snapped loose, hanging limp against my head by a flap of skin.

The convulsions grew worse. My arms wavered like a bowl of Jell-O. Nevertheless, I grabbed the butter knife from the table and aimed it for Betty's screaming voice. Its dull, serrated edge scraped against the divot she'd made in my brain, back and forth, back and forth. Once the job was done, I dropped it to the table and caught myself on the table's edge.

Betty's upper segment writhed in a puddle of my blood. I wanted to say, "Choke on it," or anything that would signal the finality to this damned situation. But the longer I stared at her—slowly dying, moving less and less as the seconds passed—I found my finger pointing to her head, pressing down until my fingertip found the surface of the table. After she stopped writhing, I threw her remains into the embers of the fireplace and watched her body blacken, shrivel, and burst into flames.

With Betty gone, the Silence vanished.

"There. It's finished," I said.

And I believed it. That is, until the front door opened and the old woman and little girl entered, arms filled with firewood. The moment they saw me covered with blood, hovering over a blood-stained knife and hatchet, the little girl gasped and the old woman dropped all but one log. She came at me in a flash. I barely had time to say, "It's not what it looks like," before the log swung like a bat at my head.

Homerun.

I woke up in Patches' bed covered in blankets, next to a crackling fire. The second I tried to sit up, the little girl yelled for her grandma. The old woman rushed out from the kitchen, wiped her hands on a towel, and considered me thoughtfully.

"You're awake now, are you?"

"You'd be a better judge of that," I said, collapsing back to bed.

"How's your head feel?"

I reached for the part of my skull that I'd cracked open like a boiled egg and tapped a finger on the spot. To my surprise it held in place, though it still felt a little tender.

"Don't go messing with that yet. May take months before the bones knit together properly."

"I guess I owe you my thanks."

"Yup. Care to tell me what happened?"

"I'd rather not. It's a long story."

"Figured. Would you at least care to explain what happened to Patches?"

I reached up and stroked my beard. "Sorry, ma'am, I had to kill him."

The little girl squealed. She rounded on me with fierce eyes, and those red hammer hands returned to her sides. Lucky for me the old woman held her back.

"Go play with your grandpa."

"But—"

"Now!"

The little girl hauled herself out of the room, stopping at the foot of the stairs to toss a withering glance my way.

"That was her dog, you know," said the old woman.

"So I gathered. Just so you're aware, I had a good reason to kill it."

"Oh, I know all about that dog. I only kept him around for Sandy's sake, against my better judgment. It's my fault, I suppose, for not keeping a closer eye on it. In other words, we're good, but I think it's time for you to leave."

I nodded and stood. The room reeled, but it soon stabilized after a few earnest blinks. Once I got dressed, I put foot after foot, stooping beside the doorway to pick up my belt, hatchet, and pack.

"Thanks again," I said and closed the door behind me.

Outside, the sun bathed everything in vibrant light, reflecting so bright and pure off the surrounding Wilderness, it felt as if the world had been made new in my absence. Or maybe I was just elated to see another day.

Once I hit the street, I gazed into the distance, imagining the old bones of cities spanning the horizon, wrapped in the tangled branches of the Wilderness. For a moment, I wondered if there was anything left out there for me beyond bitter memories and a never ending cycle of retreats. Still, as my dad liked to say, "It isn't the place itself, but the getting there that matters." In other words, my journey had only just begun.

With that, I set off down that great asphalt roadway, humming a merry tune. And the Silence, warded off by the sound of my voice, trailed behind me like a weak and wounded puppy.

JOSHUA was born and raised in Alpine, California, a little unincorporated town within San Diego County. He was 19 when the world changed. Within the first several months, the Quiet Folk destroyed most of his community and he fled north soon after, with only the clothes on his back and his father's hatchet.

SAMUEL MARZIOLI is an Italian-Filipino author, born and raised in the drought-ridden state of California. His work has appeared or is forthcoming in numerous publications, including *Apex Magazine*, *Shock Totem*, and *Intergalactic Medicine Show*. He currently resides in Oregon with his family. For more information about his upcoming works, visit: marzioli.blogspot.com.

THE MEN ON ELDAMA RAVINE

An account by Jaclyn Maise,
AS PROVIDED BY B. T. JOY

1 *7.5.17- Eldama Ravine- Kenya.*

I killed the children today.

I'm not telling you this to salve my conscience, but you should know that they died peacefully.

I took each one to the nurses' station and administered an intravenous dose of potassium chloride. The resulting cardiac arrest lasted only a few seconds, and I'm almost convinced there was no pain. Though with a dozen infants to euthanise and since I only had the courage to begin around noon, it took until well into the evening to finish the job.

I've left two of the infants alive. One male and one female.

If you're reading this, I only wish that you could try to understand. If what I've done's wrong, and if even these two I've saved grow up to hate me, just try to think if you could have done any better under these circumstances. I'm alone and there's no one and nothing left to guide me.

The fifteen of us stood no chance of survival. Even as it is, there's still three mouths to feed, and we're down to our last six months of supplies.

✪

18.5.17

I've decided to keep adding to this journal. It at least gives the illusion of conversation and fills in an hour after the sun first goes down. That's the worst time, I think: the nights.

Today I put on the hazmat suit and left the surviving babies in the neonatal unit for an hour. I'd just fed them and put them down to nap in their cribs, so they were safe enough.

I checked the suit a dozen times, I think. The pathogen still has around a 25% index in the area, and after seeing those pictures from Nanyuki, I'm not taking any risks. There was no help for it though. I had to go out. After yesterday, it was all I could do to take a black dive into my bunk and try to forget all those needles and children's faces.

I admit that I've been drinking a little, and it took me the best part of a bottle of Glenfiddich to bring on even a broken sleep. Ironically, whiskey is the one commodity we're in no shortage of.

I'd tied the kids' bodies in separate refuse bags and stowed them in the freezers. Technically, it was the best place for miles to keep them, if the object was to stave off decay, that is. But somehow it seemed too perverse to sit eating our pork chops knowing they'd been preserved next to all those human remains.

I made a tough decision, one of many, and took the bodies out onto the grass by the complex. I suppose I was doing all this more for psychological than practical reasons, but you shouldn't judge me like that. If you've survived and you're reading this, you must have dealt with the strain that followed the collapse too. You must know what it's like for me now. You must know that, these days, anything that gets me through is okay by me.

I stripped the kids and laid them out on the grass. Much like T cells are reprogrammed to attack cancer, so someone had programmed the pathogen to seek out and destroy only cells containing Homo sapiens DNA. As a result, when the human species vanished, they left a garden behind them, a massive wilderness of nature not only untouched by the disease but thriving in its presence.

There's a pack of jackals I hear every night from my bunk. They've moved into the ravine since the traffic to the hospital has disappeared. With any luck, they'll be around again tonight, and by this time in a few months, there won't be anything left to say there even were children here. The jackals will eat the meat and scatter the bones and, in time, I'll be allowed to forget.

I hope it happens like that, for all of our sakes.

On my way back to the hospital buildings, I stopped in the deserted parking lot and made a pile of the kids' clothes.

I covered them in lighter fluid and set them on fire.

21.5.17

One of the kids sleeps so well and the other one won't stop crying whatever I do.

The pair of them are chalk and cheese in so many regards.

I never had the mothering instinct, which was ironic for a woman who'd chosen obstetrics as a career path. Still, I always thought having kids would only result from meeting the right man, and I never really did. And now, given the fact that I'm nearly fifty, and that even the most eligible men of my age are cancer-filled corpses littering cities on every continent, I shouldn't really get my hopes up at this late stage.

I took the crying one to the station where my little lamp was lit, and I spent the time sending out signals on the radio that I'd set up in there. Same message every time: *SOS. SOS. We are survivors living in Eldama Ravine Missionary Hospital. One boy, aged six months. One girl, aged six months. One doctor. Send help.*

These two kids had been half the age they are now when I started making that call. Though then I was more desperate and I actually expected a response. These nights, I just carry it on to pass the time. You'd be surprised how much of the human social instinct is based on language. Even though I know I'm talking to dead air, somehow just speaking that short m'aide message a couple of times a night makes me feel a little less alone.

And keeping this journal too, just speaking inside my own head, even that gets me through. And anything that gets me through is okay with me.

I hit a lucky blow on the boy's back at one stage and he let out a bellyful of trapped wind through his little throat. *Poor little tyke*, I remember thinking. That's why he was screaming.

He settled down after that, and I got him to bed by around two in the morning.

By the time I made it to my own bunk, I was too exhausted even to drink. I lay there in my clothes until I fell asleep, just listening to the silence and imagining those tiny dead bodies on the earth outside.

22.5.17

The male baby is making a real effort to get onto his stomach and crawl. He has this look of steely determination on his face, and I can't help but think: *poor little bastard. You don't know the world's ended.* Everything's over and he was just getting ready to flip onto his stomach and start crawling.

I've been avoiding this. But he'll be walking in a few months and she won't be far behind him. Then there'll be talk and questions, and judgement no doubt for the little holocaust we've had round here this week.

I decide there's no help for it. If I'm going to try to save us, I need at least to know who we are. I decided to name them.

Christ, you've no idea how hard that was.

When the pathogen hit, and we were sealed in neonatal, some of the older babies already had names, of course, but later, when the disease spread, when I was the last civilian in the town, and then the last adult, I decided not to name any of the younger kids and to try to forget that the others had names to begin with.

Part of me knew the cold mathematics of the situation. Fourteen infants and myself living in a hospital with only weeks of supplies, and all around us a wasteland of intense heat and predatory animals.

All it would take was for something to pick me off during one of my fruitless expeditions in the ravine, and they'd all have had to suffer slow starvation.

I never named them because I never wanted to push a hypodermic full of potassium chloride into the veins of something with a name.

Still though, things were different today. The boy was trying to push himself onto his belly. He was trying to crawl. And, if he could try, so could I, I guess.

I called him Mohamed. And the other, the girl, I called her Fatima.

They had been the most common names on the continent before the collapse. It seemed a good way to choose what to call them: by chance and by lottery. Maybe in my own way, I was still trying to avoid becoming too attached.

23.5.17

Mohamed sleeps better these nights. Fatima sleeps as well as before.

I'm writing this from my bunk. Yes, I've had a drink.

This is where I first heard the jackals howling. You can hear them through the ventilation system that hangs over the bed. The first night I heard them, I'd nearly pissed myself. They sounded so like human beings and getting up, to go outside, I made such a bloody row that I woke the children. I'd left them crying too (it was for the best), and I pulled on the hazmat and got outside into the ravine as quick as I could.

Christ, how dark it gets. Like nights before people came. And it was only when I shone the torch out into the wild grass and saw those rows of low green eyes that I knew it hadn't been a rescue party, just a crowd of scavengers whose numbers were rocketing and had been sustained on the bodies of the dead.

I'd gone back inside that night, and I'd remembered the pictures from Nanyuki. All those strong military men coming out in black tumours faster than the camera could record it. Hyperactive malignancy. Ultra-aggressive cancer.

I remembered the days that followed. The Kenyan and the world news had reported it as a biological attack by an Islamist group on the British military presence in Kenya. It seemed plausible, given Nanyuki was the target.

But within the week, the reports changed as the airborne pathogen crossed the border with Uganda and, days later, as South Sudanese civilians started to die in Juba and surrounding towns.

In the western media, Africans of all nations were depicted as zombified monsters. The sea and airports closed overnight. There was a lockdown of travel and immigration that made Ebola look like a free-for-all.

It didn't stop the pathogen.

A month later, less really, there were isolated cases of infection and fatality in Athens, Naples, and Marseilles.

Within the year, I was here alone watching the last of society reporting its own extinction through an increasingly frantic media.

Then the media stopped altogether, and the air went silent, and I heard nothing again but the sounds of animals around the hospital.

Not tonight though. Not yesterday either.

I'm lying awake for all the hours I would've done while Mohamed screamed. And while Mohamed sleeps, I wish I could hear just a sign of movement through the vents.

I want the jackals to come. I want them to eat the children.

24.5.17

I've decided only to eat every second day. With a steady course of vitamins, I should be able to manage it without losing much strength, and the extra food can be stored for use later.

Until now, I've been telling myself that it's all useless anyway. I was getting ready to exhaust the food supply in around six months. It would give Mohamed and Fatima time at least to become toddlers and experience a little of the world before I'd have to put them to sleep. I'd decided the surest death for me would be to fill a bath with warm water and open my veins with a razor. The drugs could fail. There was a chance. But if I cut myself right, and with no one to help me with the wounds, there was no possibility of me surviving.

In the past few days, though, I've been thinking differently.

When I watch the babies on their play-mats, so blissfully ignorant of being members of an endangered species, and of everything I've done in the past week, I begin to hope maybe there might be another way out of this.

We had survived this far. The military, with Nanyuki being so close, only three hours away by road, had focussed their attentions on the Missionary Hospital. They'd set up decontamination tents over the most important areas, the centre being the neonatal ward. They'd screened the staff for the pathogen, and they'd found a handful of us clean. I, being one, and besides an obstetrician, was put in charge of the unit.

I took many of the kids to the plastic screens to see their parents as they died of cancer. Each day they came back weaker, and then they never came back at all.

The army were infected to a man and soon left to battle the spread. They'd all be dead now for sure.

But *we* survived. And if it was possible for us, then maybe more people, farther north, had also found a way to combat the disease. Maybe beyond the wild jungle that remained of Africa, there were still pockets of human life in Europe, and America, and Asia.

I decided to try.

I fed the kids their dinnertime baby food. I played the aeroplane game and ate my vitamins.

Later, when they were sleeping, I swilled the entire stock of whiskey down the kitchen sink before going to bed. I can't help what's already happened, what's done can't be undone, but I'll need all my wits if I'm going to stop it from happening again.

As I write this—you'll think I'm an idiot, but I think it's a reward—I hear a dry snuffling and the sound of paws through the ventilation shaft. One jackal yipes and the other snaps at it with its powerful jaws.

They're scuffling in the grass outside, just where I left the dead babies.

Tomorrow I'll go out and check how much is gone.

25.5.17

No time to write.
Huge development.

There may be more survivors in the ravine!

28.5.17

Today I blocked up the ventilation shafts so I can't hear the noises from outside.

I've moved Mohamed and Fatima's cribs into my bunk room, and we spend most of our time in here. They still don't know what's going on, and that's for the best. Christ, I wish I had their ignorance sometimes.

I've pushed a filing cabinet against the door, because I've no way of telling what's out there.

The hospital's so huge, and there are so many points of entry.

29.5.17

I've been avoiding this.

No—not avoiding it—I've just not been able to write it.

Even in my own head, I can't put it into words. Every time I try to conceptualise what I've seen, I find myself in a loop. How can I explain? It's like trying to define a colour on paper. You just can't. There are no words except *red, blue, green*, and unless you've seen what they refer to, those words mean nothing.

Christ! I'm sorry. I'm babbling.

I'm just writing whatever comes to mind.

No—no I'll try—I'll slow down and I'll try.

It happened four days ago. I'd gone out early in the morning— around sunrise—to check if the jackals had been eating. What I found confused me. There were a series of skittish tracks around the bodies of the kids. Their skins had dried out horribly in the sun and, if I'm truthful, it was difficult to look at them straight in the face.

The spoor said that they'd been there, the jackals, and I knew they had taken to eating human flesh, but not one of the children had been so much as scratched and, somehow, I'm not an expert, but the paw prints left behind told of animals in a state of frenzy or distress.

I had begun to feel distressed myself. My heart rate had increased noticeably and my skin was prickling. However—looking down at the faces and bodies of the kids, as I was—I remained totally ignorant to the reasons for my anxiety.

Then I saw it, just a shimmer like heat haze in my peripheral vision, and when I looked up: there they were.

Two figures were standing out in the open grass. The topography of the area is such that they might have been half a kilometre away, but I could still see them. Two shapes that, due to their hairless silhouettes, I took to be men rather than women.

I left the kids' side and started screaming. I waved my hands in the air and called to them across the long distance of the grass.

They both remained still. Breathlessly still. Neither one moved.

I screamed to them to stay put. I shouted that I had babies here. I said we were running low on supplies.

I ran back like the clappers to the parking lot and jumped inside the jeep that I'd kept fuelled and primed for just such an emergency.

But by the time I got back round to the road running through the grassland, the two figures had gone. I looked everywhere across the levels and inclines of the country, and nowhere was there a single projection that wasn't obviously an acacia tree.

I spent the rest of the day scouting all the roads within an area of five square miles. Travel is dangerous with the disease still at 25%, but the prospect of finding more survivors had made me daring. I came back intermittently to feed Mohamed and Fatima, and only stopped when the lights went out.

I set an alarm for sunrise the next morning. Maybe they lived a long way off and had gone for help. Maybe they'd heard me calling about the babies and would return to save us. I fell asleep that night, and I dreamed the first good dreams I'd had since—

I need to stop writing. I heard something moving in the corridor.

30.5.17

I know they're in the hospital now, and I know what they are.

I've been doing their job for them. Up until now, I watched Mohamed and Fatima play and gurgle, and I thought they were ignorant just because of their infancy. It isn't the case. It's just their feelings are still human. It's just those things never spotted them out there on the ravine and started their mind control.

Of course there's no reason I should've killed all those babies. Of course there isn't.

I could have tried! I could have tried to save them, but I just led them to the station, made them form a fucking line, and shoved a needle into their arms.

I've murdered twelve children.

They had seen me scouting round the hospital, looking for sources of food I hadn't thought of yet, and they'd planted those homicidal thoughts in my head.

When I went back out, on the morning of the 26th, they'd been there again. Just standing like a pair of fucking scarecrows in the middle of the grass. I shouted again and waved my arms, but this time I forgot about the transport and just started to run in their general direction.

I screamed as I went; I screamed and shook my arms over my head.

I'd heard once that when the ships from Spain first grounded in the New World, the Native Americans read the sails as clouds and so completely edited out the vessels as a passing weather pattern. I'd always doubted the human mind was capable of such subjectification.

Now I know it's true, because this *is* the New World and those shapes—the men on Eldama Ravine—those are the conquistadors. And so what does that make me? An ignorant native, squawking and jumping on the spot, because I see men standing in the grass.

When I got close enough, I realised they'd not been men at all.

Their necks were insanely long, they had no shoulders, and the appendages that curled out from under those necks were not arms or feet but both members contained in one. There's no way to put into words what I saw. These are the simplest and most straightforward aspects of their anatomy. Their faces—

Jesus. Oh Jesus Christ.

They were trying to push that image back into my head. The image of euthanising children as though they were dogs.

They'd heard me. They'd heard me screaming about Mohamed and Fatima. They were trying to brainwash me again, to make me go back to the hospital and finish the job.

31.5.17

I know what we're dealing with now.

It all makes sense.

For months, I've been wondering what terrorist organisation could ever conceive of a pathogen designed and engineered to target all living human cells. I knew the technology existed, but I'd never dreamed it would become so horrifically efficient in my own lifetime, and I doubly never imagined that there was a group insane enough to let it loose.

For a while, radical Islam seemed the surest culprit. Only a man who believed firmly in an afterlife could act to so utterly annihilate this one. But even then I had my doubts.

Now I'm sure. Everything's become clear. It all makes sense.

A virus created for the destruction of all Homo sapiens DNA is only insane if the creator is human. The target being Nanyuki had nothing at all to do with the military. From their perspective, it was just a geographical location through which the equator passed. It was like dropping a bomb into the middle of a sphere for maximum impact.

And now the cleanup crew has arrived. Just as contingents of the British and the Kenyan and the US militaries had swarmed through the country after the attack trying to kill off the pathogen before it spread. Now, in the same way, they had arrived—the men on Eldama. They'd come ahead of the rest, and their orders must have been mechanically simple: *Find the ones who aren't already dead, and make them so.*

1.6.17

They bleed a kind of grey grease the consistency of wood glue, and I think the stuff is so loaded with ultra-efficient leukocytes that they probably heal a lot faster and better than us.

The one I clipped is still one of the pair that have invaded the hospital. They only move in the early morning and after sundown, which leads me to conclude two things: 1) they either don't sleep at all or sleep in very minimal rotations, and 2) they don't function in the daytime temperatures and UV levels at these latitudes.

I caught one of them sliding its underdeveloped hand or over-developed foot (or whatever the fuck it is) in beneath the plastic of the decontamination tent. When I shot at it, it sent a pinwheel of that pressurised grey blood jetting all over the floor and up the opposite wall.

As it retreated, it tore the wall of the tent completely away, and so I'm sure the unit is swarming with the pathogen now. I'm definitely infected, and though I've kept Mohamed and Fatima safe inside my bunk room, I'm sure they must be infected too.

I'm writing this from inside the bunk room. Mohamed and Fatima are here. The voice in my head keeps telling me to kill them.

They're dead anyway, it says. *If you let them live, they'll only suffer. Remember those poor bastards in Nanyuki: tumours blooming out of their eye sockets and blocking their respiratory canals.*

But no. I won't listen. I can't help what I've already done, but I can make sure it doesn't happen again. I've gathered all the arms and ammunition that the army left behind. In this small room, it looks like an entire arsenal's worth.

I've still got the double-barreled rifle I used on the thing earlier, but right now I feel the need for more lethal protection. So I'm holding a 9mm submachine gun, loaded and ready to be discharged the second that filing cabinet I've blocked the door with hits the ground.

It seems a laughably ironic way for a medical doctor to end her life. Blasting wounds in something organic to save something that's dying anyway.

But then again, maybe that's all disease and cure really are. Us and the pathogen and the things that made it, even the jackals out there on the grasslands, all creatures unable to coexist and vying with the others to be the one to survive.

All I can hear are the babies rocking on their backs behind me in their cribs. All I can feel is the cold metal of the MP5 in my small hands. The room's close and dark, but I know that outside the sun is beginning to fall.

They've started stirring again. I can hear them in the halls.

JACLYN MAISE was born in Bury St Edmunds, Suffolk, in 1968. After excelling in her secondary education, she went on to study for her MD, with a specialisation in obstetrics and gynaecology, on full scholarship at the University of California. After graduating, in the 1990s, Maise would later join Médecins Sans Frontières and would work extensively in Dadaab, Kibera, and a dozen other towns and cities throughout Kenya affected by HIV/AIDS and tuberculosis. She would later settle in Kenya, where she worked as chief obstetrician in the Missionary Hospital at Eldama Ravine. According to army reports, she was still there when the pathogen hit Africa.

B. T. JOY is a British horror writer whose short fiction has appeared within the printed pages, internet presences, and podcasts of markets such as *Static Movement*, *Surreal Grotesque*, *James Ward Kirk Fiction*, *Human Echoes*, *MicroHorror*, *Flashes in the Dark*, *SQ Magazine*, *Forgotten Tomb Press*, and *Chilling Tales for Dark Nights*, among others. He is also a practicing poet and his poetry can be found in magazines and anthologies produced worldwide. He is currently working as a high school English teacher in Heilongjiang, China. He can be reached through his website: http://btj0005uk.wix.com/btjoypoet or on Tumblr: http://btj0005uk.tumblr.com/.

NOT EVEN A WHIMPER

An account by Irvin Murphy,

AS PROVIDED BY DUSTY WALLACE

"Here?" I asked. It was a trivial question, given what he'd just told me. When a white man in a suit shows up on a black man's farm in North Carolina, well... it's usually for nothing good. But he wasn't a lawyer, detective, or IRS agent. Doctor Steven Parnell was a physicist.

"Yes, sir," said Dr. Parnell. "I believe the last atom in the universe will cease to exist somewhere on your property."

"That sounds like a whole lot of pigshit, which I've got plenty of already. Keeps the fields fertile," I said.

"Mr. Murphy—"

"Please, call me Irvin."

"Irvin. You wouldn't be the first person not to believe me. I spent a long time trying to convince my colleagues at MIT, wrote letters to CERN; they all laughed at me," Parnell said.

"If you can't convince your peers, then why would I let you move in?" I said.

"I'm not trying to convince *you*," Parnell said. "There's a suitcase filled with hundreds in the trunk of my car."

"Jesus. Are you a scientist or a gangster?" I asked.

Parnell chuckled, "Depends on who you ask. But I promise you this is legit. That money represents the liquidation of every asset I had. I'd like to move in and start my work as soon as possible."

Janice would take some convincing. Having grown up poor and black, asking her to live with a white man could be a hard sell. But after forty years of marriage, I could play her like a kazoo.

"Give me tonight to discuss it with the missus, and I'll see what I can do."

The candles I'd lit were still burning, the ribeye steaks eaten, wine bottle emptied. That's when I broached the subject, slick as a greased pig.

"A hundred thousand? Of course you let that crazy man move in," Janice said. "Why do you even need to ask? Once he figures out ain't no rapture 'til God decides, he'll move on and we'll still have the money." Then my beautiful wife cocked her head, and I thought I heard a cog click into place. "Wait a minute. Is that what all this romantic nonsense is about? Does every gesture you make have to be selfish? Praise Jesus, I thought you were trying to butter me up for some hanky panky and it turns out to be about money."

Not quite how I pictured it, but at least she agreed. It was time to clean up my mess. "Of course I wanted to get physical. I'm sixty-seven years old, woman, I got to have a little romance to get things working."

"So you're telling me this had nothing to do with the scientist?" Janice asked.

"Not at all. I just figured if a man's gonna move in our house, we ought to discuss it," I said.

"You better prove it to me," she said, her voice deeper, teasing and sultry.

"Meet me in the bedroom in five minutes," I said. Then, as she stood and made for the door, "Better make that twenty. Need time for my blue helper to kick in."

Janice said, "Gets me all excited when you talk dirty like that," then sashayed her way to the bedroom.

After taking the blue pill I took two brown ones. Didn't want to be sore in the morning.

I called Parnell after the post-dinner love dance. He arrived at six the next morning with suitcases. There was other luggage, too. Odd-shaped leather cases with steel handles. Most of them featured a "fragile" sticker but gave no other hint of what they held. I helped carry them into the guest bedroom anyway.

Janice shook Parnell's hand as he crossed our threshold for the first time. "Nice to meet you, Doctor," she said.

"Steve's fine, ma'am," he said. "Lovely place you have."

"It's quaint but keeps us warm and dry," Janice said. "Your bedroom is the one on the left. There's still some kid stuff in there—posters of baseball players, action figures, stuff like that. We didn't have the heart to box it up after Junior moved out. But I'll put it away since you're here."

"No need to do that ma'am. Either way it goes, I won't be here long and I don't want to intrude on your memories," Parnell said.

"Either way?"

"If my hypothesis is wrong, I'll be moving on. And if I'm right, it won't matter anyway," Parnell said.

I'd been listening from the bedroom where I'd left some of Parnell's bags. Now I came out to preempt a disaster. "Steve, we don't mind you doing your work. We don't mind you living here, feeding you, or helping you with anything we can. But we're Christians and believe that only God can end the world. First he'll take the believers and then he'll send the fire. So we'd love it if you didn't bring up your hypothesis any more than absolutely necessary." Janice gave me a nearly imperceptible nod of approval.

"Mr. and Mrs. Murphy, I understand that completely and didn't mean to disrespect your faith." He'd worn a smile since he arrived, but now it disappeared. Replaced by something darker, more sincere. "I'll play with my instruments and record my findings in a notebook where they belong."

"Thank you, Doctor. My husband and I really appreciate it," Janice said.

"No problem. And if I can be of help with anything around the house—cooking, cleaning, laundry—you let me know," Parnell said.

"Once you try my wife's cooking, you'll never offer to help again," I said.

The smile crept back into Parnell's lips. "That good, or that bad?" he asked.

"Like you said. Depends on who you ask." That earned me a swat on the shoulder from Janice before I scampered out the front door. I don't know about hell's fury, but that woman's scorn kept me working in the fields on many occasions.

I was driving the corn harvester the day after Parnell moved in. Used to be Janice would drive the tractor with a bin in tow. But last year I'd invested in a newer machine that had a bin built-in to the back. Took me a while to figure it out, with all the levers and flashing buttons on the dash. It seemed like something NASA might build.

Watching Parnell set up his equipment near one of my silos, I felt like the harvester was a child's toy. His equipment was as tall as two men. Taller if you counted the dish on top. It started spinning when Parnell plugged it into a panel he unfolded on the ground.

Ten minutes and countless wires later, he was sitting at a plastic desk plucking away at a laptop. A printer underneath spun out a ribbon of paper not unlike an EKG I'd once had. For me the diagnosis was angina. It could have been worse. Hopefully Parnell could say the same about the universe when this was all done.

"What does that thing do?" I asked, parking the harvester near the equipment.

"Do you mind moving that a little? It's casting a shadow on my solar panel."

I pulled up a few more feet, stepped down, and approached Parnell. "That looks like something from Battlestar Galactica. The original."

"It helps me keep me safe from Cylons," Parnell joked.

"What does it really do, Starbuck?"

"I didn't think you wanted to hear about any of this," he said.

"I don't want to hear about the world ending. The equipment, however, is fascinating," I explained.

"Okay then. It's a clock. A timer, really."

"Seems a little fancy for a timer."

Parnell said, "The government broadcasts radio frequencies from atomic clocks. What I'm doing is comparing the speed of those clocks with the timer I've set up here."

"Looking for what, exactly?" I asked.

"Inconsistencies. Something that might indicate time dilation, which can be an indicator of warped space," Parnell said.

"Couldn't dilation just be the result of special relativity?" I asked.

The scientist grinned and cocked his eyebrow. "I thought you were a corn farmer."

"I occasionally open a book," I said.

"Time dilation can be caused by several things. But the timers I'm comparing are on the same planet, in the same gravity, and moving at the same relative speed."

"Okay, so how does warped space relate to, you know, Armageddon?" Janice would not have approved of this question.

"You'd have to crack open a few more books before I could explain that one, Irvin."

I said, "Well, if you figure out the farmer translation, let me know. Just not while the missus is around."

Parnell nodded, turned back to his computer screen.

"Dinner's at five," I said and climbed back into the harvester.

Janice and I were already at the table when Parnell walked in. "My goodness, that looks and smells delicious," he said, looking at the deep fried entree, collard greens, and cornbread. "What is it exactly?"

"Pork," Janice said. I had to fight back a grin.

"Let me wash my hands and we'll dive right in," he said.

Janice blessed the food. Parnell seemed comfortable around praying folk. I wondered if he were raised religious.

"My goodness," Parnell said through a full mouth. "This *is* delicious. What cut of pork is this?"

"Chitlin," Janice said.

"Come again?"

"These are chitlins, Mr. Parnell. Stewed then battered and fried. Just like my momma made 'em," Janice said proudly.

I thought he might throw up. But I guess white scientists from the north don't even know what chitlins are. Because all he said was, "You'll have to write down that recipe for me."

In the following days, Parnell unveiled equipment that put his fancy clock in perspective. He attached some sort of array to the top of a silo, turned a camping tent into an observatory, and set up microscopes to examine core samples he'd taken from our fields.

At first, he seemed content in his scientific labors. He came in to dinner every night in a good mood. He loved trying new food—beef tongue, black-eyed peas, livermush sandwiches. I began to suspect he had southern blood in his lineage.

Then one night he showed up and pushed food around his plate in silence, eventually excusing himself to his bedroom.

"You better go see what's troubling that man," Janice said.

"He's probably got an upset stomach from all the new foods he's tried," I said.

"My cookin' ain't never upset no one's stomach, Irvin Lloyd Murphy."

I knew I'd better not argue when she used my full name. The look in her eyes was an unnecessary confirmation. I wiped the grease and crumbs from my face and moped down the hall.

Parnell had closed the door. He probably didn't want to be disturbed, but Janice would be furious if I didn't check on him.

I knocked three times. "I'd like some privacy," Parnell said through the door.

"Well you ain't gon' get it. Remember, I got the key to this door. I don't know where it is, but I'll find it if I have to," I said. My son had heard the same threat growing up.

The door swung open. "I'm sorry Mr. Murphy, I'm just not in the mood for chit-chat at the moment."

"You sick?" I asked.

"My health is in good order," he said.

"Is it about your research?"

His face paled.

"You found something then," I said.

"Nothing you want to know about," Parnell said.

"Don't treat me like I'm stupid."

"I… I'm sorry," Parnell said. "My research has been disturbing."

"How so?" I took a seat in a wooden rocker. Parnell sat on the bed facing me. The "Say Hey Kid," Willie Mays, struck a pose on one of Junior's old posters behind him. I should have called my son the day Parnell showed up spouting his crazy theory.

"I was right," he said. "Mostly. Only thing wrong in my hypothesis was the timetable."

"So things are gonna end a little quicker than you thought? How many years do we have?" I asked

Tears started pouring from the scientist's eyes. "We'll be lucky to make it to the end of the day."

"That's impossible," I said. "You said we would be the last ones left. I haven't seen anything on the news about other places falling apart."

"That's because those other places don't exist," he said. "This isn't the fire you thought God was sending down. It's like we're the last two digits on a hard-drive waiting to be wiped."

"That doesn't make any sense to me," I said.

Parnell tried a different analogy. "God's pulled the thread and we're on the sleeve, the last part to unravel."

"But there's still television being broadcast," I pointed out.

"I noticed the TV in the kitchen. It was local programming. Probably came on when the parent station's signal went out," he said. "It won't last much longer."

Janice, from down the hallway: "Honey, when you're done in there I need you to check the cable connection. Nothing but fuzz on." Then the power blinked off.

Now it was impossible to dismiss. I could only hope Parnell was pulling the most elaborate prank in history. "What do we do?" I asked.

"You go tell Janice you love her," he said.

"That can't be all there is. We're just gonna blip out of existence? I'll believe it when I see it," I said.

"Go see Janice. Pray with her. That's all that's left to do."

I got up and stumbled out of the room. Parnell was an ass. Some crackpot with money who thought he was a real scientist. That's what I tried to tell myself.

"Janice, we need to kick out—" I stopped when I saw her staring through the window. She didn't even turn around when I spoke.

"It's black out there," she said.

"Just a new moon," I said.

"No. I don't think so."

Janice had a candle lit on the kitchen table. Her features danced when she turned to see me that last time. I saw her as she'd been when we met—young, fit, and full of fire.

I stepped forward and reached out. She put her hand in mine, soft and delicate. I pulled it to my lips for one last taste of her. But it was already gone. Her image existed only in my mind then, for however long that lasted.

It didn't happen quite like the Bible said. Still, I saw the fire. A cold flame. Painless. Pleasant even.

IRVIN MURPHY lives a quiet life. A hard-working man in North Carolina, Irvin wants nothing more than to tend his crops and grow old with his wife, Janice. Irvin Murphy would be satisfied with the life he'd lived if the world ended tomorrow. And it just might...

DUSTY WALLACE lives in the Appalachians of Virginia with his wife and two sons. He enjoys reading, writing, and the occasional fine cigar. Find him on Twitter: @CosmicDustMite

DOWN THERE

An account by an unnamed survivor,
AS PROVIDED BY MJ WESOLOWSKI

"**D**id you know, *back when*, they used to use words like '*Polar Vortex*' and '*Weatherbomb*' when it snowed?"

I already know that. I also already know that they used to take photos of the snow and share them with each other.

To be honest, I'm 99.9% sure Sol's lying about that one; why would you do that when you could look out of the window?

I say nothing though, I let Sol go on, let him talk. The wind's starting to blow harder, snatching at Sol's elaborations the moment they leave his lips and hurling them back behind us onto the dismal furrows of the frozen fields. He's already told me seven times that something called "corn" used to grow here. How the hell does he know that?

"You weren't there *back when*," I say.

Sol won't hear that, he's striding away a few feet ahead. Head down to the wind. There's a screecher coming.

Great.

There are a few things I remember from *back when*, they come back at inopportune moments like when I'm pissing or hacking a hole in the ice or something—flashes of memory—smells, images—my father's breath steaming in the air, the smell of wind in his beard, the wicker of a bird, wellies squeaking against snow.

I sometimes want to ask Sol if he knows about stuff like that—when the snow was soft, when you would throw it for fun—but I daren't, I daren't in case it never really happened.

There are other things I won't allow myself to recall very often, things that are so fragile, if I speak them or think of them too hard, they'll shatter.

Green grass. Christmas.

That's enough for now.

"Look." Sol points ahead, but all I can see is the usual grey whirl of endless distance, the land rising before us like the belly of some vast, pale creature.

There's trees too; the sight of them sends a little flurry of panic into my stomach. Anything that looms unexpectedly from the pale nothing is danger. The wind's getting stronger, and the trees are waving back and forth across the dirty sky, bending almost double in agonised choreography.

"Sol! Stop."

I've seen a screecher tear trees right out of the ground, hurl them into crowds of folk, roots and branches snatching them like tentacles, blood on the snow.

Sol opens his mouth, and for a horrible moment, I think he's going to tell me some fact, like the one about how birds used to live in the trees in nests made of mud and sticks and spit. If we heard the sound of birds now, it would be terrifying, some terrible, squalling thunder; folk would scream, run.

"Bunker!" he says, instead.

I follow the way his finger is pointing, but I can't see anything, my eyes flicking back to the trees, imagining them flying toward us, bouncing off the frozen ground, what it would feel like, would we feel anything at all or would we just lie here broken and bleeding until we joined the ice, vanished beneath the snow?

That's enough of that too.

"Come on!" Sol's off again, and I follow. I can hear the wind's empty wail whipping against the remains of crumpled frozen monoliths up ahead. This is going to be a big one. It'll start sleeting soon, a hail of broken glass flying toward you, your eyes, your face.

I've seen what a screecher can do to a face. I tap the plastic of my goggles and adjust my snow-scarf over my mouth. Leather.

Back when, they used to exchange stuff for money.

Thanks Sol.

There's an orange sign a hundred meters or so up ahead. Like the trees, the sight of it peering from the thorns of a dead hedgerow rattles at my nerves. I look back the way we have come, nearly invisible now, just the ever-decreasing frozen mud, occasional piles of stone.

"Did you see a vent on the way up?"

I shake my head. Of course I didn't. If I'd seen a vent, I would have said.

"That means it's been hooded."

I know that as well.

I also know that means that the bunker's been used.

Or is currently occupied.

We'll have to uncover the door. Sol's already taken off his backpack and unfolded his spade. One end spade, one end ice-pick. Cost us all sorts, that one. I scuttle toward him; the wind is either getting stronger or we're on high ground. I don't need Sol to tell me which one; they built the bunkers on top of hills. If we're lucky, this'll be at least a two-down. The vents used to be easy to spot—a hole in the ice, melted by the steam. I wonder how many vents are frozen over now, how many people below the ground in its halls, dead of thirst, skeletons in tombs.

Enough of that as well.

I pull out my own spade, it's really more like a trowel but I join

Sol in hacking at the ice. The faster we go, working together in our solemn clockwork, the warmer we get. There's a bunker down here too, just pray it's not tombed.

We're getting closer, moving quicker, the wind's starting to sting my face and I can smell myself.

Nice.

My coat is a good one—a really good one—fur-lined, some sort of animal skin, at least I hope it's animal. I keep it filthy—spattered with shit, piss, and blood when I can get it. There's those out here that'd kill for this coat. There might be those that'd kill for this coat down here.

A memory comes back as they tend to do at times like this, flittering from the first flecks of sleet riding the tendrils of wind over the hills.

School.

Dad always used to laugh when I called it that. *School*, he would say, *you mean government-brainwashing children-farm.* I had headphones on, mittens, I was holding a tablet, the thrum and clank of the heating, chattering teeth and the reek of soaking clothes. Old HD archive footage, flat vids of the icecaps, great shards of them collapsing, crashing into blue liquid they used to call the "sea."

It's all bullshit. Dad used to say, *propaganda, they did it on purpose.*

We've cleared most of the ice now, a great pile of it behind us. I can hear sleet rattling against my goggles.

Another one out of the blue. Knocks me for six—Dad running forward through the snow, crying and screaming—*A house! A house! Look, look, we're safe!*

No, please. Not now. Not this one.

I remember the cottage on the top of the hill, walls like logs, a red-tiled roof, orange lights flickering behind glass windows, figures moving back and forth.

Music.

Dad running toward it.

"Done."

We stop; our efforts have uncovered a hinge. Sol looks up at me.

"Fuck's sake."

"Hang on." Sol measures out the point where the handle will be and we start again, faster this time, *clock-thomp, clock-thomp*. When we're done, I pull my bunker key from the layers of stench beneath my coat. It's on a chain around my neck and that's where it stays, Sol or no Sol.

"I remember when I got given my bunker key…" Sol says.

"Shut up, no you don't."

I push the key between the rubber lips of the lock and twist. I actually *do* remember the day the bunker keys got given out; crowds hemmed in around the civic centre, police, hats and scarves, gloves and red cheeks. It was the second month of snow, great halogen lamps to keep the ice away. "There's enough for everyone, please do not push." Over and over again through the loud-hailers. We were some of the last to get one, because of our surname. They were right though, there was enough for everyone.

But all that was before the APs came.

"Stand back." I pull open the bunker door and turn my head away. We've never encountered a bunker that's been tombed before, but we've heard the stories—the snow filters, the heating, it becomes filled with CO2, they say a tombed bunker doesn't smell, but we stand back anyway, just in case.

"Thank *fuck*." The entrance is just a slim, circular tunnel, rungs leading down into blackness, the rubbery prongs of a sort of brush to keep the wind out. Sol reckons they used to use these on people's letterboxes *back when*. The lights that circle the hole glow green. Everything's working.

No APs.

Sol goes first like usual, disappears down into the hole. I follow, pulling the door closed over my head. Hear it click. The outer world is silent now; there's just us and green-tinged darkness.

Eventually, we reach the floor. Compared to outside, the bunker's like a furnace; Sol's pulled out his wind-up lantern and placed it in the middle of the airlock, he's searching for a handle.

"Not bad." I hate this part.

Bunker airlock chambers are like purgatory; you're not out *there*, but you're not safe *down there* either. I still have dreams about the one we found a few months back; I went down first and felt something brittle beneath my boots, heard the empty clatter of bones as I dislodged fingers from the ladder. When we got the lantern going and looked around, we wished we hadn't. The airlock was torn to pieces, the door to *below* shattered, it stank of blood and shit down there in the dark. We both heard something rustling, and when we got back to the surface, we didn't stop running for hours.

This one's alright.

So far.

Sol's found the power wheel and I can hear the *scrick-scrick* as he winds it. There's no smell at all in this one. The longer Sol winds, the wall lamps begin to go from nothing to a soft phosphoric yellow. Maybe we've struck gold? Maybe we're the first. It's impossible, utterly unfeasible, but is it, really?

Of course not, what am I thinking. The hooded vent, the…

"Stop!" My voice wavers, almost a scream.

Sol stops winding.

Oh shit. Oh god.

This isn't happening.

"What?" Sol hisses, but I don't need to speak, I point instead to the far wall.

"Oh…" Sol's mouth hangs open.

Stencilled on the far wall of the bunker airlock, over the revolving rubber door that leads down to the halls is a symbol.

"That's a…"

"Stop it." I say and point back to the ladder.

Sol shakes his head. "We can't," he says.

I want to argue, but there's no point. It'll be dark by now, that eerie, fleeting gloom that will have descended up there while that terrible wind whirls.

We stay here, or we die.

"Maybe, if we just stay up here, in the airlock." My heart is hammering and my mouth is dry, I already know that this is futile. "We'll be ok?"

Sol shakes his head. He looks from that symbol to the doors. "Get behind me," he says.

I do it.

There's a comms unit next to the airlock door; Sol's winding has illuminated the speaker and receiver, two compound eyes. Green LCD letters roll along beside it. We read them as we wait.

Bunker 8674-NE66-5-ST.

5ST, five floors—that means they'll be right down on the very bottom. What was I even thinking? A place like this unoccupied? Far too good to be true. Rookie mistake.

Sol and I stare at the comms. Any second now.

When it bleeps, I jump.

"I'll…" Sol moves forward.

"No." I push him in front of the door.

I walk over to the comms and stare down into the mic, thousands of tiny metal holes. I'm shaking like a fucking leaf now, trembling, I feel faint. Please, just don't pass out, if I pass out we're fucked.

It bleeps again, an irritable, impatient sound, the blue light flickering. I look at Sol, but he's staring at the door. Ready.

I touch the screen.

"Yep…" My voice sounds ridiculous, like a child's. "Just two of us. No harm, we don't want to come in… there's a screecher…"

"Shhh…" The voice clips a little, so far underground. "Someone will be with you shortly, please wait."

"NO!" My hands are shaking. "Please! We don't need it, we don't want…"

The comms goes dead.

"Shit."

Sol still stands before the door. I crouch into the corner, pull up my knees. My heart is still hammering away. We could brave the screecher or stay here. Either way we're fucked.

"Sit down."

Sol slumps. I can't look at him, if he starts with one of his facts…

Another memory. An apt one this time. Dad's phone making the retro *bing-bong* doorbell sound, his face creasing.

"You expecting anyone?" I was about ten.

"Shh." I could tell he was scared; there was a strange light in his eyes as he beckoned me across the hall. "Qui. Et. Ly."

We took it in turns to peer through the spy-hole and look at the man on the other side. I wished we hadn't. That man stayed in my dreams until I was at least 16.

"One of those nutters," Dad said, after what seemed like a hundred thousand years, when the slow *clop-clop* of that man's shoes had disappeared down the stairs. "My dad used to call 'em 'god botherers.'"

"What's *god-botherers?*"

"That's a bit tough for you to understand. That whole 'God' business was a long time ago."

I thought of the man who stood before our door; there was a pained smile on his face, clean-shaven and wrinkled skin, a great mane of pale dreadlocks, huge puffa-jacket with a fur-lined hood made him look like some sort of bear. His neck, hands, and all the way up behind his ears filled with those snowflake tattoos, some big, some small, none of them the same.

"These ones though, these ones are worse."

I remember the man had pushed one of his flyers through the door; Dad scanned it with his phone, chucked it up on the TV, and we looked at their site together.

"Look at this, *mental!*" The website looked ancient, like something out of the nineteen nineties—a great backdrop of snow, ice, trees with blackened branches. Great big letters, interlocked icicles "THE GREAT MELT IS COMING." A sub-heading "Will you be prepared?" That symbol, the same as the one above the airlock door twenty years later.

Who would have ever thought that it was this lot who were right all along?

"They think they're immune to the APs." Sol says, and I peer at him. Sol doesn't usually say stuff like that. His voice is all slow and weird, it sounds horrible.

"Don't be stupid." I can hear Dad's voice in my own, a far away echo. "The APs don't give a fuck, it's all meat to them. Just... stand there."

I remember the temples that began to sprout from the remnants of towns like the tips of weeds through the snow—corrugated iron, old fridges, bits of car—the huddles of people fighting their way through the streets to get to them, to pray. Most of the world was under water by then.

Feet on the stairs from down below, *clop-clop*, those boots they wore, their stockpiles of coats and picks and masks. *Bow with us and await those that emerge from the great melt.*

Newscasts, holo-casts on the kitchen table, Antarctica—that ice falling away in great rifts to reveal a vast, swollen black place that looked like a wound. The hiss of breath from the camera-man as those great swarms emerged from that wound, silent scurrying legs over legs over legs over...

"Get up."

"Shit!" I scramble to my feet.

A figure stands before the airlock door, impossibly thin, hair matted in great wiry strands, tied back from his face.

A priest.

Sol just stands there, unmoved. His head tips forward, chin on his chest.

The priest makes a symbol with his hands, thumbs interlocked, fingers wriggling. Dual snowflakes in black ink on the backs of each.

"Ave Polaris," he says.

"Ave Polaris." I don't remember removing my mittens, but I mirror the man's sign. He seems appeased. The words come out blunt, through my teeth. I want to curse them.

"What about him?"

Sol is still standing there. Still.

"Oh." I walk over and open Sol's jacket. The man looks for a moment then nods.

"You know he cannot join you then, below."

"Please." I don't want to sound too desperate. These fuckers love that sort of thing. "Please, we don't want to, we don't want any trouble, we just want to wait here until the screecher passes." I nod at Sol, "He's all I've got."

It sounds pathetic.

The priest takes another look at Sol's chest and cocks his head, back and forth, Sol to me, me to Sol, his top lip curling. In some ways he's beautiful, fine features, cheekbones, just don't look into his eyes.

"You say you don't want to come below when all you have left in the world is an..." The words with unbounded disgust. "... an Erot-o-bot."

"No." I am starting to panic now. "He's not an... well, not any more... he's been modified... somehow... I think... his programming has malfunctioned... he's not... *that*... anymore."

Sol's jacket hangs open—his exposed chest still reads, in garish, looping letters on the black metal, "Oh-Tommy-Tom! 3X15." A phallic trademark stands out in bright, metallic pink. Sol's my friend… I want to say… sort of—he's sort of my friend, I found him in the wreckage of a tower block when I was nineteen, after Dad died, he's all I've got. I try not to remember the skeleton who held him, small. Smaller than me. I try not to remember pulling those arms from around Sol's chest, the *skrick* sound of the fingers, picked clean.

This heartless, soulless, malfunctioning Erot-o-bot is all I've got. Surely you, of all people would understand that.

I don't say anything.

"What about your parents?" The priest says.

"Dad's dead." A sudden anger fills me. "The APs got him."

Something flickers on the priest's face. "How?" He licks his lips.

"I don't remember."

I'm not telling him the story, no way. I'm not telling him because I know he'll enjoy it; he'll then want to start telling me about the fucking APs' divine "intelligence," and I'll want to vomit that back right into his face.

He cocks his head again. "Where are you going?"

Now I want to laugh. Play it cool. I look at my feet. "Dunno."

The fucking Araneae lot always ask that—that was their fucking trademark *back when*, Dad said. They would come up to you in the street and ask you where you were going, no, but where are you really going? Simple but effective.

If you were stupid.

But they were right.

All along.

"We have a…" He licks his lips. I don't like it. The beauty in his face, the swollen insanity in his eyes. What the fuck has this guy seen? "… sanctuary here in Bunker 8674-NE66."

Right you do, I want to say, right you do. How many of them have you got here? I want to shout it in his face. How many? What are you trying to fucking *do*?

"Please..." I say, maybe I'll break through and find any sort of humanity left in him. Maybe it'll all go differently? "Please just... just let us go... I promise, I won't tell, I don't even know where we're going... we just need..." I look at Sol, still slumped. "... some power... some water and then we'll be on our way... *please?*"

The priest smiles, and I wish he wouldn't. "Tell me how they got him. Your father. How he was *chosen.*"

I lift my hand to punch the wall, think better of it. "Please..." Don't beg... *don't beg.*

"It's okay..." The man shuffles forward and I flinch, if he touches me I'll scream. "... just tell me... I will be able to help you... *understand...*"

I do understand, I do fucking understand. I understand just like you understand, even with that thrumming madness that's seeping from you like a fucking smell; I understand what they are, those horrors that swarmed from that hole in the ice. Where they'd waited.

I understand what they do, how they hunt.

"I don't remember..."

But I do; that cottage, stood like a fucking *beacon* in the snow. Was there music coming from it? Orange lights flickering in the windows, pale figures like ghosts moving back and forth. It was ludicrous, like something out of a film.

"We're saved!" Dad shouted, and for a moment, I nearly believed him, nearly didn't see the utter stupidity of what was happening. I didn't have the voice to call him back.

Dad called it government propaganda when we got taught about the APs in school; they taught us how they work together in a silent, collective consciousness to assume the form of anything. Cars, buildings, even people.

He must have known, how *didn't* he know?

The only creatures on earth with any comparison to the APs were spiders, they said, their silent webs a primitive version of these faceless creatures that had waited, beneath the ice. That's where they got their names AP—Araneae Polaris, polar spiders—but those silent pale things are worse than spiders.

A thatched cottage in the snow, like something out of one of Dad's fucking books.

"We're saved!" and he ran toward it; I watched it cave in around him, consume him like a fucking *mouth*.

I didn't stay to watch them feed.

"We have sanctuary here..." the priest says, and his eyes roll, tongue protrudes slightly, and all I can think is that he's in some kind of terrible ecstasy. Here in the dim light of this chamber. "We have hot food, water, this is a place of love..."

His words are caustic, especially that one. The L word. It takes everything for me not to laugh in his face.

I know what you are.

He moves closer to me and I'm shaking, I'm fucking *trembling*, but I hold it together. The man extends his arms, and as his sleeves ride up, I can see more of those snowflakes tattooed on his bare skin; they cluster over lumps of scar tissue, great long scratches, deep where it looks like hard pink plastic has bubbled out of the wounds. How many do they have down there I wonder?

"A place of love..."

He is so close now I can smell him, a reek of meat, tinged with a sort of citric sweetness. His pale eyes whirl in his skull, that tongue protruding farther, and I can see his lips are moist. How many do they have down there? By his scars I reckon more than one.

By the time the floods came, most people had joined the Araneae Cults, bunched up together inside their temples and just *waited*. I thought we were different; Dad made me believe we were better— rucksacks filled with tins, laminated maps, bunker keys around our throats. There were still people who believed the snow would stop, we would survive.

Even when the birds left the skies and the last dog had been eaten. "Sol! Now!"

The priest flinches at my shout, just for a moment, but that's enough. I duck beneath his arm, pivoting on my hips, and catch him in the ribs, just under the arm. There's a slight *hiss* as my palm-blade pierces his coat; it rattles against bone, sending a little shiver through me.

"You little…" He pitches sideways, but it's too late. Sol's lumbering frame reaches for him, that little pink phallus glowing on his chest. His arms strike out, twin snakes.

"Oh *baby*! I *like youuuuu!*" The ridiculous porn-star voice that crackles from Sol's mouth never fails to make me smile, especially now in this terrible contrast, the yellow light of a bunker airlock, the highest floor of an Araneae temple, and O-Tommy-Tom! has one of their priests in an unbreakable lover's grasp.

The priest is spitting and snarling, eyes rolling back into his head. The rest of them won't come up here, they never do; they always send a priest, their faith as blind as *back when*. *Back when* they worshipped an invisible, uncaring God.

"Let go! Let go of me!"

But Sol is grinding against the man, his limbs hissing and creaking with a terrible, mechanical hunger. I waste no time and stab the priest a few more times, stomach and chest before slashing at his throat. He screams, a horrible, piercing shriek that dissolves into gurgles as blood fills his throat.

"Oh yeah, baby… you're *so hot right now!*"

There are times when I'd like to meet that fucking maniac who programmed Sol and give them a hug.

I move fast; we can't stay here forever, the rest of them down below will, no doubt, become suspicious about what happened to their priest. That said, they very well might have forgotten he's even come up here. I think of the knotted scars on his arms, they've got at least two or three of them down there, they won't forget.

"Please... I..." He manages, his teeth look bright against the blood that fills his mouth. Sol squeezes harder and I hear muffled *crack* sounds as his ribs break.

"Shut up," I mutter.

Sol is squeezing the last breaths from the spider-priest as I root about beneath his jacket. His coat's nowhere near as good as mine, but we could take it to trade; it'll replace the tatty old thing Sol wears anyway.

My hands close around what I'm looking for, it's warm from his death throes, and I yank it from around his neck. Another bunker key. Bingo. That'll get us meat and a bed. At least.

Sol releases the priest from his embrace, and his body slithers onto the floor. I glare down at him with nothing but contempt, nothing. I feel no remorse for this fucker. I hack up a greener and gob it onto his face.

There is silence for a few seconds. Then I hear my breathing, Sol's hydraulics.

"Did you know, *back when*..." Sol's voice is Sol's voice again. "... they used to take photographs of themselves and share them online? They used to call them *selfies*."

"Shut up Sol." I mount the ladder and begin climbing. "Your motherboard's malfunctioning again. You're talking shit."

Sol follows me. Screechers don't last very long, and we'll have a brief window of almost clear sky before the snow resumes. We can make some progress then, Sol's solar panels will be able to get some light into them, and my face will be free from the bite of the wind for a glorious hour.

When we emerge from the bunker, I let Sol fasten the trapdoor, bend the handle, collapse the bolts, make it impossible to be opened again. I take a can of smart paint from my inside pocket and spray a black cross on the orange bunker sign that protrudes from the hedge, just in case anyone else comes along.

"This way." I point to the horizon; the frozen fields leading upward.

Most of the trees have been half-uprooted, and I want to get away from here just in case another one comes. Sol strides along beside me, new jacket in hand, solar panels glinting in the pale half-light cast down from the sky.

I still have one of the old maps Dad gave me. I have a bunker key in my pocket, and I'm hungry.

"Come on slow-coach..." I say. There's a spring in my step.

I can almost taste pit-grilled long-pig, smell the reek of old foam beneath me, a scratchy dog-skin blanket, Sol's shadow cast over me as he stands guard and I sleep.

And I forget.

And I dream of what we were.

It's just us **SOL**, me and you.

The only way is forward. Walking onward. That's the way it has to be. That's the only way it can be. We don't look back; we can't, we won't. To look back is death.

There used to be a story about that didn't there, back when? Dad told me it once.

Stop it.

You're looking back, you're staring into death. The stories, dads and mums and sons and daughters, they're all gone.

We were all wrong.

And they were right.

And now it's just us Sol, me and you.

MATTHEW JOHN WESOLOWSKI is a writer from Newcastle-Upon-Tyne. His first ever book, written and illustrated by himself at age 11 was entitled *Attack of the Killer Flytraps* and whilst his writing style has possibly matured since then, his themes and content almost certainly haven't.

His short horror fiction has been published in *Ethereal Tales* magazine, *The Midnight Movie Creature Feature* anthology (May December Publications), the *22 More Quick Shivers* anthology (Cosmonomic Multimedia), the *Short Not Sweet* anthology (Iron Press), the *Kitchen Sink Gothic* anthology (Parallel Universe Publications), the *Selfies from the End of the World* anthology (Mad Scientist Journal), and the *Play Things & Past Times* anthology (Great British Horror)

His debut novella, *The Black Land*,a horror set in the Northumberland countryside was published by Blood Bound Books in 2013.

You can find Matt on twitter: @ConcreteKraken

He blogs about horror, books and strange things at mjwesolowskiauthor.wordpress.com

ART BY Amanda Jones

AMANDA JONES is an illustrator based in Seattle. She likes reading horror stories, binge watching seasons of her favourite sci-fi/fantasy shows, and everything *Legend of Zelda*. She focuses on digital portrait painting and co-creates the webcomic *The Kinsey House*. You can find more of her work on Tumblr under 'thehauntedboy'.

DOG YEARS

An account by Skye,
AS PROVIDED BY KRISTOPHER TRIANA

Last spring there were only three graves in our backyard.

Mom and Dad were buried side by side beneath the tallest sycamore, and Pete, who was Bobby and Julie's cousin, was placed closer to the house so Julie could visit the grave without getting too close to the fence. She liked to make wreaths for the dead from time to time by gathering dead brush. Being 12, she was the youngest, and we didn't want her going too far from the house, even if we did have pretty good security. The fence itself was only wood, but Dad had lined the top with razor wire when things had started to get bad, and soon after he started on the booby traps. It all had seemed pretty paranoid to me at the time, but it sure don't now.

Back when the poison really started to affect the adults, Dad went into overdrive. He was always the survivalist type though. He was into the NRA and all that kind of stuff. There were always guns and knives in the house. He liked to hunt a lot and would skin his own deer. But on top of that, he stockpiled canned goods, water, and batteries and always had a different kit for any emergency you could imagine. That was *before* all the adults started dropping dead. Once the poison spread, he really went apeshit.

He put bars on the windows and extra locks on all of the doors. He bought weird weapons like crossbows and swords because he said they were reusable, and he made Mike and me learn how to use and clean every one of them, including all the pistols and rifles. I was anti-gun then, not like now, and when I would argue with Dad, he'd tell me it didn't matter that I was a girl and that I couldn't count on men to do everything for me. Suddenly it was Mike and me who had to clean all the game and gut all the fish. He made us learn first aid and had us study the U.S. Army Survival Guide. He stocked up on lighters, toilet paper, soap, vitamins, peroxide, charcoal, and canning supplies. His most paranoid fantasy was coming true, and he knew it, even if all of us thought he was overreacting, including Mom, who kept insisting they'd find a cure. But Dad was right in the end, and the proof of it was those two graves beneath the sycamore.

"What do you miss most?" Bobby asks me.

He does this a lot. Bobby's the sentimental type. I've always said he has the heart of a poet. Hell, that was why I'd fallen for him in the first place, back when all we'd had to worry about was curfews and math tests.

"I miss music," I say.

All of the phones and mp3 players are long dead now, but we have my Mom's old boombox from the attic and a bunch of her tapes. But there's no radio signal anymore, and of course no power. We have to use batteries to use it, and so we don't do it often. Batteries are for flashlights and other more important things. Music's a luxury. We save it for holidays and birthdays, or at least what we estimate them to be. We've been reusing the same calendar.

"What do *you* miss most?" I ask him.

My head is in his lap, and I'm staring up at the sky, which has fallen to the soft lavender of noon. The atmosphere is still changing in spooky ways.

"I miss my hair," Bobby says.

But he's joking.

Granted, his whole head has turned white, but at least he hasn't lost it yet. It's only natural for him to have gone grey by this point. He's 17, after all.

"What do you *really* miss?" I ask.

He thinks about it for a while.

"The internet, I think," he says. "We got so used to having all that information right at our fingertips. Can you imagine how useful it all would be now?"

I can. I think about that all the time, like when I'm struggling to repair the house or trying to prepare squirrel meat so that it's stripped of parasites and not overcooked. The internet would be a tool for me now, as opposed to the toy it had been to me back when we all had it. It occurs to me then just how much time we all wasted in the old days—with our eyes glued to our phones and most of our communicating done through social media. It was such an artificial way to live.

Bobby takes my hand, and I notice the protruding veins on his. He looks down at me, filling my head with warm memoires of hayrides and dances that happened only two years or so ago, and yet now it seems like nothing more than a girlish fantasy I'd had.

"What else do you miss, Skye?" he asks.

Whenever this topic comes up, we have an unspoken rule about not saying we miss our parents. That's a given, just like our health. We don't talk about how we missing running water, air conditioning, or heat that doesn't rely on fire. We don't mention a good steak, cheese, or ice cream. The point isn't to get depressed. It's just to be nostalgic—to try and recapture some of what we've lost.

"I dunno," I say. "Maybe chapstick."

With Pete dead that left four of us.

Mike was the oldest, but he wasn't in charge anymore because his mind was going. Most people didn't live too far past 19, and Mike was almost 21. He was still in fairly good shape and was active, but his mind was going. Most of the time he seemed to have it together, but he often forgot where he was and what was going on. Sometimes he'd even talk to me like I was Mom.

That left me as the head. It was a responsibility I didn't care for, but it was our family's house after all. Bobby was one year older than me, but he'd be the first one to tell you that I was better with guns, traps, stitches, and the like. His Dad had been a photographer, not a militia nut, so most of what Bobby knew how to do I had taught him. It only made sense that I led the way, but I never bossed Bobby around or anything like that. I always thought of him as a partner, not a sidekick. There was just a dynamic to our group that made everyone turn to me. I was never appointed our leader or anything like that, and frankly I didn't want to be. Whenever we encountered other gangs, it was always best to have one of the males step forward and do the talking. Almost all gangs had male leaders in the dog years.

We called them that because that's what our lives boiled down to.

The poison made people rapidly age, basically at the same rate as a dog: seven years of age for every calendar year that goes by. When it first spread, the elderly just crumbled like dust, and everyone our parents' age started to wither away. It didn't take but a few months for my parents to mirror my grandparents.

It was weird though.

The poison would rot your organs, so you'd deteriorate, but it didn't make you age like normal. Your bones would stay strong because they're not old and your skin wouldn't wrinkle and sag because it hadn't had enough time to. But your eyes would get milky with cataracts, your hearing would fade, your breathing would fall short, and for whatever reason, your hair would go ghost white or it would fall out altogether. Then your organs would start to go and soon enough you'd just go toxic and shut down.

There were other effects of the poison too, such as the girls never menstruating. Before you'd be old enough to have sexual desires, you would've already hit menopause. If you were a dude you'd be shooting blanks. That was a particularly grim effect because it spelled the end of the human race. The babies that had been born before the poison were going to be the last ones on earth, and they would last less than a quarter of a century.

I go inside to check on Julie and see that she's still sitting on the couch where we left her. She's drawing more of her pictures—illustrations she wants to put into a time capsule along with her journal entries, just in case mankind springs anew and wants to know what we were like. I don't have the heart to tell her how unlikely that will be or that all her pictures will have rotted and vaporized by the time new life could form.

Napping beside her is our dog, Teddy. He opens his eyes at the sound of my voice and his tails gets thumping.

"Where's Mike?" I ask her.

"Upstairs, resting."

My big brother does that a lot these days.

"It's a nice day outside," I say. "Bobby and I thought we could all have a picnic."

That just means a blanket and a very small portion of food. But it also means taking advantage of the warm weather season, which gets shorter each year.

"Okay," she says and gets off the couch.

She goes into the kitchen to put our lunches together. Everyone in the group has their own duties. I go to walk outside and Teddy leaps up and comes to me with his tail wagging. For him, nothing much has changed.

Mom and Dad got him for me when I was 12 because I'd been begging for a puppy for years. They'd finally felt I was old enough to handle it. He's 4 years old now. If you'd told me when I got him that he was going to outlive all of us, I'd have said you were crazy.

Bobby had started to go downhill early, all things considered. He'd always been more prone to illness though, even before the poison. He used to carry an asthma inhaler around, and he took prescription meds for his nasal problems. But once the dog years came, he had to go without it. I know that wasn't what really broke him down though. It was just the poison itself. Not just what it did physically, but also what it did to him emotionally. It just sort of chewed him up inside even more than the rest of us, which was damn plenty, I'll tell you. He tried to hide it from me, from all of us, but I loved him and knew what was in his tired heart.

He was a poet. Sensitivity ran in his family.

He wasn't a high school football hero turned apocalyptic warrior like Mike.

He wanted to see the good in the world.

He just couldn't seem to find it anymore.

When I come out, Bobby's on the porch starting off into the woods. I come up next to him and see that he's watching the birds spin and bleat in the bare branches. I step into him, and he throws his arm around me.

"Betcha nobody ever thought we'd live out our golden years together, huh?" he says.

I pat his chest and ask, "How are you feeling?"

He had a rough night last night, coughing and sniffling beside me. He's phlegmy all the time now and hacks up a lot of blood. He always tries to hide it from me, so I don't say nothing. What's the point?

"I'm feeling better," he says, but I know he's lying.

I stand there and just let him hold me, knowing it won't last any more than anything else but wishing it could go on so much longer because it's one of the few beautiful things I have left, and definitely the sweetest. It's not fair that he doesn't have good genes like Mike and me. But then, seeing how Mike is at his advanced age, maybe it's better to go young. All I know is that I wish it was me that was fading away instead of him. I prefer dying to going on without my Bobby.

"Birds seem happy today," he says.

"Damned poison only affects us humans."

"The change in the sky and trees seemed to throw them off for a while, but I think they're used to it now."

"Yeah. So am I."

"It's nice to see some beauty left in the world."

He leans in and kisses my forehead, letting me know, like he always does, just how beautiful he thinks I am and just how treasured. While everything and everyone else has changed, Bobby's still the same. He's my Bobby—the same boy who used to skip rocks on the lake when we were in camp, and the same boy who first kissed me on the floor of the roller rink after he'd helped me up. Just like then, when I feel like I have nothing left to hold on to, I just take Bobby's hand and suddenly it all doesn't seem as difficult as it was a moment ago. Somehow it all seems so, so easy.

I felt worst for Mike.

He had bailed us out of so many dangerous situations when everything had first fallen apart. He'd done a lot of killing, and I know it haunted him. He had been not just our leader but also our hero. He'd fended off people who tried to steal our food and weapons. Later, when times got much darker, he kept the gangs away. He wouldn't even think twice, and he was a great shot too. He taught Bobby how to fight, and he taught me to use a rifle even better than I already could. His word was the code we lived by, and he had never steered us wrong.

But once he'd gotten past 20, even he was well aware that he wasn't fit to lead us anymore. He was forgetful. He would often confuse dreams with reality. He would sometimes talk about people and things from the old days as if they still existed. There were moments of lucidity, but with each day they seemed to lessen in duration.

Mike was the last family member I had left. We would care for him to the bitter end, dementia or not. But there was a hollowness to his eyes now that was at best sad and at worst frightening. His eyes had gone black and wild like an animal, so that they seemed to look past you, through you—a look that reminded me way too much of how Dad's were in the end.

Julie comes out of the house with a full tray and begins tapping the rain barrel to fill the tall cup of powdered milk. She comes to the ground where we're sitting in the pale light of the sun and stirs the milk into the oats, and then she opens up the single cans of tuna and pinto beans. For dessert, we each get a spoonful of peanut butter. Tea that she has made from pine needles fills three cups. Teddy stands beside us the whole time, drooling. There will be no scraps for him, no matter how much Julie wants to sneak him some. He eats his dog food in the morning and at night only. House rules.

"I'm gonna make rabbit stew with the hare Mike shot yesterday," she says.

It had been a good round of hunting in the brush, even if we hadn't spotted any deer. One thing that hasn't faded in my brother is his killer instinct. He's like a damn wolf. He goes all still and stops breathing, and then he loads the crossbow so quietly you'd think he was a ninja.

"Did you bring him a plate?" I ask her.

"Yes, Skye. But he's still sleeping. I left it on his night stand."

The oats get soggy because I try to savor them, but I ain't about to waste a drop. The tuna is an old standby that I'm sick of, but I gobble it down too, wishing I could have some more. Funny how I used to be vegetarian. I sure wish you could grow something in this soil. At least we still have plenty of canned vegetables and fruits.

"I think we'll have some peaches tonight too," I say, thinking of them.

There's not much else to look forward to but meals. We play board games and read old books. We sing songs and tell stories. We get a little buzzed on whisky but never too drunk to shoot. Most of all we sit by the fire to stay warm and hope to make it through another night without any trouble.

This must be what it was like in the old west.

I take it back.

Mike wasn't the one I felt worst for. Julie was.

In a few years I knew Julie would be barely 15 and on her own. Every day Bobby and I would teach her new things and help her practice the old ones. He was so good with his little sister. Made me sad to think what a good Daddy he would've been to our babies. Julie had become a good cook by then—far better than the rest of us. I'd taught her to take down a squirrel at fifty yards, and she and Teddy were a solid duck-hunting duo. She could find water by following animals at night, and she could identify edible nuts like acorns. She could sew clothes and stitches, build a fire and shelter with sticks, mend a fracture and treat a burn, and she knew how to make Teddy attack as well as back off. These were all skills that Dad drilled into Mike and I and we passed down to the others.

But what Julie did best was draw and write, so we saved our paper and all writing utensils for her. She became lost in those imaginary worlds, and who could blame her. The end result was always impressive too. She'd come up with short stories about explorers, ghosts, and princesses that she'd read to us by firelight, and she'd decorated the house with portraits of each of us, as well as the still life drawings and landscape pieces. My favorites were the ones she did of Teddy.

Her one wish was to have a guitar. She had used to take lessons and she still has several guidebooks. There's nothing but time for her to learn to play guitar. If any of us had felt it was safe enough to travel into the city anymore, we would have tried to find her one.

The sky is turning red, meaning that the afternoon storms will be coming soon. We all hope it will be more rain. Lately it's been mostly heat lightning and hail. Bobby enjoys the show, but I find each one of them scarier than the last. The weather's gone strange. But it ain't storming yet, so we stay outside a little longer. Bobby and I are alone, and he has his hand under my dress. Julie is in the front yard playing Frisbee with Teddy. In so many ways he's become her dog now, and I'm okay with that. He'll be beside her when we're all gone, and that makes me feel a little better about things.

Bobby and I lift up our heads when he starts growling.

He never growls at any of us.

He goes silent around critters because he's a hunter.

We know damn well what his growling means.

The garage was our storage shed and where we kept our emergency getaway mini-van. Bobby and I had the master bedroom, and Julie and Mike had a bedroom each. We had a kitchen and a living room, and with Pete gone, the dining room had become just a big, empty space. We had two bathrooms, but we relieved ourselves outside and only used the tubs for our monthly baths, recycling the water from person to person, the girls going first and the boys last. The only part of the house that had changed drastically during the dog years was the attic.

It had a low ceiling so you could only crouch or sit. Up there we kept some extra supplies, along with Pete's old mattress. It was laid out facing the wood blinds of the attic's window, which faced the front yard. It was there to keep your elbows comfortable. Propped up before it, with the barrel just poking out of the window, was the semi-automatic rifle with the telescopic sight and the hand guards attached to the front of the receiver.

The attic was our sniper tower.

I'm headed inside while Bobby is running to the front yard, going for Julie. We both know the drill. Only this is *not* a drill. I can hear the wood of the front gate cracking, and Teddy is barking his head off now. I'm so glad we keep guns on us. Bobby has his .38 and Julie has her .22. I've got my Glock 19, my personal favorite, but that's not the gun I'm going to get behind.

I'm the best shot of the four of us.

By the time I reach the living room, I can see that the front door is open, and I can hear the trusty shotgun being pumped on the front porch. Mike is awake and he's ready. I glance outside as I head upstairs and see that he didn't even waste time putting on clothes.

I listen as I make my way to the attic.

"Best turn back now," Mike warns, his voice full of gravel.

"We just wanna talk to you," one of them says.

"I let this shotgun do my talkin' for me, boy."

I'm wondering if they saw the bear trap before one of them could step in it.

"A storm's comin'," another voice says. "We need shelter."

"There's no room at the inn," I hear Bobby say.

I open the attic door, climb up, and fling myself onto the mattress. The rifle is always loaded.

I open the window so I can see, and put my good eye at the scope. I see three boys at the foot of the driveway, past the gate that they've busted open. Two of them look about fourteen and the other one looks about ten. But we all know this trick. Hiding behind the fence are two older, bigger boys; at least 17. I can see them just fine and can pop them from here, but I wait. I'm not like my brother. I hate spilling blood when it ain't necessary. But every one of these bastards has a weapon. The boys behind the fence are packing a rifle, and probably more. One of them has something strapped to his back, but I can't tell if it's a sword or rifle or god knows what. The boys inside hold a machete and a lawnmower blade that has been fitted with a handle, and I can see one of them has some sort of weapon in his pants. Even the little kid has a kitchen knife and what looks like a pipe sticking through his belt.

Mike takes a cue from Bobby's biblical reference.

"You boys are gonna learn about the power and the glory in about two seconds," Mike says.

The wind has picked up, and his long, grey hair and beard spin in it, making him look like a crazed, bare-assed wizard. Bobby has tucked Julie behind him, but her gun is in her hand and I'm proud of her for it. Teddy is roaring like he's rabid.

"We're hungry," one says.

"Learn to hunt," Bobby tells them. "There's no food we can spare."

Seeing that their ruse isn't working, one of the older boys creeps forward. I see the other one has a revolver, but he's still hiding, so I keep my sights on the one with the rifle.

"There don't need to be no trouble," the rifleman says. "We just think y'all should share."

"We ain't got nothin'," Bobby says.

"Well, maybe you ain't got food and water, but I can see you've got a woman behind you."

My blood burns with anger. I want to shoot him now but don't want to set the others off. My group is outnumbered, after all. They don't know about the fifth boy.

"She's just a kid, you bastard," Bobby says.

"Old enough to spread her legs," the pistol packer says.

To my surprise, Bobby shoots first.

"Kill it," Dad had said.

We were standing in the woods in knee high snow. I was numb from the cold and all I wanted to do was go home, but we had found a deer after hours of hunting and there was no way Dad would let us leave until this was finished his way.

"Shoot it now," he whispered.

The deer was about fifteen feet away, slurping at the creek. I had it in my sights, but I was having trouble seeing because of the tears that kept filling my eyes.

"This is a rite of passage, Skye. You have to learn to kill if you're going to survive."

I didn't want to kill anything, especially not an innocent fawn that only wanted a sip of water. My hands had begun to shake.

"Forget about what you'll do for food," Dad said. "What are you gonna do when someone tries to rape you or kill your brother?"

I fired, sending the fawn tumbling into the rocks of the creek bed. The water ran so red you'd have thought it was full of salmon.

A bloodbath unfolds.

Even Teddy gets into it. He lunges at one of the middle-aged boys, grabbing the arm that held the lawnmower blade. The one with the rifle is winged by Bobby's shots, but as he steps up to shoot, Mike blasts him, pumps again, and blasts a second time before the bastard can even hit the ground. The blood spatters against the fence and the yard is soaked in seconds. Mike moves forward while Bobby holds back, firing from the porch as he makes himself into a human shield for his little sister.

The youngest boy tucks behind the older ones, crying instantly. The pistol packer moves from behind the fence to try and surprise everyone. He takes quick shots at Mike just as I take my shot at him. Mike spins as a jet of blood spurts from his shoulder and the shotgun falls. But my bullet lands in the center of the pistol packer's chest, and he hits the ground screaming. By now Teddy has shredded the other boy's throat. It's wide open, and he's bleeding out quickly. His face is so slick with red that I can't tell if he's alive or not.

The machete boy actually jumps into the air like a gymnast and comes at Mike with all he's got. The awning blocks my shot but I see

Bobby run to Mike's aid. He fires a round, misses, and then he's out of bullets. But Mike's got the lawnmower blade now, and he's raving like the lunatic he has surely become. The boy is faster than Mike, and he manages to block a few swings with the machete and even slices Mike across the chest. But Mike doesn't even seem phased by this. He swings the blade down like a sledgehammer, and it bashes through the boy's defense and sinks about 7 inches into the spot where the boy's shoulder meets his neck. His cries remind me that he's really just a kid. He falls with the blade still in him. Mike takes the machete from him and starts hacking away. Teddy runs in circles around this terrible scene, barking and barking with his fur on end. I can hear Julie screaming somewhere, and the little boy at the front of the gate is paralyzed by his fear.

I think the war is over, but then Mike does something even crazier than the butchering of the kid who lies in pieces in the dead grass.

He starts to run toward the little boy, the machete high above his head, glistening with blood. Bobby sees this and chases after him.

"Mike! No! He's just a kid!" he cries.

Mike reaches the little boy, and just as he's about to chop him in two, Bobby tackles him. They tumble to the dirt, and the little boy finally comes to his senses, drops his knife, and runs out the gate and into the street. Mike gets back up before Bobby can, pouncing like a gorilla. Through my sight, I can see the animal look on his face that has frightened me this past year whenever it has come across him. He's under the hold of his madness now and clearly doesn't even know who Bobby is as he comes down with the blade.

My shot echoes in the dusk as the top of my brother's head comes off. He folds like a raggedy doll and hits the ground, finally at peace. Bobby is covered in blood that is not his own, and Julie, seeing that the coast is clear, runs to him, brave considering the brutality of what she's just seen. Her love for him just overrules any other feelings she could have, just like it does for me.

I trot down the stairs and make my way out into the yard. It's all far more ghastly than it looked from the attic. There are severed limbs and guts thrown about like yesterday's trash. Blood is absolutely everywhere and bullets and the break-in have all but ruined the fence. Bobby is shaking when I reach him, and Julie's sobbing into his stomach—the most that I have seen from her since her mom died in her arms.

"Are either of you hit?" I ask.

"Huh?" he says.

His hearing had gone bad already, and now he's half deaf from all the gunfire.

"Are you okay?" I ask, louder.

He nods and pulls me in close. The three of us huddle into a hug for a moment and close our eyes against the awfulness all around us.

"Let's get inside," I say.

The rumble of thunder groans above and as I turn to go into the house I see the flash of steel poking out of the gate. I jump on Julie, pushing her to the ground.

"Duck!" I yell to Bobby, but he's too deaf and slow.

The little boy had a gun after all. What I'd thought was just a pipe was a little, one-shot zip gun.

Julie and I scream as Bobby falls to his knees and leans forward, clutching his belly while blood starts to trickle out of his mouth. I've drawn my gun, but I hear the boy's feet running up the street as he vanishes into the sorrow of the dark alleys. I brace Bobby and as he falls backward, I see that there's an oozing hole in his stomach. He heaves a bit and struggles to speak as the tears pour down my face. Beside me, Julie is a mess. Her face is in her hands and Teddy is beside her, whimpering and trying to comfort her with nuzzling.

"Take care of her," Bobby tells me.

"I will, baby."

He manages to smile, and my mind reels with late night kisses when he would sneak into my room, the Christmas when he saved up his allowance to buy me the necklace, cuddling through the carnival's cheap tunnel of love, and his gentle touch when he took my virginity on that summer night while we watched the fireflies come out.

"Don't you let this break you..." he says through the rising blood.

"Oh, Bobby," I cry. "I love you. I love you."

He's the only boyfriend I've ever had or ever will have.

"I love you too, Skye. I always will."

Tears roll down the sides of his face, and he winces from sadness as well as pain. Julie comes closer and collapses into him, and he manages to turn his head and kiss her cheek, leaving a little smudge of blood. He looks up at me, and I lean down and kiss him one more time. Above us, the red smoke has begun to separate and drift away, and now the stars are fading in against all that black. There's the beginning of a rainbow forming in the night. We get these now and then. It's like aurora borealis—rippling beams of multicolored light that make our world gorgeous, if just for a little while. Bobby always says that it's the only good thing to come out of the dog years. He loves watching them grow stronger and form into a lovely, wavering festival, but this time he's never gonna see it come.

There are five graves in the yard now, and Julie makes them new wreaths every few weeks. Summer's ending quickly, and the cold is getting stronger. In the living room, Julie and I have set up the old bed Bobby and I used to use so we can sleep by the fire. It's better for both of us this way. I hated rolling over and not feeling him there, and Julie doesn't want to sleep alone anymore. She has so many bad dreams. I hope they'll go away in time, just like I hope mine will. They say time heals all wounds, but that's something we don't have a lot of. All we have is a sisterly bond, a good dog, and enough ammo to take down anyone else who comes near our property.

We're celebrating my seventeenth birthday today, and we're treating ourselves to a feast. With our group cut in half, there's a lot more food to go around, so we're eating better, even though we wish we still had the boys to share it with. I've got one of Mom's tapes playing, but Julie says she has a new song for me. As it turns out, what was strapped to that one boy's back was an acoustic guitar. Tonight we're going to use one of the tapes to start recording them to add to her time capsule. As for the boy and his friends, I did what Mike had always wanted to do. Their bleached skulls are on spikes out front.

SKYE is a teenage girl, doing her best to survive in a world without adults. Her love for her sick boyfriend and remaining family carries her through the bleakness of their new world and keeps her finger close to a trigger. In her heart there is a wealth of compassion, but in her mind is the terrible knowledge of man's primal nature. This is her story...

KRISTOPHER TRIANA is the author of *Growing Dark*, and his novel *The Ruin Season* will be published in 2016. His work has appeared in countless magazines and anthologies. He is also a professional dog trainer and runs the popular horror webpage Tavern of Terror, where he rambles on and on about how much he loves 80s horror and forgotten VHS treasures. He lives in North Carolina with his wife.

STREETCLEANER

An account by Sara,

AS PROVIDED BY NATALIE SATAKOVSKI

Mama walked between me and the border, using her body as a shield when I tried to see past her.

"Don't look at them," she muttered, tugging me along by the wrist.

It was hard not to. It had been weeks since the last inundation was admitted to the city, and refugees infested the beach right up to the cyclone fencing. Tarp hovels and shopping bag tipis patched the shore, and the air stank of them. Through the wire, they watched us like animals hungry to break in, until a crack made everyone turn.

Smoke shot into the sky, rising from our side of the fence and tracing an arc toward the ocean. More people emerged from their hollows, looking between The City and the flare. Farther down the path, a citizen stood flailing in the direction of the fence.

"You're all going to die!" His eyes were livid, his voice urgent. "Go home! Run!"

The man looked as if he'd been whittled down to a skeleton. When several coast guards jumped on him, I heard bones hit the pavement, navy uniforms smothering his screams.

Mama's fingers dug into my shoulder.

"Who's that?" I asked as she dragged me away. I was straining over alternate shoulders, trying to watch as guards kneed the man to the cement.

"Nobody. And none of your business." She was patronizing me again.

"Why was he saying that?" I whined. "Just tell me."

Her lips made a line while her eyes remained directed ahead. "Because *they* ought to go home. Queue skippers, plotting a take-over. You know that."

I shook my arm free but quit dragging my feet, dissatisfied as we marched on.

When I went back to the beach the next day, it was deserted. Abandoned shelters flecked the sand like crustacean husks waiting for new occupants. The night before had been an admittance.

I went up to the chain-link and hung off the freezing steel, battling the gale to peer through. The unsewered beach reeked of sulphur, and junk flapped in the wind.

Someone shouted, "Hey, you."

I sprung off the wire guiltily. To my right, a sentry was yelling from his tower—but rather than scolding me, he was calling me up. I approached the watchtower, a sparse construction of recycled iron. The frame's paint job had been ruined by teenage scrawlings—tags and lovers' names in hearts. I climbed the stairs, watching the sand retreat on either side of the rail.

The coast guard crouched at the landing, offering me a toasty hand and guiding me into his cabin.

"Cold out there, isn't it?" he chuckled.

The first thing I noticed about him was his hair. It wasn't cropped and combed like that of other men but smoothed back and tied into a low pony tail. It looked silly.

He introduced himself as Marco. "Would you like to see the beach?" he asked.

Because I wasn't tall enough to see out the window, Marco slipped his hands under my arms and helped me onto his desk. The glass window went all around the lookout, revealing everything from the horizon on one side to the metallic storm-resistant city on the other. A nearby billboard depicted a caricature of three ravenous refugees, scaling the sides of a not-to-scale version of our island-city. Atop it, three victorious civil servants—the coast guard, the police, and the escobita—were blocking, kicking, and crushing them respectively. The coast guard looked nothing like Marco; the escobita looked nothing like Papa.

Near the water, a pair of guards dragged an abandoned vessel from the swell. Others traipsed the shoreline, each footstep sinking into black sand.

I hopped off the desk and stood in the centre of the cabin, in awe of the strange space. Beneath the glass, a rifle and binoculars hung from one wall, from the other, charts and crayon drawings. Looking closer at the latter, the pictures were of spidery yellow suns, crude fences, and smiling twig-people.

My thoughts returned to what had brought me to the beach. "Did you see that skinny man yesterday? Yelling at them to go home?" I asked.

Marco's gaze flittered, as if he was thinking of what to say. "Yes."

"Why did he do that?"

He reached for his open windbreaker and zipped it up. "Not everyone agrees with the escobitas."

That confused me. Without the streetcleaners, The City would be no better off than the mainland. We'd seen aerial videos of the crime and chaos, greedy mainlanders fighting for food. When the sea levels rose and the weather turned against us, the whole world turned to mayhem. Only we were safe in our island cities, where the citizens were kind and intelligent and helped each other survive.

Marco looked me over. "How old are you?" he asked. "Seven, eight?"

I frowned, though it was nothing new to be mistaken for younger. "Ten," I stated.

"Ah, I should have known. I was thinking 13 because you seem so clever but…" His words were blatant flattery but effective nonetheless.

School started in the weeks that followed, distracting me temporarily from what I'd seen on the beach. I was too awkward to blend with the other children and spent recesses by myself between the main building and the gymnasium. There I sat in a nook that I'd staked out as my own.

I crouched against the brick as usual and started unpacking my lunch when a pong of tobacco made me look down the corridor. A number of voices were giggling behind the wall. Eventually two girls emerged and I quickly looked out at the playground, embarrassed at being caught alone.

One of the girls walked straight past. The other stopped about a foot away, towering over me.

"Hey, shorty," she said. I recognized her as an older girl and a student representative, but she was no A-grade pupil; her class had voted her in for her looks. Maria Alejandra.

"Aren't you the cutest thing I've ever seen," she said.

I rolled my eyes; we were about to go through the *how-old-are-you* routine again.

"You look just like my baby sister…" She trailed off oddly, then said, "You look bored, why don't you come hang out with us?" She reached down and flicked her knee which was stained and flaking with grass. "—just for today."

I spent that recess with Alejandra, the other smoking girl, and two boys—one of the few mixed-gender friendship groups at our school—all 12-year-old seniors. When the bell rang, these kids were in no hurry to get back to class. I lingered anxiously, torn between seeming cool and avoiding my teacher's reprimand.

One of the boys, Daniel, turned to me. I marveled at his frames, antique alternatives to contact lenses. "Ever stayed up past curfew?"

"No."

"If you do, we'll let you hang out with us again. The beach is full and there's going to be an admittance this weekend. Come back on Monday and report what the escobitas do. That's how we'll know you did it."

On admission nights, a switch somewhere would tick over, and the air raid sirens would sound. In our coastal district, there were measures "to prevent damage from flooding," and when curfew commenced, the external staircases automatically retracted, leaving no access to ground level. Shutters clamped down over windows to protect the glass, eliminating any possibility of viewing the night outside. When Papa left for work and Mama went to bed, I snuck out onto the rooftop.

The city was unlit, neighboring edifices barely visible by the light of the gibbous moon. A clatter resounded in the distance. By the beach, the horizontal beam of the border gate rose, glowing under a lonely street light. I heard them before I saw them. The murmur below was like a festival but dim and tinged with confusion. I sensed them pouring into the streets, seawater on a sinking ship.

A rattle of steel and aluminum echoed through the air, rebounding off brick and asphalt and dissipating into the sky. It was the sound of the station's garage doors opening. Several blocks away, the stark ray of headlamps illuminated a corner of the city. Myriad heads appeared below, grey and gold pebbles. From that pocket of glowing light, an engine roared as loud as a low-flying plane, chugging and snorting like a Trojan horse of monstrous mechanics.

All down the street, people clawed at the walls. One man scrambled upward, trampling on the ear of the woman next to him, ripping at featureless brick with nothing to grasp. Another man, standing atop anonymous shoulders, made a futile leap toward the retracted staircase above.

The escoba emerged from its cave, roaring down the street, headed in my direction. I squinted through the rapidly spinning lasers, a disorienting display above the headlamps. Smoke stacks protruded hornlike from the vehicle's roof, and giant propellers at the front of the truck made steel sounds as they hacked the air.

Refugees could barely run at first with the crowding so dense, but their movements soon synchronized into a stampede. With the powerful light of the headlamps thrown over them, the refugees streamed through the street. About a block away, another swarm was being herded from behind, headed toward the first and on a path to collision.

Something caught my attention on the adjacent building. For a moment, lights continued dancing in my vision and I couldn't quite see. Then the flickering shapes became Alejandra and Daniel, pointing at me with wide eyes. They scattered. A thick palm settled on my shoulder. The guard was barely a silhouette in the night, his face masked by two alien eyes protruding from a respirator.

I felt her behind me as I ran to my room. I threw myself onto the mattress, the impact causing briny vomit to rise into my mouth.

"Sara, staying up past curfew, you know better than that," Mama said.

"How can they do that?" I screamed into my pillow.

"You're a big girl now. Think. What would happen if the refugees grew so many they could take over? There'd be nothing left for us *or for them*. It wouldn't help anyone."

"But I thought they were building underground?"

The mattress compressed, and her gentle hand touched my back. "They are, chiqui, but it isn't enough."

My throat stung. "It's not fair."

"Shh," she said. "Your grandparents were refugees too. We were lucky enough to get a home here. Now let's do our best to keep it."

The man on the beach had been trying to tell the refugees the truth. I didn't know how my father could do what he did. I would rather face deportation than perform duties as an escobita. No matter how bad conditions were on the mainland, I'd have preferred to starve.

The beach was littered with encampments, and a cluster of black boats floated on the horizon. Marco lifted his hat and hooked it over my head. I had to hold the too-big cap down so the wind didn't lift it away. I told Marco what I had seen.

"Doesn't anybody care? Why won't someone stop this?" Suddenly shy, I removed the cap and fingered the 'rising city' badge. It reflected a golden orb onto Marco's uniform.

"Come," he said.

Inside, Marco spread a newspaper across his desk, pushing log books and charts away as if they were scrap paper. He placed a hand down on the page he wanted me to see. There was a photograph of a man. Handcuffed and held before the camera by two military police, his shirtsleeve was held up to reveal a tattoo on his bicep: an ornate boat, with a ribboning flag across it—the white banner of peace. The headline read, "Subversive Underground Foiled by City Intelligence."

Marco explained the meaning of "subversive" and "underground," both saving me the embarrassment of asking, and making me feel adult enough to know—worthy. A veil was raised from my eyes.

"See," he said. "Some people are doing things."

"Like the man on the beach?" I asked.

"Exactly. This group believes in a *policy of disclosure*. They want The City to tell The Mainland that we're not letting refugees in. Why would mainlanders threaten our home if there isn't enough room? This group wants The City to help the mainland stabilize from economic devastation. Through our assistance, less boat people will arrive on our shores."

I took in these new concepts. Marco was so different to my parents, not just in the way he thought, but in the way he treated me. Despite the weight of our conversation, his eyes creased into a calm smile. I wondered how old he was. No older than twenty-five I hoped, because that would mean he was only 15 years older than me and maybe, one day… No, I was kidding myself. He had to be at least thirty.

"What about you?" I asked. "What do you think?"

His grin melted but his eyes stayed the same. "I think you know what I think."

We were made to stand in a line—Alejandra, Daniel, and myself. Our principal was a man who should have retired years ago but for The City's limited resources. Señor Zapata's jacket bore insignia that showed that he was ex-military. His powerful voice almost threw us against the wall.

"This is not acceptable," he boomed.

Alejandra and Daniel were red-faced, staring at the carpet. Neither of them had spoken a word to me since arriving.

"Curfew time is when refugees are admitted and when escobas prevent our streets from devolving into madness. If you want to know more about refugees, just watch the news, read the papers. You'll see greedy, evil mainlanders who just want to steal your home any chance they get."

I said, "But we were all refugees. At one time." It was out before I realized what I was saying.

The others sniggered. It was as if I'd admitted a truth about my family that didn't in fact pertain to everyone. But even the history taught to us corroborated the fact. The City was built on a high-altitude plain as it slowly grew isolated from the rest of South America. We were the same, mainlanders and citizens of The City—did that mean nothing to them?

Sr. Zapata huffed. "This is a serious offence. If you were any older, you'd be facing charges for being on the roof after curfew. And anything more serious would see you deported."

I thought of the subversive photographed in the paper, and that harbinger of truth, the skeleton I saw that day on the beach. All of them would be gone by now.

"As punishment, you three will stay back after class to clean this school from floor to ceiling."

Alejandra and Daniel looked up simultaneously, shooting me venomous looks. For some reason, they blamed me.

Between The City and the border fence, artificial trees lined the footpath, huge cylinders hailing the sky. As I walked, they whirred and sank into their rinsing chambers, preparing to scrub more CO_2 from the air. On the other side of the fence, refugees stirred, looking on with curiosity. A tiny boy shrieked with excitement, squeezing his hand through the wire and pressing his face into the diamonds. A pair of children about my own age ran from the beach. They were a girl and a boy, reminding me of the friends I almost had. Uninterested in the trees, they locked eyes with me and towed along the fence, following as I passed in imitation of my gait. I thought, *these people aren't bad, they're just kids.* I had to do something to save them.

I waited a week before I returned. The beach was half full, many of the boat people camped up by the fence, others spreading out toward the shore. Several hundred meters to my right, a guard loitered by a gate, to my left, a watchtower. I couldn't see its sentry from this distance, but I knew he could see me. I fingered the folded paper inside my coat pocket. Could I approach the fence with a semblance of innocence, coming near enough to another child to pass it through? The watch of the guards prickled over my skin. I stepped toward the fence.

Instantly, the guard to my left marched toward me. I turned, and instead of going through with my plan, continued down the path.

The paper in my pocket was softening with sweat. I came to the tower with the silvery graffiti on its columns. Marco peered out over the beach, his head haloed by the sun. This was it, my chance.

I snatched up a rock and inside the thin cover of the staircase, I fixed it to the note with my hair-tie. Before reaching the top, I had the little message-grenade hidden in my pocket.

Marco greeted me with a light pinch on the shoulder. I shifted in my coat, feeling the preliminary itch of guilt. How would he feel toward me if he knew what I was doing?

"I've been waiting for you to visit. I found another newspaper clipping…"

As he moved to the corner of the cabin, I made as if to amble to the balcony and stood outside by the barrier. Then I took one last glance back at Marco leaning over his desk.

I pulled the rock from my coat and threw.

A shout. Marco whipped his rifle from its hook and bounded toward me.

"Get out!" He yanked the gun up, peered through the eyepiece.

I turned and rattled down the stairwell. From the beach, I heard howls of fear and pain. On the ground, a troop of guards entered the cage before the border gate, waiting for it to open. I didn't wait to see what happened. I ran all the way home.

That night, Mama and Papa's spoons clinked against the crockery while I sat tearing up my bread rations. The sound of sirens made us look up.

"Curfew tonight?" said Mama.

I realized I was unconsciously clenching my jaw. Blood began to vibrate my chest.

"You're not at work, love?" she said to Papa.

He shook his head, eyes slanted in confusion. "I didn't think the beach was full—"

I could almost hear their minds click; something had gone wrong. The refugees were being admitted before the beach was full, The City didn't *need* all its escobitas on duty.

My face was getting hot. Mama glanced at me, then silenced Papa with a piercing look that meant *Let's talk about this later.* How I hated their condescension at that moment. But I hated my own naivety even more.

A knock on the door. It was the police.

I was seated at a table and made to face a policeman. Mama and Papa stood behind. Good citizens of The City, they believed in assisting the investigation any way they could.

"We want to ask you some questions about your friend Marco," said the policeman, tapping the button on a recording device. "You know Marco, don't you?"

"Yes," I answered.

"Now, Sarita, Marco is a bad man. You're a lucky girl to be safe with us. Marco has done some terrible things. Do you know what they are?"

"No." If they thought Marco had been responsible for the note, I was going to have to confess.

"Marco is an enemy of The City. Did you know that he wants to give your home away to boat people? He wants to let them in by the hundreds, free to steal all your food and toys. If that happened, our city would become like the mainland. That's why we need your help. We want to ask you some questions about Marco, to help us stop people like him. Okay?"

"I don't know anything," I said.

He disregarded my statement. "Did Marco ever tell you about his... plans?"

I was preparing to confess but struggling for the words. "No."

The policeman tilted on his seat, reaching into a back pocket. Casually, without even looking at it, he placed a Ziploc bag onto the desk, my cursive on a ragged paper within.

"Let me ask you another question," he continued. "Did Marco have any *markings* on his body? Anything you can think of, scars, lines?

"Not that I know of."

"Tattoos?"

Silence. A clock's ticking resounded through the room.

"Can you describe Marco's tattoo?" he asked.

"No."

"Well how did you know there was a tattoo when I asked you to describe it? Why didn't you say, *what tattoo?* Surely you must know about it, but you don't want to say anything because you know that tattoo represen—*means* something bad."

So Marco was a member of the dissident underground. But if they already knew this, why were they asking me? Marco was in serious trouble and I was responsible. Not because of the note but because of the attention it had drawn to him.

The policeman continued. "We know that you threw the note. It's in your handwriting and we have your fingerprints on it." He touched the bag. "Do you know how serious this is? It's illegal to communicate with refugees through the fence, you know that. And you know what happens to people who commit crimes, don't you?"

"Yes."

"What?"

"They get deported."

"That's right," he smiled evilly. "Deported. Sometimes, even whole families, if they're trying to put The City at risk, like you did."

Mama and Papa were huddled in the corner. Had I betrayed everyone in my life?

"But we also know that you spent time with Marco and that he influenced you. We know you saw his tattoo and you wouldn't have thrown the note if he hadn't told you to. If you're honest with us, we can prove you're innocent and that you were manipu—tricked by him. So I'm going to ask you again. Did you see Marco's tattoo?"

They already knew about Marco. They probably had him locked up somewhere. All they had to do was search him to incriminate him. If I didn't make my false confession, they'd find a way to pin him regardless and we'd all get deported. At least I had a chance to save myself and my family.

"Did you see Marco's tattoo?" he asked, louder this time.

A warm droplet slid off my face and onto my hand. "Yes."

"Can you describe it?"

"It's a ship," I said, "and a flag."

"Did Marco tell you to throw the note down?"

"... Yes."

The policeman sat back as if sated by a good meal. He flicked the device off with a lazy arm and rose from the table. He turned to my parents, and as if I wasn't even in the room, said, "We've got it. The boys will go pick him up."

I was removed from my usual classes, made to watch history videos and sit tests about the state of the mainland, the privilege of our home. The rest of the time, I had to join the special needs children, regurgitating what I was being taught.

When I saw Alejandra again, she was leaning on a bathroom basin, smoking shamelessly. "Retard," she laughed, "refugee baby."

Time after time, I was singled out.

The profesora would address me in class. "And Sara, are refugees good people or bad people?"

I peered out with as much contempt as I could muster. "Bad!"

And I was made to feel ashamed.

I didn't make any friends that year, or the year after. But I made a promise to get my last one back. If he was on the mainland, I would find a way to save him, or failing that, I'd save others in his honor. Deportation, I realized, was probably just another state lie.

I drew sigils on my skin, of boats and sailing ships and flags, hoping that one day I'd find the others and join them.

SARA is a civil servant by day and member of the dissident underground by night. Since having a transformative experience as a child where she lost her best friend, she's been on a life-mission to restore socio-economic stability across the mainland and open the privileges of The City up to all.

NATALIE is an ex-English teacher who's turned to copywriting to support her fiction habit. Her fictional work has appeared in *Infernal Ink* and *AntipodeanSF*, and is upcoming in the anthology *In Sunshine Bright and Darkness Deep*. She loves reading all things creepy, from southern gothic to the new weird.

THE STORY OF AFTER

Letters by Co,

AS PROVIDED BY ALEXIS J. REED

Dear Em,

I've got to be honest with you, the apocalypse beat is getting me down. You'll probably think I'm being selfish, that there were hundreds of applicants for this position, and I should be grateful. I am, don't think for a second that I'm not thankful. It's just that I'm struggling to maintain my distance.

It's been so exciting, I know it has. Over the past year and a half, I've seen earthquakes and tsunamis tear apart Thetis 5. I've watched as an asteroid collided with Farkalia, exploding in the atmosphere, raining down the end. I've stood idly by as the citizens of Palereos 9 destroyed each other with bombs that burned white hot, melting the skin from the people, leaving them as posed shadows on the ground.

I've reported it all with suitable reverence and objectivity. Stood in front of the iriscams as the calamity unfolded behind me. I just kept on staring straight ahead into Je's eyes, into those minuscule cameras, and I knew I was really looking at you. Hoping you'd absolve me, lessen the suffering caused by my own indifference.

The viewers have loved it though. Me blasting into their homes as they watch the carnage unfold. They gasp. They may even cry, but then they go to bed and they know they're safe. If there's one thing I've learnt on the apocalypse beat, though, it's that none of us are safe, not really. We're only secure until we're not. We're only alive until we're not.

We arrived at the latest scene a few days ago. Third planet in the Persepha Sphere. It's beautiful, Em, you'd love it here. Mostly water with some magnificent mountains, vast deserts, blocks of ice rising out of the sea like leviathans. There's so much life here, it's hard to fathom really. The dominant species are a lot like us. Bipedal, primate origins. But violent. God, you wouldn't believe the brutality.

We met Ti on the surface after the camo surgery. It's started to feel less strange, wearing an alien face. It's like they become a part of me. This time, the feeling's even more intense. By putting on this disguise, I'm becoming more of myself rather than less. At least I got to stay as a woman this time. Their genders are very similar to ours too.

Anyway, where was I? Oh yes, we met Ti on the surface. He's been here for the past seven years, working on a book. He's even married a local. You might have read some of his articles on the Lines, he's a good writer, really shows the essence of a place, you know? He's distraught about all this, but he says that our projections are dead-on. The plague or "flu" as they call it here has already begun to spread across some of the less wealthy nations. It seems strange, this concept of rich and poor. It might be something for our own economists to study.

Their technology isn't able to provide a cure for this disease. We project a massive 80% of the population succumbing to it. I don't know what will happen to the remaining 20%. I'm already thinking about staying on, after it's all over, to chart what happens "after the apocalypse." Maybe that wouldn't sell. Would you miss me if I stayed? Would you join me? You'd love all the blues and greens. Anyway, got to go.

Love,

Co.

Dear Em,

Have you seen my reports? I bet you have, you always said you were my biggest fan. Je got some great footage of that medical centre. He was so happy with it, muttering about how it's going to win him the Terragia Award. It was some of his best work, I'll give him that. I was with him, of course, as he made his way along the lines of beds. We couldn't tell who was alive and who was dead. It's hard to know for sure with these aliens. As Je walked through the ward with his eyes slowly panning around, I sat next to a woman and gave her some water. She choked it back, but it seemed to soothe her. You're going to think that I don't sound like myself. Getting involved with the subject matter like that. I couldn't help it, these people are just so interesting. Water is everything here, it's their world, it's them, it's even in the air they breathe. The woman nodded at me and rested back on the pillow. I felt a hand on my shoulder. It was the man in the bed opposite. He was sitting up, looking at me with bloodshot eyes. He spoke so quickly that it took the translation matrix a dot longer than usual to decipher it.

"Where's Harry? Have you seen him? Do you know where he is?"

I told him that I hadn't seen Harry but that if I did, I'd bring him over. This seemed to placate the man, and I eased him back down onto his bed. He fell asleep. For a second I thought he was dead, but then I saw the characteristic rise and fall of his chest, indicating life. I turned back to the woman. She was staring at me.

"Harry's his son. Seven years old. He died day before yesterday," she said.

"Oh, I'm sorry."

"You ought to be careful in here. Don't they give you them protective suits?"

"Not anymore."

"Who would have thought I'd die from a cold?"

"Cold? Would you like a blanket?"

"No... a cold. You're not from around here are you?"

I gave her some more water and settled her under her sheets. I sat watching her for some time, how her nostrils flared as she breathed in, the way her eyelids flickered. When I turned back to the man, his chest had stopped rising and falling. I covered him over with a blanket. That's their tradition here. The living don't want to gaze at death. But these days they've not really got much of a choice. The ones in the ward were the lucky ones. I'm sure you've seen Je's footage of the outside. The corpses in the street.

When Je found me, he was frantic, thought I'd gotten lost. He didn't understand why I had sat with the people. What could I possibly gain from talking to them? He didn't understand. Do you?

Ti left this morning with his Earthen wife. Don't know how he'll explain that one to the ethics committee, but I wish him well. I thought about asking him to take me along, but I can't leave Je on his own, and I can't leave these people. Not yet.

Do you think it's right? The Codicil of Non-Intervention? I used to believe in it completely, and I think that was a better time. A time of total faith, total confidence. Now, I look out of this hotel window at the ragged death below, and I'd do anything to stop it, to make it better. Don't tell anyone I told you that. I know you wouldn't, but still.

Love,
Co.

Dear Em,

I'm sure you've been following the casts. Headquarters say that this is the most popular apocalypse in recent memory, and that the viewing figures are enormous. They're even talking about the film rights. Who do you think should play me in the film? Someone gorgeous, obviously.

God, it feels ridiculous to be talking about movies. Je and I are holed up in a hotel. The last time we went out was when we got the film of the riot. We managed to get some good shots I think, don't you? Je was particularly happy when that bald-headed man beat that smaller man to death with that stick thing (known here as a "baseball bat").

So much of the population is dead now, and it seems that the whole planet sings with the stench of decaying corpses. It's amazing how quickly the surviving populace becomes immune to the bodies of their fellow humans just littering the streets. Some make fires to dispose of the carcasses. I don't know which smell is worse, decaying flesh or cooking flesh. Mostly, they're taken away by carrion-eaters. The people just walk on by as the cadavers get eaten away at by rats or dogs or birds. Maybe that's what survival is, not looking at anything too long. In which case, I'm screwed because I gaze at all this suffering, I stare. And I don't look away.

I want to go back out onto the streets, but Je says it's too risky. He's been spooked ever since he got elbowed in the face at the riot. He was a mess afterward, couldn't quite believe he'd been touched, let alone hit by one of the subjects. Then he saw the footage and was pleased with it, a slow-motion elbow coming right at the cameras. So now we're hiding in this hotel with a pathetic barricade at the door. We're using the drones to gather film for the reports. I look at the people out there, how hardened they are, and then I think of Je and his bleeding nose, and how he thought it was the end of all things. It wasn't. We're softened by watching it all on our screens from a distance. Hell, I'm softened even reporting it because we never get consumed by it, we never really feel it. But we're not immune, Em, no one is.

Love,

Co.

Dear Em,

Je's gone. I'm sure you've heard by now. Last night, we were asleep when we heard voices in the corridor, followed by the sound of someone trying to push the door open. Je was up so quickly. He grabbed his pack.

"We're going," he said. "Emergency evac."

He nodded at me as he disappeared, 'ported back up to the ship. I think he expected me to follow, but I didn't. Instead, I inserted the iriscams he'd left behind and waited in the dark for the marauders to break down the defences. They didn't. Whoever they were, they must have grown bored and moved on. I thought about comming Je, telling him to come back down, but I didn't. Instead, I waited for probably another hour, my legs growing numb from being crouched in the half-light. Then I got up, packed my bag, and started to disassemble the barricade. Moving the bed was the hardest part, and I was worried that the noise would attract others. The hallway was pitch black, and the stench was a visceral assault on the senses. I used my light, but even with that, I tripped a few times on soft things that lay in the dark. By the time I reached the stairs, I had to vomit. An interesting sensation. Not at all pleasant, but weirdly I felt better afterward, as though I'd released some of the poison in my system.

I met no one on the stairs, or in the lobby. The water feature now a stagnant pond, growing ever-greener. Outside, the sun was starting to come up as I walked down the street. I crunched on broken glass, finding bodies here and there with their eyes just staring out at me.

It's so hard to tell if they're alive or dead, Em, you wouldn't believe it. I saw a few pillars of smoke rising up into the air, and they reminded me of the spiralling cerulean nebulas of the Sparses Sphere. Only these were grey. A different shade of grey to the sky but grey nonetheless. I avoided them, not wanting to know the destruction that caused them.

I know I should have gone back to the ship, but I just couldn't. If I went back to the ship, I'd have to return home and then, in a few months, there'd be another apocalypse, another slaughter. And I just can't watch it again. I can't keep reliving extinction. So I'm going to stay here. I'm on a road at the moment, and I'll be sending footage when I can. Maybe I can start a new story. The story of after. I hope you can understand.

Love,
Co.

CO is an apocalypse reporter for Feed One, the main news channel on her home world of Metis. Her reports on planetary catastrophes have earned her numerous awards and accolades. Opponents to her approach call these broadcasts voyeuristic and ghoulish while others feel it is important for the people caught in these devastations to be remembered. The programmes have made some call for the Codicil of Non-Intervention to be rescinded in extreme cases. Her wife, Em, lives in the Acaste region with their two pet sylogramanders.

ALEXIS J. REED is a UK-based writer who self-published her first novel, *Searching For You*, in 2012. Two of her plays were performed in festivals in London and Cambridge. She has also had two stories shortlisted for the International Aeon Award for speculative fiction as well as having short fiction published both in the UK and abroad.

IN A MANNER OF SPEAKING

An account by Soshi Patel,
AS PROVIDED BY CHARITY TAHMASEB

I use the last of the good candles to build the radio. I still have light. The fire burns, and there is a never-ending supply of the cheap, waxy candles in the storeroom. I will—eventually—burn through all of those. My fire will die. The cold will invade this space.

But today I have a radio. Today I will speak to the world—or what's left of it. I compare my radio to the picture in the instructions. It looks the same, but not all the steps had illustrations. This troubles me. My radio may not work.

I crank the handle to charge the battery. This feels good. This warms my arms, and I must take deep breaths to keep going. I shake out my hand and crank some more. When buzz and static fill my ears, I nearly jump. That, too, sounds warm. I am so used to the cold. The creak and groan of ice, the howl of the wind. These cold sounds are their own kind of silence. They hold nothing warm or wet or alive.

I decide on a frequency for no other reason than I like the number. I press the button on the mouthpiece. This, according to the instructions, will let the world hear me.

"Hello?" My voice warbles and I leap back, as if something might spring from the speakers.

Nothing does, of course. In fact, nothing happens at all. It takes more than one try to reach the world.

"Hello? Hello? Is anyone there? Can you hear me? I would like to talk to you."

Perhaps I should try another frequency—or try a little patience. If someone is out there with a radio, might they right now be cranking a handle to charge a battery, or sleeping, or adding wood to their fire? This last is something I must do and soon. The embers grow a bright orange, but the chill has invaded the edges of the room.

That means venturing outside. Of all the chores, I like this one the least. The trek to the shed is short, but nothing lights my way. The dark is just that: dark. While the cold is fierce, I know nothing can lurk outside my shelter, waiting to pounce. And yet, every time I collect wood, it's as if a predator stalks me. I anticipate claws digging into my shoulder, sharp teeth at my neck, my spine cracked in half.

But the only thing outside my shelter is the cold. But it is the cold that will take me in the end. So in a sense, I am its prey and it is stalking me.

With my parka buttoned tight, I clip myself to the rope between my shelter and the shed. Wind tears at me, and I plod to the shed. I pat the pile of wood, reassured that yes, it is substantial. For now. With my arms full, I push against the wind and spill into the shelter.

It's then I hear something. At first, I don't recognize it because it's been so long since I've heard that sound. Then the notion of it lights my mind. I fly across the room, wood spilling from my arms, the wind banging the door behind me.

It's a voice.

I grab the mouthpiece, my thumb clumsy through wool mittens.

"Hello! Hello! Are you there? Can you hear me? Hello?"

The wind screams at my back. The door slams against the wall, the noise like a death knell.

"Please. Talk to me."

My small space is chaos. Whirling snow, slamming door, biting wind, and scattered wood. It is too loud and too cold for anyone to hear me over the radio, and I have foolishly let the heat escape. It will take hours to warm the air to the point where I can sit without my body convulsing with shivers.

I have been so very foolish.

I fight the wind to shut the door. With it latched, I turn to inspect the mess. Stoke the fire first. Perhaps by the time I stack the wood and sweep the debris, the flames will throw enough heat that I can sit, crank the radio, and try again.

After I clean, after I heat my insides with broth, I crank the handle and try the radio again. I send my voice into the endless night, into the world, maybe even the universe. My voice could go on forever, long after I am gone. But that doesn't seem to matter.

No one answers.

When I wake, my nose is chilled, but only slightly. The air holds enough warmth that I can move and think. The fire is hungry, I can tell, but content to give me heat for the moment. Last night's folly has not ruined anything. My gaze lands on the radio, and I wonder. Is it more of a curse than a possible blessing?

I will try again today. It will not hurt to try. It will keep me warm and keep me busy. As long as I don't hope too much, it cannot hurt me, either.

After I eat a can of peaches for breakfast, I set to the task of cranking the handle and giving the battery a full charge. I debate switching frequencies. I wonder if that voice I heard was merely wishful thinking. These thoughts do not stop my thumb from pressing the button.

"Hello? Are you there? I think I heard you last night. Well, it's always night here. I mean, before. I heard you before."

Even now, without the sun, I still think in night and day, breakfast and dinner. I could have broth for breakfast, but I never do. I could reconstitute eggs and eat them for dinner, but again, I never do. I am a creature of habits. Now, these habits are all I have left.

"Is there anyone there?" I speak slowly, in case these words must fight the static to reach whoever is on the other side. "Should I change frequencies?"

This seems to be a silly question. If no one has answered my other calls, I'm not certain why this would compel them to. My fingers touch the dial. I'm about to spin it when something crackles over the speaker.

"No."

I stare at the space in front of the radio as if it's possible to see the owner of this voice.

"No?" My reply is a tiny thing.

"Don't... don't change the frequency... there's a good girl. Hold tight, I'm having some technical difficulties, but I'm here."

"I don't understand. You can hear me?"

"I can hear you."

"You have a radio too?"

"In a manner of speaking. I have a way to talk to your radio, at least."

Again, I stare at the space in front of the radio. I even wave a hand in the air. The voice is so rich and deep and clear. Yes, there is no static on my frequency. I wonder if that is something this other voice has done.

"Are you a man?" I ask.

"In a manner of speaking."

I laugh. The button on the mouthpiece is still depressed, so this voice, this man, hears my laughter. His own in response is as rich as his voice.

"I don't know what that means," I say.

"I don't either, except that I was a man, once—or male, at least. If that makes sense," he says, his reply filled with both humor and sadness. "Now I am, perhaps, less than that."

I still don't understand, but I'm not certain it matters. Not when there's a voice on the other side of this endless night, not when that voice wants to talk to me.

"I'm Soshi," I say, a strange, unaccountable shyness invading my voice and heating my cheeks.

"It's a pleasure to meet you, Soshi. I am Jatar."

I like the way his name feels in my mouth, and I say it out loud. "Jatar." Yes, it is delicious. Speaking is delicious. I touch my cheeks. The skin burns hot, but my fingers are like ice. The fire. Too late, I realize I've let it die down far too much.

"Oh, no," I murmur. "I forgot about the fire."

"Go, go. Tend to your fire. Then fix yourself something to eat, and come back and charge your battery. I will be here, on this frequency."

"Always? When I call, you will be there?"

"In these times, Soshi, there aren't many things I can promise. But I will promise you this. I will always be on this frequency, and I will always hear your call."

Jatar won't talk to me until I've assured him that I've fed myself, tended to the fire, and the other chores. How he knows I need to do these things puzzles me. Of course, I did fling my words into the darkness before we found each other. So I ask him.

"Yes," he says. "I did hear you. I have trouble on my end. Your radio is nothing like the device I use."

"You still have trouble?"

"Had. I mean, I had trouble. But you can hear me now, yes?"

"Yes." Sometimes I want to nod or smile, but I know he can't see these things. We have nothing but voices to guide us—their tone, their thickness or thinness. How a smile makes the throat warm and disapproval has an edge.

"You are not on earth," I say, "are you?"

The frequency carries his sigh to me, and the sound holds reluctance. "No, I am not."

"You are lucky then."

"I don't know about that."

"Where are you?"

"I don't know about that, either." By the way he says this, I know he wants me to laugh.

I do, but I also want to know the answer. "Where are you?"

"I'm not certain *where* matters all that much, not anymore."

"But you must be somewhere."

"Must I, dear girl? Must I really?"

I don't know how to answer that. I crank the handle to charge the battery, just so I don't lose the connection. I hate that, every morning—or what I call morning—charging the battery, sprouting sweat, and praying that Jatar's voice will come over the speaker and fill my little room with warmth.

"Maybe you are in my radio," I say now.

This time, he laughs. "What I wouldn't give to be there, living inside your radio."

"You would have to be very small," I say. "Smaller than a mouse."

"You wouldn't need to feed me very much."

No, I wouldn't. A thought seizes me. I think of small things, tiny things, mouse-sized things. I think of their absence.

"I killed them," I say. The confession both lifts me up and weighs on me. I know its truth.

Our frequency is clear of buzz and static. So when there's silence, it stretches long and empty.

"Who do you think you've killed?" Jatar says at last, his words quiet and low.

"The mice. When I first… found this place, there were droppings everywhere. The food is in metal containers and on metal shelves. But I stopped leaving crumbs. No more crumbs, no more mice."

"And it's you, not the lack of sun or heat that's responsible."

"I don't need to eat every last crumb."

A few nights ago, I left a bit of cracker on the floor, deliberately. I placed it well away from my sleeping pallet. My first nights in this space, I was consumed with the fear of mice, of rats, crawling over me in my sleep. I jerked awake so many times, breathing hard, cold sweat washing across my skin that I almost gave up on sleeping. But this time, when I woke, the crumb remained, untouched.

"Oh, dear girl, you did not kill the mice. They no doubt went elsewhere. They are resourceful creatures. Besides, they carry diseases. They could contaminate your food, your water…"

Jatar's voice fades, either from the buzzing in my head or failing battery power. I remember standing over that crumb, then falling on my knees next to it. For how long I stared, I don't know. Here's what I do know:

I picked it up and ate it.

"I can't talk now, Jatar," I say into the mouthpiece.

"Soshi, please. Listen to me, you did not kill the mice." Jatar's voice fills the air. He does not stop talking, not even when I refuse to respond. "You'll lose me soon if you don't crank the handle." He knows the life of the battery—or at least how to gauge it. "Crank the handle, at least. Tell me you're still with me."

But I don't. I sit, curled by the fire, chin on my knees. I could've captured a mouse, tempted it with some crumbs, built a home for it, close enough to the fire so it would always be warm. We would dine together, morning and night. I could spare what it would need to survive. I would have given it a good mouse name.

But I don't have a mouse. Something about that makes me clutch my legs to my chest. Salt from tears irritates my cheeks, but it's only later, when the tracks have dried, that I scrub my face with my palms. I've forgotten to eat, and the fire is low, but it's the radio that I reach for. My chest heaves as I crank the handle.

"Jatar," I say when there's enough power to carry my voice. "I want a mouse."

"I know you do, dear girl. I know you do."

He is there; he is always there. Maybe he does live in my radio. Maybe Jatar is my mouse.

"I know you do," he says one last time. His sigh carries so much weight I'm surprised the air isn't thick with the sound. "Your fire," he prompts.

"I should stoke it."

"Dinner?"

"Not yet."

"Tend to your chores. I'll be here when you're done."

"You will?"

"Where else would I go?"

I have found a rubber band, one that feels stretchy and fresh in my fingers. Its edges have not rotted away. It is strong, and when I wrap it around the mouthpiece, the button remains depressed. I love my radio, but now I am no longer tethered to it. I can use both hands while talking to Jatar.

Not that he can see my hands. But I can stoke the fire, feed myself, and crank the handle. I can fall silent, and he will not worry—too much. He can hear the rustle of my boots against the floor, the whisper of the broom, the crack and sizzle when I stoke the fire.

"Have you gathered wood recently?" he asks now.

"Last night… yesterday. It's stacked high. I don't dare bring anymore in for a while."

The air is too dry; sparks from the fire have too great a range. The thing that keeps me alive can also kill me. At least then I'd be warm, I tell myself. I don't speak these words to Jatar, but my laugh gives me away.

"That sounds morbid."

"It is," I admit. "I was thinking about the fire, how it might kill me before the cold does."

"I wish you wouldn't—"

"It's like that poem about the world ending in fire and ice. And I think it could be both, couldn't it?"

"I suppose it could, and suppose we change the subject?"

I agree, but don't know what to say at first. Jatar does not talk much about himself, although I wish he would. That doesn't stop me from trying.

"Can you see the stars where you are?" I ask.

"On occasion, yes, I can."

"Ours left. Actually, that's not right. I'm guessing they're still in the sky."

"Your guess would be correct."

"We blotted them out, all the stars, our sun, and now we have nothing. You know, when I first found this place, you could still see the stars from here. I thought: *oh, I am so lucky.* There used to be a stream. It even had fish, although they swam funny, so I never ate them."

"That seems like a wise decision."

His words have a teasing quality that makes me want to talk more so I can hear the humor and approval in his tone.

"It must have been a beautiful spot, with the mountains and the woods. I wonder why no one else ever came up after I did. Was it just too late?"

"Perhaps they weren't as smart as you."

"I don't think that's it. I think something happened, but I just don't know what that something is."

"Hm." Jatar sounds as if he's giving this much thought. "It's possible that the only thing to happen was self-inflicted, especially with the cities, as crowded as they were. Disease, fighting. It's hard to say."

"The cities *were* crowded. It's why we left." I nod before stopping myself, since Jatar can't see me. I may be the only witness to these things, and yet, I might as well be blind for all I've seen. Self-inflicted. The phrase makes me think of something else I found along the stream, something else I witnessed, and yet didn't.

"I'm wearing a dead woman's boots," I say.

I must shock Jatar with this confession. Silence greets me, and I wonder if I need to crank the handle again. At long last, he coughs.

"Dear girl, Soshi... I don't know what you mean by that."

"When there was still some sunlight, when I could walk along the stream, I found a body, a skeleton, really. Small, like me, so I'm guessing it was a woman. She was mostly bones, but the gun was still in her hand, and for some reason, nothing had chewed away the boots on her feet. Thick leather. They're heavy, but they are very good boots."

"The boots on her feet." Jatar says these words slowly. "Your boots?"

"I had to shake her bones from them, but yes. I took her boots."

"Did you leave her gun?"

"By that time, there was nothing left to shoot. I didn't see the point, even though I was still scared. I didn't think anyone would climb up this high in the mountains, not if they hadn't already."

"So you left the gun." Jatar's voice is tight as if this is something he absolutely must know.

"I left the gun," I say. "What would I shoot at? The wind? What would that do? Maybe cause an avalanche?"

"Yes, I suppose it could." He clears his throat. "I don't like this subject either."

"Then you tell me something about you."

"I am not that interesting."

"Are you a scientist?"

Jatar is intelligent; I can tell he holds back in saying things, perhaps so I don't feel bad for not being all that smart myself.

"A scientist?" he says. "Is that what you think I am?"

"You are very smart."

"I don't know about that, but you could call me a scientist, in a manner of speaking."

I sigh. The radio carries the sound to wherever Jatar is, and he laughs.

"What do you study? Planets? Stars? Solar systems?"

"Yes, you could say that. I… take the temperature of things. Some of those things include stars and planets."

"Earth?"

There's the slightest hitch in our frequency, the slightest bit of hesitation in his voice. "No, actually, Earth wasn't something I monitored."

"But you are now?"

"On my own time."

"You must have a lot of time."

Here, he laughs, the sound so clear and hearty, I can't help but laugh as well.

"Oh, yes, I do," he says. "I have time to spare."

"I wish I knew what day it was," I say.

I am trying to draw Jatar out, get him to respond. Today he has been so very quiet.

"I always know what day it is," he says.

"Somehow, I don't think it's the same as mine."

"It is, and it isn't."

"Because if I knew what day it was, we could have a party."

"What kind of party?"

"Well, that depends on the day. See? It's important."

His laugh filters through the speakers.

"It could even be my birthday."

"Oh, dear girl, it certainly could. You deserve lots of birthday parties."

"Would you get me a present?"

"As many as I could carry to you."

"Like what?"

"How about a mouse?"

"I would very much like a mouse. I would name it Jatar."

A harrumph comes from the speakers, one so strong the radio seems to vibrate with it.

"I think," Jatar says, his words slow, "that I should be offended."

Before I can explain that having a mouse named after you is an honor, the floorboards shake beneath my feet. I give a little cry, no more than a yelp from the back of my throat, but Jatar hears.

"What is it?" he demands.

"I don't know. The house is…"

I can't find words to describe the tremors that run through it. It's like my house has suddenly caught a fever and is shaking with chills. Then there's an awful groan.

"Oh, dear girl," Jatar says, and now his voice is low, but taut, as if it were nothing more than a rubber band stretched to its limits. "Stay by me—I mean, the radio. Stay by the radio. Do not open the door. Do not go outside. Stay as still and as quiet as you can."

I retreat to the radio, grip the mouthpiece, although I don't need to. Another groan sounds. It is like nothing I've heard, not even in the days when we fought to leave the city, and certainly my mountain has never made such noises.

"What is it?" I whisper, my lips only a breath away from the mouthpiece.

"I have heard this sound before."

"Will it eat me?"

"No." This word is not quite as tight as all his others. It almost sounds like he wants to laugh. "It won't eat you, dear girl."

The roar comes next, so loud it steals my breath. It reminds me of the few trains that still ran, back when we were walking, back before I was alone. We'd follow the tracks, and the roar would sneak up on you. Someone always kept watch.

Or did. Because, of course, the trains stopped running after a while. We still followed the tracks. They would lead us somewhere important, somewhere safe. I'm not sure how true that was, because they didn't lead me here, to my mountain, where I've been safe.

Until now.

The floorboards jump beneath my feet. The force knocks me into the wall and knocks embers from the fireplace. I claw my way across the floor. Before I can cup the glowing ember in my hands, I jerk back. I glance around, but the world shakes too hard, and my feet are too unsteady. Already smoke rises from the wood slats. I bite my lip and sacrifice the back of my left hand and shove the ember into the hearth.

I must scream. My throat aches as if I have. Jatar's voice pours from the speaker in response. He must fight to be heard over the roar and rumble and chaos that have swallowed my house.

Then, everything is quiet. The world. Jatar. So quiet I can hear the fire sputter. My gaze goes there first. Build the fire back up, make it safe. My left hand is nearly useless. If pain could scream, it would fill this space, this mountain, this world. I worry that I have done more damage than I can repair.

First things first. The fire. I build it up. I don't know if it's the stoked fire or if my hand makes me feel as if I'm on fire, but the air is warm, warmer than before. I glance about, knowing I must dig out some first aid supplies, perhaps scoop up some snow or ice from outside.

"Jatar?" I say, hoping to hear his voice.

Nothing.

Panic seizes me before I remember: the battery. It's an awkward thing, cranking the handle with my right hand, bracing the radio with my left elbow, but I manage it.

"Jatar?" I say, before I even have a full charge.

"Soshi? Dear girl, are you okay?"

"I burnt myself, but that's better than the house burning down. I'm going to get the first aid kit."

Actually, in the storeroom, I have many first aid kits, more than I could ever use.

"And maybe some snow," I add, making my way across the room. My legs wobble, and I take unsteady and erratic steps.

Behind me, Jatar is saying something, but he sounds so very far away. Shock, I think. How do I cure myself of that? Hand first, then the shock. I open the door to the outside. All I want to do is grope around, grab a handful of that sharp, crystalized mix of icy snow, and cool the fire of my skin.

At first, I don't understand what I see. I can only open the door part way. Something solid, cold, and white blocks its progress. The rope lifeline that leads to the woodshed is gone. That is no matter. Because my woodshed is also gone. Either that, or it's buried beneath a mountain's worth of snow.

Why the avalanche spared my little house, I do not know. But it has. And yet, it hardly feels benevolent. I do not feel grateful.

For a very long time, I do nothing but stare at the snow. Then I shut the door. I throw the deadbolt.

I will never open it again.

I use the last of the dying embers to light a cheap candle. The flame throws little light and even less heat. A couple of them on the hearth chase away the worst of the dark—if not the cold. Jatar is speaking to me now, urging me forward. Before the cold can steal all my rational thoughts, I scrawl *Crank the handle* on any surface I might chance to look at—the floor, the walls, the plastic tub that once held the blankets and clothes I stumble around in.

My fingers are black from the burnt bit of wood that was my makeshift pen. I use as little water as possible to wash, although this is from habit. I will run out before the water does.

"The storeroom," Jatar says. "You can navigate in the dark. I'll help you. Don't take a candle."

"All right." I push to standing.

"Go straight back and then to your left."

"My left." I don't say it as a question, but that's what it is.

"That's the hand with the burn." He never scolds, even when my words come out stupid.

"On the shelf, above your head, there will be another bin of blankets and things to keep you warm."

Halfway inside the storeroom, my mind blanks. Everything is dark, but Jatar's voice echoes behind me.

"A few more steps, dear girl. Just a few."

How he knows what I need to do, I can't say. Perhaps, before the avalanche, I spoke of these things. Yes. I nod to myself. I did. I told him where everything was and now he's telling me. I lug the bin from the shelf and emerge into the dim light of the main room.

My movement causes one of my candles to sputter. It gutters and dies. Maybe it's the cheap wax, but it sounds like someone drowning.

"Soshi? Are you there?"

"Yes, I'm here."

"That noise?"

"One of my candles," I say. "The flame went out."

"It sounded horrific."

"It sounded like someone's throat being slit."

Jatar's voice fills the speakers, but I don't understand him. His voice has a musical quality to it, as if he uses notes rather than words. But I recognize the tone.

He is scolding me.

At last he comes to himself, the notes fading into lyrics I understand.

"Soshi, please."

He doesn't call me *dear girl*, and I think that hurts more than anything else. That makes me rush to explain before the cold steals this piece of me as well.

"I said that because I know what it sounds like. I've heard it before. It's why I left the group. They weren't collecting children because they were kind. They were collecting children because they were hungry."

Jatar is silent.

"I ran away," I continue. "I'd rather die alone than be someone's dinner. I left the group, stopped following the train tracks, and found my mountain."

"I had no idea, dear girl, no idea. You've never… I mean, I didn't know."

"I don't like to think about it."

"Then we won't speak of it ever again. Go on, open the bin. There are warm things inside."

I pull the items out, one by one. They are heavy in my hands, thick wool coats that might weigh more than I do at this point. There are light things as well, down-filled jackets and sleeping bags that sprout tiny feathers when I squeeze them. At the very bottom, there is something furry and soft. I don't recognize it, and it isn't something you wear. It almost looks like…

"Jatar! I have a mouse!"

"Do you now?" He sounds amused.

"Yes! Did you… did you find a way to send me a mouse?"

"I did, dear girl, I did."

"Is it my birthday?"

"I think it might be."

"I should have a can of peaches then."

"You should have two."

"Oh, I don't know if I could eat two whole cans." I am not as hungry as I used to be. Sometimes Jatar must bully me into eating.

"Try," he says now. "Pretend I'm there, and the second can is for me."

In the end, I manage to eat one and a half cans. This gives me energy to make tea. The drink heats my throat, my stomach, and for a few moments, I can pretend I feel warm.

"You know what you should do, now that you have a mouse?" he asks.

"What?" I am amazed that there's something I can do, so he has my full attention.

"Build a nest, one you can share with it. You can keep each other warm."

I do as he says, piling the heavy coats along the floor and against the wall near the hearth. I move the radio within arm's reach. I can keep the candles lit from here. I curl into the blankets and pull the mouse to me.

"Would you mind," I ask, "if I called him Jatar?"

"I would be honored."

Crank the handle.

I know the words mean something, something important. I know there's something I must do, but can't remember. When the last of the candles dies and the dark erases the words, it's almost a relief.

I pull my mouse to me, cuddle him against my neck. He is so soft.

"Don't be scared," I whisper.

Because he is scared, of the dark, of the cold so sharp it feels like a knife's blade. I dig us further into our nest.

"Close your eyes, Jatar. Go to sleep."

I shut my eyes. The sound of a voice pricks my ears, but I think this voice is in my head, not in my house. It is a rich voice, amused and musical. When I try, I can make this voice laugh.

And in that laughter, there is warmth.

It's the silence in the end that's the worst, when Soshi's voice no longer fills my shuttlecraft, when I know she's alone, in the dark. She has her mouse, I tell myself; she has her version of Jatar. She is not alone. This thought offers nothing, not even a cold sort of comfort.

Earth was never in my sector of responsibility. Before Soshi, I knew very little of it, just that it was another small, life-bearing planet. Enough small, life-bearing planets implode on our watch that one more hardly makes a difference.

Except, of course, when it does.

As always, the jolt takes me unaware, throws me into the control panel. Pain shoots along my extremities. The grind of metal on metal follows and what sounds like a ripping. I brace against the floor, the craft shuddering beneath me. I count to three.

And then it ends. Everything is solid around me. Everything is as it should be. Everything is the same.

"Hello?"

Including Soshi.

"Hello? Hello? Is anyone there? Can you hear me? I would like to talk to you."

Why my communications system picks up her transmission, I don't know. It hasn't failed to yet, just as the crash never fails to surprise me, never fails to injure. I push to stand, then fall back. I strain and stretch, manage to press a button, call out a few words, although they are rough. My memories are intact, but each time, I must relearn her language. In those precious moments, it is easy to lose her.

"Hello! Hello! Are you there? Can you hear me? Hello?"

I can't find the will to move. I'm not certain I have it in me to live through this again—I've lost track of the number of times.

"Please. Talk to me."

If I lie here and soak in my own juices, what good will that do? But if I claw to stand, lock onto her frequency, what good will *that* do?

Every time is different. Every time... breaks me a little more. My sigh comes across the frequency, changes her thought or her footfall or something, and I open up another vista into her soul. Just when I thought I knew all of Soshi's trials, she tells me of shaking bones from a dead woman's boots and those who collect children in order to eat them.

I spend this time between her first call and that last, desperate one deciding. Earlier, I researched. While Earth never was in my sector, our information is complete, and what's stored on the shuttlecraft is more than I'll ever need. Quite against my will, I've become the foremost expert on hypothermia in humans.

When the end is near, I coax her into burrowing, better that than paradoxical undressing. I know when the avalanche will strike and her best chance to survive it. Once she stepped outside and it took her. I listened to icy silence until the battery on the radio finally died.

I have a complete mental inventory of her storeroom. What she finds in the bottom of that bin, I'm never certain. A child's toy? A fur-lined glove? A hat meant for an infant, perhaps, with whimsical ears.

"Hello? Are you there? I think I heard you last night. Well, it's always night here. I mean, before. I heard you before."

My strength returns, but so does my resolve not to answer. Does it matter, one way or another, if I'm there for her? Must I bear witness? She dies. She always dies. Once, I'd like that not to happen.

"Is there anyone there?" Her words are slow, deliberate, plaintive. "Should I change frequencies?"

Her question holds humor, as if she recognizes that it's a somewhat ridiculous thing to ask. The first time I heard it, I launched myself to my feet, smashed into the control panel, and opened a communications channel. Now, I hesitate, but thoughts cloud my mind. She will not find her mouse without me. She will step into that avalanche.

She will die alone.

I propel myself off the floor. I land with a crack against the control panel. I still ooze, and I coat the surface with what can only be described as slime, at least in human terms.

"No." It's more of a cough than a word, but it crosses space and time and opens her up to me.

"No?"

Her voice is filled with so much hope, choking out a reply is almost impossible. The panel is such a mess that establishing a permanent link is, also, almost impossible.

"Don't... don't change the frequency... there's a good girl. Hold tight, I'm having some technical difficulties, but I'm here."

I'm always here.

In a manner of speaking.

Before the collapse, **SOSHI PATEL** attended Fremont Middle School where she was an honor student and ran on the cross country team. Her favorite poet is Robert Frost. She has always liked mice.

JATAR is, among other things, an expert on avalanches, hypothermia, the complete works of Robert Frost, and the nutritional value of canned peaches.

CHARITY TAHMASEB has slung corn on the cob for Green Giant and jumped out of airplanes (but not at the same time). She's worn both Girl Scout and Army green. These days, she writes fiction (short and long) and works as a technical writer.

ART BY **Shannon Legler**

Information about **SHANNON LEGLER** and her monsters can be found at shannonlegler.carbonmade.com.

APOCALYPSE IN AN ARMOIRE

An account by Charles Rankles,

AS PROVIDED BY HERB N. LEGEND

My world did not end with a bang nor a whimper. At the end, the end of it all, as the ceiling crashed down in large molten chunks all around me, there was only a kiss.

Most of the night had been uneventful. The most interesting thing had been the sudden and inexplicable flurries of pristine snow dancing gracefully down to earth like celestial teardrops. At the beginning of the snowfall, everyone had been dumbfounded. Most of us had grown up in the Midwest, so we weren't strangers to the occurrence, but never had any of us seen it come down like this in the middle of July.

Eventually, freak snowstorm or not, the lure of intoxication and the hope of rekindling old high-school flames ushered us back to the basement. I can remember half-mindedly chatting with a few old friends I'd lost touch with. The usual conversations arose—the comparing of carnal collegiate conquests, our school's respective football standings, and all the other trivial matters that I couldn't have cared less about. It was odd, usually I loved these talks. The looks on the faces of the guys from high school when they saw some of the pictures of the girls I'd been with made my awkward virginal years seem like a past life.

But even then, that night had felt different. Whether I was conscious of it or not, there was a sense of urgency in the air. The universe was shouting its last call, and as I downed the cup of beer in my hand, a part of me was answering it.

My body moved across the room of its own volition, weaving easily through the different clusters of laughing friends who'd grown apart and navigating around the trampled Solo cups that littered the cement floor. I found my way to her, Janice Lanza, where she sat immersed in her phone like a moth finds a flame.

"Candy Crush got you stumped too?"

She looked up, her eyes wide. I could tell I'd just snatched her back from some faraway realm. "No," she giggled, more for my sake than because she actually thought the joke was funny, I think. "I was reading."

My stomach sank, and I fought a smile from forming. The thought set my palms sweating. Out of the hundred or so generic "Don't Change!" signatures that I'd scrawled in yearbooks, the only one I could say that I actually meant it to was Janice. And she hadn't. She was still the timid bookworm that she'd been in high school. It seemed not even the raucous reputation of her college could take that away from her.

I sat down on the couch next to her. She was sitting with her long caramel legs on the couch, so her black flats were almost touching my jeans. Almost.

"Anything good?"

"A collection of T. S. Eliot's poetry." She smiled. "I know it's nerdy and I'm at a party, but I've just been obsessing over his stuff lately."

"You're right. It is pretty nerdy, but it's the cute kind of nerdy."

She locked her phone and turned to me, brushing her wavy black hair over her ear. "So, what have you been up to lately, Charlie?"

"The usual. Looking for a summer job, planning my classes for next semester." I paused, wondering if I should say the next thing in my mind. There was an inkling, something niggling in a part of my brain I'd never felt before, telling me that it was time. "… and hoping to make up for mistakes made in the past."

"Ah, that sounds a little bit more than the usual, but also like it could have some interesting consequences. Any mistakes in particular?"

"Yeah. There's this big one that I've never really forgiven myself for—" I wiped my hands on my jeans, ready to take the step. After six years—four in high school and two in college—I'd finally tell her.

"I've—"

"Oh my god! Jan-nnyy!" An annoyingly shrill voice called. "You've got to come see this!" I shook my head as Trisha, Janice's nuisance of a best friend, drunkenly made her way over to the spot where we were sitting, effectively ruining the moment.

"Uhh, Trish can we have a—"

"Charles! Charles Rankles? What are you doing here, cutie?" She winked at me, knocking her glittery fake eyelash off-kilter.

"Umm… this is my party, Trish. But, like I said, I'm trying to talk to your—"

"Right!" She blurted out as recognition or a faint memory passed across her mind. "I came over here to get you! You have to come to the window! It's the most amazing thing ev-er!"

Janice and I shared a look. Clearly Trish was drunker than a Catholic freshman in a frat house, but there didn't seem to be any reasoning with her. Janice silently mouthed a *sorry*, as she got up and let Trish lead her away to the front windows.

I stood up, kicking a crumpled cup and sending it skidding across the floor. Then I went to get a cup of beer to forget about yet another lost opportunity. As I pumped the tap, I wondered why no one was manning the keg. That was unusual.

Looking around, I realized that the whole basement was empty, except for a half-clothed couple on a couch who seemed too preoccupied with one another to realize anyone else existed. Grabbing my cup, I bounded up the stairs and found everyone staring in awe out the front windows again.

"Come on guys, it's just snow. It's not that interesting."

Janice turned her head and motioned me over. I smiled because Trish was nowhere in sight and maybe I'd be getting another chance. I squeezed through the orgy of bodies centered around the radiator in the front room until I found Janice. In the mess of limbs and flesh, we were pressed against one another comfortably.

"It's not even snowing anymore. What's the big deal?"

She grabbed my chin in her hands and tilted my head skyward. At first, I didn't see anything. I was too focused on the softness of her dainty hands, and then an explosion of light commanded my attention.

It was like the coolest display of fireworks I'd ever seen. There was no sound, just an array of dancing colors writhing across the dark night sky with the largest moon I'd ever seen as a backdrop.

"Is this the Northern Lights?"

"Nope," she answered with a smile that rivaled the phenomenon overhead. "The colors are too complex."

She was right; looking up at the sky, there were millions of different hues, swirling and twisting into one another seamlessly. Purples became greens and oranges became blues. There were even other colors, unnamable and completely new, yet somehow innately familiar to me.

I don't know how long I stood there slack-jawed in wonderment, but eventually I realized that seeing them through a transparent pane of glass wasn't good enough. Numbed by the alcohol and fueled by the beauty I'd just witnessed, I grabbed Janice by her hand and whispered in her ear.

A few seconds later, we were in my backyard, hand-in-hand, looking up as vibrant angels waltzed above us. We sat side-by-side in the snow, even though Janice had on a skirt. She didn't seem affected by the cold at all, and my brain couldn't be expected to register things like temperature. Not right now, at least.

It was perfect, we were all alone under the most romantic night sky I could have ever hoped for. I was close enough to lean forward, pull her hair out of the way, and place a kiss on her lips. *Would she kiss me back?*

There was only one way to find out.

"Ohhh my gaawd!" I clenched my fist into snow to keep from cursing. "Guys, what are you doing? It's so cold out here!" Trish stumbled outside, shivering and groaning each time her stiletto-clad foot stepped into the snow.

She stood next to us for a while, singing "Janice and Charlie sittin' in a tree" and making kissy noises—being a nuisance as usual. But finally, like a tiring child, not even she could resist the allure of the unfiltered spectrum of lights above us. Her annoying voice silenced, and I heard her sit down next to us, only offering the occasional sound of amazement.

I wondered if they were looking up at the same night sky I was. And if they were, were they seeing the perfection of it? It was unexplainable.

Every word I couldn't formulate and every feeling I'd never expressed to her was playing out in the sky before my eyes. It was as if God's paintbrush skirted across the starless canvas, capturing my desires and reproducing them beautifully.

"Well, I gotta pee, guys!" Trish said with a giggle. "Don't look Charlie," she said with a wink that almost made me puke. "And don't have any babies while I'm gone!" She yelled from where she was squatting into the bushes.

Time may have passed, or maybe in that moment the sands of the hourglass stood just as still as we, mesmerized just as wholly as we. I can't recall when it happened, but soon the colors grew more vivid, bleeding through the canvas. Hues began to disappear, being overtaken by violent colors of neon orange and scarlet, and it was as if someone had pressed *unmute*, bringing thunderous terror back to our perfect silent movie.

Nothing could be heard but the shrieks of the angels that were now hurtling down toward earth. We were unable to move, stuck in some paralyzing trance until the first explosion rang out from somewhere near. The ground shook beneath us, an intense heat turned the air muggy and humid, and nothing could be heard but a ringing in my ears.

It took me a while to catch my bearing with the incessant high-pitched squeal blocking out my thoughts. Even after reality had caught up with me and I was sitting only yards away from the indisputable truth, I couldn't form a single thought. There, at the back of my yard, sat an enormous, smoldering black orb of some sort. It was shiny, and metallic looking, and much too perfectly circular to be just a comet.

My heart dropped as the true tragedy of the situation struck me. The *thing* had crash-landed exactly where Trish had been just a second ago. Whatever it was, it took up a third of my backyard. There was no way she'd survived. And even more disturbing, by some unfortunate random occurrence, Trish had been the one to get hit, when it could have just as easily been me.

Or Janice.

There was no time to waste. I grabbed Janice's hand and led her into the house. Even as we crossed the threshold, her eyes were still locked on the heavens, engulfed in whatever that had been. Things— fiery, enormous, murderous *things*—were crashing down on us with no rhyme or reason. Nowhere seemed safe, but the basement was our best bet.

As we ran down the stairs, Janice finally cognizant and sensing the urgency, we saw that half the partygoers were already huddled under objects—pool tables, propped up couches, folding chairs, whatever they could get their hands on. We rushed through the room looking for shelter.

I paused for a fraction of a second as my eyes glanced over the couple on the couch. They weren't even half-clothed anymore as they held on to one another, rocking back and forth to a rhythm of their own. I wondered if they even knew what was happening.

Janice yanked at my elbow. "Come on!"

I followed her to the corner of the room where an empty armoire stood that had once held my extra sheets and pillows. We both climbed in and closed the doors behind us.

Utter darkness amplified the sounds all around us. I could hear everything: Janice's ragged, scared breathing and racing heartbeat. Whispered prayers and whimpers from the other people scattered around the room. And not too far off, more thundering explosions as *things* crashed into the earth one after the other.

Reaching blindly in the dark, I found Janice, and pulled her close to me. There was no thought needed, no second-guessing, no awkwardness. With the same natural form of magnetism that had led me to her earlier, we found each other's lips. And there, in the lightless confines of an abandoned armoire, just as a *thing* crashed through the ceiling, I saw God for the second time that night.

CHARLES RANKLES was born in Schererville, Indiana, to a pair of loving and moderately affluent parents. Charles worked hard in school and after graduating in the top ten of his class (#10), he received a partial scholarship to the University of Iowa. College was a time for Charles to blossom, finally coming into himself, gain some confidence, and learn how to actually hold a conversation with the fairer sex.

HERB is a budding, twenty-year-old African-American wordsmith from Chicago with a penchant for fiction, poetry, music, and trees. Perhaps you've seen him—a skinny red-eyed kid sipping a scalding cup of tea, completely engrossed in a paperback or tarnished notebook. Or maybe you've read some of his previously published works, which include a self-published collection of poems—but let's be honest—you probably haven't. One thing's for sure, whether or not you've heard of Herb or not, he's an author to keep your eyes on.

SOUL JAM

An account by Jim Davis,
AS PROVIDED BY NICK NAFPLIOTIS

Used to be when someone walked into my shop, bells would ring. Wasn't something I really thought about much—just picked out the cheapest sleigh bell door hanger I could find and put it on the inside doorknob. That way if I was in the back, I'd know a customer came in. I also just liked the sound of it. I'm not some old timer who gets completely befuddled by technology or nothing—used to have a decent security system with cameras and motion sensors and all that. I suppose I could've set the system to beep when someone opened the door, but I always felt like the sound of bells ringing was more personal somehow.

Maybe that's the real reason They took it from me.

The world's gone grey ever since the Great Old Ones showed up. Not like the color of my hair (though the sky ain't blue anymore), but bland. A lot of folks died during those first couple weeks. The few who're left walk around like they're in some sort of trance. They come in, get their groceries, pretend to pay, then leave. Don't know why they even bother with the money part. Maybe it's just an old habit, like the supply truck drivers who still make me sign for deliveries. Used to shoot the shit with them when they dropped stuff off. Now they just stare at me until my pen scratches the paper.

One time, I asked the Wednesday delivery guy how his family was doing. He just blinked and asked me to sign that everything was correct. That's when I finally decided to say something.

"And who should I call if the order of canned crap they got you bringing me ain't right?" I asked, trying to smile so he'd know I wasn't mad at him. It's wasn't his fault that this canned stuff is all we get to eat anymore.

His eyes got real wide, like I'd said the most profane thing he'd ever heard. Then he clammed up and turned away without saying a word. Nearly ran out of the damn store. Wasn't long before I realized everyone but me was acting the same way. That's also about the same time everything B.Z. had been yapping about the last few months finally made sense.

I met Barnabas Zann around a year ago, almost nine months before everything went to hell. A pasty white German kid with a weird name really stuck out in a mostly black neighborhood like this one, but it never seemed to bother him. Said he moved to New Orleans because of the city's rich musical history. Can't really argue with that.

He was a real good kid, too. Started off as a regular customer. Always friendly and polite. One day, he heard me playing a little in the back right before close and asked if we could jam together. He came back with his bass after I locked up, and we got to it. Shit, that kid could play! I kept telling him he needed to go out to the clubs and start making a name for himself, but that wasn't something he even thought about.

"I've got much more important work that can be done right here," he'd say in that weird accent of his. Kind of a weird answer, but I left it alone. It was nice just having someone to play with again.

We started jamming a few times a week after that. Once B.Z. and I got to know each other a little better, he told me that his great-great-grandfather, Erich, had created some of the most important music ever. I didn't have the heart to tell the kid that I had no idea who the hell Erich Zann was. Neither did Google or Wikipedia, for that matter. But whoever gave that kid his musical genes had to have been damn good, because B.Z. could play just about anything.

Some nights he'd bring in a saxophone or trumpet—wailed on them as good as anyone you'd ever hear at the top clubs. Then there were a few weeks he brought in a banjo. His fingers picked the strings so fast I thought they might start smoking. Sometimes I'd put down the guitar and groove with him on the drum kit I keep down in the store's cellar. (Wife never let me keep it in the house before she passed, and I just couldn't bring myself to move it back into our house.) I'm pretty decent for a guitar player, but when B.Z. took a turn on the skins, it was like watching Buddy Rich reincarnated—without the whole "being a complete asshole" part. That was another great thing about B.Z.—he was one of the kindest souls you could ever hope to meet.

After a while, we spent almost as much time swapping stories and laughing as we did jamming. Turned out he'd been all over the world, living off an inheritance his father left him before dying in a boating accident a few years back. It wasn't lottery type money or nothing, but he lived as modestly as possible to stretch it while taking odd jobs where he could. It not only allowed him to travel, but also let him do his main thing, which turned out to be composing.

He never let me see what he was working on, though—said I would probably hate it. I told him he'd be surprised at how much different stuff I liked. Of course I was into jazz, funk, and R&B like every other old timer around here. Even a little hip hop, depending on the artist. But I dig the hell out of Chopin and Mahler. I'm also a big Zeppelin and AC/DC fan. When I shuffle my playlist, it's as likely to land on Elvis as it is Nirvana or Alan Jackson. Yeah, that's right, I listen to country. Good music's good music—don't matter how it's made or who's making it.

When B.Z. still wouldn't budge, I decided to show him the secret shame of my music collection: the KP folder on my computer, which contains every single song Katy Perry's ever released. It's even got the Christian stuff she did back when she was Katy Hudson! I don't know man, her music just makes me feel good, you know? B.Z. gave me a little hell for that (despite admitting she had a good voice), but still wouldn't show me his music. Said it was just too personal for him to reveal before it was finished, which I could respect.

I let it go and we kept jamming, which eventually became an every evening thing. He'd compose all day, I'll sell groceries all day, and we'd rock out at night. B.Z. eventually got a job teaching private lessons to some of the band students in the area, which cut into our time since he had to make up for the lost time on his project after the sun went down. Those nights he wasn't there, I started to realize how much it helped me having B.Z. around. Hurricane Katrina took my son and lymphoma took my wife. Talking about it never helped, but playing music gave me an escape when I wasn't working. Playing music with someone else, though... that was the best type of therapy. Some days, it's like the music was letting me say all those thoughts and feelings I'd never figured out how to organize into words. B.Z. would always play a perfect answer, too, giving comfort and support that an army of good friends, family, and well-wishers had been trying to for years.

One time when B.Z. came in to get some groceries, I asked if he would like to come over to my house for a late dinner. He agreed, which I knew he would, but also said there was something he needed to tell me. I figured it was going to be that he'd finally finished his big project, but decided not to say anything and let him reveal it on his own terms.

That night, for the first time in almost three years, I left the store right at 10:00 PM and went home. It felt strange to be in my house alone before midnight. I usually stayed at the store until I could barely stay awake so I wouldn't have to be in the house alone. Thankfully, B.Z. rolled up on his bike a few minutes later. While I cooked, he sat down at Tanya's old piano and started to play. No one had touched it since Tanya's funeral. He played so beautifully that I had to pretend the onions were getting to me. I think Tanya would have loved it, too.

After we sat down to eat, the conversation started off like it always did. I told him about what the crazy lady who comes in every day at 1:00 did, he told me funny stories about his students, and we both complained how bad music is now compared to when I was a kid. Then B.Z. got real quiet. I knew he was going to tell me that important thing he'd mentioned earlier, but his change in demeanor made me nervous about what it might be.

"Something's coming," he finally said, whispering even though I don't got any neighbors that would hear him. "Something terrible that could be the end of us all. My great-great-grandfather's music is what stopped it the first time. Now I am following in his footsteps. That is what I have been working on: music to protect our world from the horrors that reside just beyond our sight."

At first I thought he was joking and chuckled. When B.Z. didn't smile, I knew he was serious—and considered taking the boy the hospital for a C.A.T. scan right then and there. First I asked if he'd been taking any drugs, which made him get mad at first before he collected himself and said he knew how crazy he sounded. Thing was, he didn't sound crazy at all. He sounded just as lucid and together as he always did; it was just the words coming out of his mouth that didn't make a damn lick of sense.

I tried asking him what the "something" was that would cause the end of the world, but he wouldn't—or couldn't—describe it. Then I tried humoring him (without being too insulting, of course).

"Alright, B.Z.," I said, "if writing this music is so important and is gonna keep the world from ending, then why waste your time messing around and playing music with a guy like me, or teaching private lessons? I know you don't charge the ones who can't afford it. It's nice you're teaching kids how to make music and helping an old guy like me feel less lonely, but if you getting this piece done means saving the world, then why—"

I nearly fell out of my chair when B.Z. slammed his hand down on the table. At first I thought he was mad, but then I saw the tears welling up in his eyes. The poor kid was upset that I didn't believe him.

"Because music is not meant to be a secret," he said, his voice wavering. "If you can create it… or even if you just love it… then you should share it. No one should compose it in a vacuum, especially for something as important as this. It would be like trying to write about nature from inside a prison cell. It could be done, but not the way I'd want. Teaching others to make music fuels me. Playing music, especially with you, fuels me. Our friendship…"

I put a hand on B.Z.'s shoulder and let him know it was alright. I think he realized I still thought he was nuts, but I hoped that he also knew I was still his friend. I won't lie and say that it didn't mess with my head, but it's not the first time I've loved a person with beliefs I thought were weird. My wife's brother, Clarence, is a Jehovah's Witness. To a guy like me (who's only considered Baptist because I had to join Tanya's church to get married in it), his beliefs sound as off the wall as the stuff B.Z. was saying. But out of all my extended family, Clarence was the one I felt the closest to. He used to visit every holiday, called every week, and spoke to me like a person rather than an egg that's about to crack. I didn't see any reason B.Z. and I couldn't still stay close, too.

"I should have never told you any of this," B.Z. said after drying his face. "Now you'll think I'm a nutbag."

I leaned down and looked B.Z. right in the eye. "Wanna know a secret about me? You know that show *The Wire*? Can't stand it. Hate it. Couldn't even make it through the first season."

B.Z.'s eyes went so wide it looked like they might pop out of his head. "*The Wire*?!" But it's one of the best shows ever. You're—"

"—crazy. Yeah, I know it's not the same thing. But listen, my wife believed in a carpenter from 2,000 years ago who called himself the son of God. Never thought it made much sense, but that didn't matter. She was still my best friend, and I loved her more than I ever thought it was possible to feel for a person. We all believe things that some folks don't understand. That's part of why music is so great; it gives those of us with beliefs that don't match up a way to find some common ground."

We hugged (which I normally don't feel real comfortable doing), talked for a little, then jammed a bit on the piano. Everything was fine after that until a few weeks later. That's when the craziness B.Z. had been talking about turned out to be real. Real awful.

First came the news reports about a massive cult that was killing people all over the world. B.Z. and I didn't jam that night it all started, instead watching the TV along with the rest of the country. It was scary enough that the cult members were kidnapping people and gutting them, but what really got everyone scared was who the killers were. These weren't weirdos or escaped mental patients. They were perfectly normally seeming folks until they seemed to just snap all at once. Doctors, teachers, police officers, secretaries—one guy got chopped up by the same dentist he'd been seeing for almost 20 years. As the police carried him off, he looked right at the camera and began speaking in some type of weird language that sounded like a car backfiring underwater. He kept repeating one word over and over again. "Ka-thu-loo" or something like that. That word must have meant something to B.Z., though. As soon as he heard it, he began muttering something about "too soon" and "not now." Then his face went pale and he ran out, claiming he would be right back. I considered going after him, but he texted me after a few minutes and begged me to stay put. About an hour later, he threw open the front door of the shop. The bells jingled as a police siren wailed in the distance before he closed the door again.

"I need to give you something!" he said, pulling out a flash drive and putting it in my hand. "This is the music I have been working on since I moved to New Orleans. You have to promise me that you will listen to all of it, no matter how bad you think it is!"

I took the flash drive and looked at him for a moment. He was frantic. "Well, if you wrote it, B.Z., then I'm sure it's good, but why—"

"PROMISE ME!" he screamed, his German accent coming out far more than usual. "Promise you will listen to all of it!"

I did. He immediately wrapped his wiry arms around me. Like I said before, I'm not real big on hugging, but I embraced him back. When B.Z. stepped away, he looked me dead in the eye and said, "I don't understand what's coming, but I know you can fight it if you just listen. Help others like you helped me to enjoy music again."

I wish I'd said something. I wish I'd at least said goodbye. But before I could say or do anything, B.Z. ran out the door.

I spent the rest of the night trying to track him down. I called and texted his phone, but it had already been disconnected. I never went to his apartment during the time I knew him, but he'd told me where it was. When I got there, police and EMS were all over the place. One person was screaming in that weird language we saw on TV while a body was being taken out on a gurney with a sheet covering it. I thought it was B.Z., but then I saw woman's hand dangling down to the side. I felt guilty about the relief that rushed over me.

After finding the landlord and describing him, I eventually convinced her to let me into B.Z.'s apartment. Most of his clothes were missing, along with his laptop. A lot of his instruments were still there, though. I guess he couldn't take them wherever he was going.

By the time I got back, it was almost time for the store to open.

I normally have the same two or three regulars there by 7:00 AM. By 6:00 AM that morning, there was a line around the block. Figured the news reports from the night before freaked people out, so I opened early. I didn't take advantage of them and jack up prices like some places did when a hurricane was coming, but I also wasn't gonna turn down the business.

Things were insane for the next few hours. I had the TV running in the background, but the store was so slammed that I barely had time to see what was going on. Between almost my entire inventory getting cleaned out and having to watch for folks stealing stuff, I would have completely missed that big ass stone city rising up out of the Pacific if the entire store hadn't gotten quiet to watch it.

Most folks left after that. The place was picked clean—even the Natural Lite was gone. For the first time since Katrina, I closed the store before noon. Then I went downstairs and cried for the first time since Tanya's funeral. I knew I should have been more concerned with the crazy shit going on in the world right then, but all I could think about was B.Z. and wondering why he left like that. After a few minutes feeling sorry for myself, I looked over next to my computer, saw the flash drive he'd given me the night before.

I plugged it in, put on my headphones, and resigned myself to letting my emotions get the best of me. To my surprise, however, that's not what happened. The music coming through the speakers (if you could even call it that) was some of the worst shit I'd ever heard in my life. It sounded like that dub step stuff that was so popular a while back, mixed with the worst nightmares of Schoenberg and Bartok. Atonal, polyrhythmic, and just plain bad.

Was this really what B.Z. was working on all that time? was my first thought. I wanted to take off the headphones right then, but the fact that it might be the last thing I had to remember my friend by—and the promise I'd made to him before he left—convinced me to continue suffering through it.

It didn't get any better the longer I listened, but I was able to understand it better, if that makes sense. From a technical standpoint, it was some pretty slick work. I'm not a music theory whiz or nothing, but I understand more about chord changes and rhythm than your average grocery store owner. A lot of it sounded like a cat walking across an electric keyboard, but it all fit into every measure and time signature change. The melodic structure seemed non-existent at first, but themes he'd been developing eventually started to reveal themselves more and more as the piece went on.

By the time B.Z.'s symphony was done, I was more impressed by his talent than I ever had been before—even if what he wrote wasn't really my thing at all. I also felt… different. I wasn't sure why or how, though. I couldn't even describe it back then if I tried. I know what it was now, though. What it still is. A gift.

The next day was when stuff got really bad. The sky went dark like it was about to storm. Then They came up out of the water and started swarming everywhere. People called 'em different things: dagons, deep ones, star spawn. Whatever They were didn't really matter, though.

Coastal cities got hit the hardest first, then everywhere else. I'll admit that I didn't fight back or nothing. I just hid. That might not might make me seem heroic, but aside from some family that don't live anywhere close, I'd already lost everyone worth fighting for. And even if I'd tried to get to Clarence, stepping outside was basically suicide… which honestly didn't seem like such a bad idea during those first twenty-four hours. The sounds of people being torn to shreds right outside the shop door was something that no amount of music will ever erase.

It wasn't until the next night that people started to figure out that

They wouldn't kill you if you didn't fight back or run. Not sure who worked it out, but when the television stations all came back on, that's the first thing they said: "Submit. Submit to your rightful Gods and you will be spared a painful death. Perhaps even be allowed to live."

It was a shitty deal, but we took it, apparently. Any time a pocket of resistance tried to fight back, the news would cut to them getting slaughtered, lingering on shots of soldiers and civilian militia members getting torn apart bit by bit until they stopped screaming.

The door to my shop flung open while they were broadcasting from Egypt. I about pissed myself... ah hell, I did piss myself. The sound of the door slamming was almost enough to scare it out of me, but when I turned around and saw those two fishy looking monsters standing there, big green eyes glaring at me like a worm on a hook, my bladder gave up along with my will.

Following behind them was a man dressed all in black, including a veil that covered most of his face. He walked into my shop between the two creatures. In each of his hands was a severed head. He tossed both of them at my feet, then looked at me. His eyes appeared human save for the irises, which were the brightest shade of yellow I'd ever seen (probably the same color as the piss running down my leg). When he spoke, it had that same gurgling quality I'd heard from the dentist on television, but it sounded a whole lot more fluid.

"You feed people."

I couldn't tell if it was a question or a statement, so I just nodded with my mouth hanging open like a dumbass.

"People must be fed to stay alive so that they may nourish the Masters. They know to go here for food. We will bring you food. You will give it to people as you always have. For this, you shall be allowed to live."

Before I could respond, he pointed down to the two heads at my feet, which were both staring up at me in a way that made it look like they were silently screaming.

"If you do not, we will do to you what was done to them. *I* will do to you what was done to them. Is this understood?"

I nodded. He then pointed to the bells on my door, which one of the fish things grabbed with its three clawed hand and yanked off the knob. Then all of them turned and walked out the door. They left the heads for me to clean up.

The first couple weeks after the Great Old Ones took over, everyone was scared. They came in the store, wide-eyed and trembling, picked up the canned stuff that now lined all my shelves, and paid for it—or like I said before, they tried to pay. Most swiped their cards like always. Some tried handing over some arbitrary amount of bills and coins. I tried to refuse them at first, but most people would insist, sometimes almost violently. They needed the routine of doing something normal more than the worthless money they had.

A few folks were still willing to talk during that first week. Some of them heard that anyone who showed any sort of rebellious spirit got sent to something called "The Feeding Pits," where the giant creatures controlling all the small ones devoured them. That didn't sound right to me, but I kept my head down anyway, especially after what happened when one guy in my store lost it. Dude starts freaking out and screaming about how he's tired of eating the processed sludge the Great Old Ones (he called them Great Big Turds) force on us. A few minutes later, this thing that looked like a living mass of oil burst in through the front door. It grabbed him by the neck, pulled him into itself, then slithered back out. You could still hear him screaming as it oozed through the door and onto the street, but it wasn't angry yelling anymore. He was being hurt in a way that his body couldn't handle, but he could still survive to experience.

I figured that's what got everyone being all docile and trance-like soon after that. Despite the sky always being grey and massive creatures patrolling the streets, some normal things from before the Great Old Ones arrived actually started up again. The first was television. That was weird. It was all the same shows and programming, but something was really off about it. It didn't take long to figure out what it was, though. You know the annoying song they use on that commercial for cat food? Gone. So were all the jingles and stupid songs they used in all the advertisements. Then I noticed that the television shows didn't have any music, either. When I tuned in to a rerun of one of my favorite sitcoms from the 1990s, that catchy theme song was just dead air.

I went to the radio and turned in on. All the news stations were still working. Even some of the blowhard talk show hosts were back at their thing. But the music stations were all gone. I closed the store early (no one had come in for hours) and walked down to the French Quarter. Used to be there was enough good live music to make up for the mix of piss and vomit that assaulted your nose. Now there was nothing but people walking by silently, half in a daze and half looking like they were gonna burst into tears. I started to run back to the store, then slowed to a brisk walk when something that looked like a cross between a praying mantis and pigeon turned and started watching me.

By the time I got back to the shop, my heart was racing. There had to still be music. They couldn't have taken away everything. I went downstairs, opened up my laptop, and started up every streaming service I had. Just like the radio and television, I got nothing but talk and static. Then I went to my music folders and opened them up. All the files were there, but I was still scared that no sound would come out when I opened them. I put on my headphones, took a deep breath, and clicked twice.

Never had a song about being a firework sounded so good.

I listened to it all the way through, then clicked on a few others, some I hadn't listened to in years. The songs took me back—not just to a time before the Great Old Ones, but all different points in my life.

To a time when Tanya and Miles were still alive. To the song that was popular when Miles went to his first middle school dance. To the first song Tanya and I ever danced to. To the song I listened to in my dad's car when it was his weekend with me and we'd drive in his sports car down the Gulf Coast.

To the times I played music with B.Z.

I must have stayed down there for a few hours. When I finally went back upstairs to lock up for the night, I almost screamed. Standing there at the counter was a man dressed in a bright yellow suit. His eyes, which peered out from a face that slipped and coiled over itself like a pile of black snakes, were the same color. That's when I realized who I was looking at.

"Have fun listening to your music, Mr. Davis?"

I'd been caught. I was sure I was going to die right then and there, but it'd been worth it to hear music one last time. To my surprise, though, the Man in Yellow just started laughing.

"Don't worry, James," he cooed in that watery voice. "If it wasn't for me, you'd have been dead a very long time ago. Luckily, you and I are on the same side."

That pissed me off. "I ain't nothing like you."

"Oh, we can definitely agree on that," the Man in Yellow replied. "Compared to me, you're nothing but an ant. But since my brother decided to make his play for this world and Barnabas Zann is your friend, that makes you a very useful ant."

The hairs on the back of my neck shot up at the sound of my friend's name. The Man in Yellow could tell I was about to ask about him and stopped me before I could. "Oh don't worry. He's fine… well, not fine, but still alive. Poor boy. He wanted to follow in his great-great-grandfather's footsteps, but that man merely prevented a small incursion with his music. What my corpulent sibling has done here was a full-scale take over—which was not at all what we'd agreed upon. And if I don't get to have this world, then neither does he."

"I don't understand," I said, trying not to stare at the black coils moving under his bright yellow hat. "You were working for him with those creatures. You killed two people, threw their heads at me, threatened to kill me if I didn't follow the Great Old Ones' commands."

"Just playing the part, James," he replied with what looked like a smile. "I did kill those people, but they didn't really matter. I've killed plenty more than that to make sure Cthulhu still believes I'm on his side in all this."

I was torn between wanting to yell at him and running away, but kept my mouth shut, legs still, and let him keep going

"Barnabas did do one thing right, though. He created that music and got you to listen to it. He tried to put it online before the Great Old Ones pulled the plug on all music, but hardly anyone would listen to it all the way through. They didn't understand it, so it was instantly dismissed as garbage. I wasn't a fan myself, if I'm being honest. But you did listen to it. That's why your mind is still open. It's what helped your pitiful soul keep from eroding into nothing when we took all the music out of the world. There are others like you out there, but not many who I specifically hid and protected. That was part of my deal with Barnabas before he headed to Massachusetts."

"Massachusetts?!" I screamed, forgetting my fear for a moment. "That place is supposed to be where the most of your people… or whatever you call them… are!"

"Yes, Barnabas is trying to meet up with others who listened to his symphony from start to finish. Unfortunately, it's quite a pitiful number. That's where you can help him… and me."

"How?" I asked, unsure if I wanted to do anything for this creature.

"One of the first things our agents did was to find and destroy every instrument and piece of recorded music they could find. Any chord or sound given rhythm or tone is suspect. You, on the other hand, are protected. I have told my agents to leave you be, and that I took care of it myself. My brother may become wise eventually, but his mindless drones won't. That means that the rebellion, in this part of the world at least, starts with you."

"I still don't understand," I said, almost pleading. "So I still got music and instruments. What do I do?"

The Man in Yellow pointed toward the door. "Start giving it back to them. How you do it is up to you, though I would recommend not doing it out here. Our agents may be mindless, but they can still hear the sickening, rhythmic sounds that your species cherishes so much. Tell people to follow you down to get something. Slip them a note. Whatever you have to do. Just start giving people their souls back. The more who remember what it feels like to be human, the harder it will be for my brother to keep control over this place."

I had about a million more questions, but before I could ask 'em, the Man in Yellow turned and left.

So that's what I do now. I got no idea if it's building something. Got no idea if I'm helping people reclaim this world again or just a small part of their lives. Got no idea what Barnabas is doing now, either.

But what I do know is that when I can get someone to put on the headphones or sit and listen to me play guitar, it looks like they woke up from a coma. Some just start smiling real big. Others start crying. A few even started dancing. A lot of them come back, too. Sometimes to say thanks, but most of the time just to ask if they can listen to some more music. I've picked up enough from them to know the ones who've woken up are planning something big. Sometimes I feel like I should be doing more to help, but one of the leaders of the resistance shot that down right away.

"You're already doing enough," she said, after going through my entire Janis Joplin collection. "You're helping us to remember why we're fighting and dying out there. The music you've still got—it's why we keep going. It's what makes us human."

Then she kissed me on the forehead, promised to come back if she was still alive, and walked out the door. There wasn't a bell there to ring anymore—just the sound of it slamming back against the frame once she was gone. She's a nice gal. Probably the closest thing I've got a friend these days. I still hope to see B.Z. come through the door again, though.

Maybe even with a bell ringing again to let me know he's here.

JIM was born in New Orleans in 1955 and has lived there his entire life. Despite showing an exceptionally high aptitude for music theory and improvisation, he went right to work after graduating high school, helping his parents run their family-owned grocery store. Jim would often take freelance music gigs at night for extra income (or just for fun). In 1997, he became the sole owner/operator of the store after both his parents passed away. In 2005, his son Miles died in the devastation caused by Hurricane Katrina. His wife, Tanya, passed away in 2006 after a three year battle with lymphoma.

NICK NAFPLIOTIS is a music teacher from Charleston, South Carolina. His short stories have been featured in a number of venues, including *Mad Scientist Journal, T. Gene Davis' Speculative Fiction Blog, NonBinary Review,* and the *Dead Harvest* anthology from Scarlett Galleon Publications. He is a television, novel, and comic book reviewer for AdventuresinPoorTaste.com. His inane ramblings on pop culture, writing, weird crime, and bizarre classroom experiences can be read on his blog, RamblingBeachCat.com. You can also follow Nick on Twitter (@NickNafster79), where he brings shame to his family on a daily basis.

LAST STOP: HANOVER

An account by Kristen Cartwright,

AS PROVIDED BY J. C. STEARNS

At a certain point, you stop responding to cries of distress. You get burned often enough, even the potential of finding another survivor doesn't outweigh the probability of them trying to rape, rob, or murder you. Unfortunately, I'm not there yet. I was jaded enough to roll my eyes before heading down the dirt road, but there was never any doubt that I'd go.

Still, when I heard the barely coherent profanity floating up from a side road, I drew my pistol before directing Andy off the main drag. Coming through the tree line, I saw the problem. There was a man in a tree, and two wild dogs circling beneath him. As I rode closer, I saw a small stick come tumbling down from the branches.

"Go on," said the man, whose voice had been the one I'd heard from the main road. "Get out of here!" He tossed another twig, which the dogs gave as much heed as a falling leaf.

I sighed and tipped back my hat, one of those flat caps my douchebag hipster ex had left behind.

"Hyah!" When I yelled, the dogs jerked back, turning to face this new threat. Some days I thought the feral dogs were one of the saddest things you could see on a supply foray. Lots of them still had their collars on even. One of my friends nearly lost a finger last year to a pug that was still wearing an "I Wuv My Mommy" sweater. Sometimes, if you could act tough enough, you could get them to back down. The moment these two stepped out of the shadows of the tree, I knew this wasn't one of those times. They were both filthy and lean, with ribs starting to show through. I knew that game in the region had been getting more scarce, but when they began stalking toward me, I realized it had to have gotten truly dire for just a pair of dogs to attack a woman and a full-grown horse.

I jerked back on the reins and Andy reared up, kicking and bellowing one of those fine, grating horse screams. The dogs decided that game wasn't all that scarce after all. I chased them to the trees, just to keep them running, but turned away once I was sure they weren't going to double back.

By the time I returned to the tree, the man was dropping down from the lower branches. After an awkward landing, he picked himself up and turned to me. He looked to be just a bit older than me, maybe nearing his thirties. He was clean too, shockingly clean. What surprised me most, though, was that he looked well-fed. He didn't just look like he'd eaten recently, he looked like he'd *been* eating. His cheeks were full, his skin had a healthy complexion, and he even had a little bit of fat around his middle. I was so astonished that I couldn't think of anything to say.

"Well look at that," he said, grinning. "A girl and her horse. Some things never change."

I frowned and turned away. "Good luck, dickweed."

"Whoa, whoa," he said, hustling after me. "Come on, I'm sorry."

I stopped and turned back to him, not bothering to turn Andy around.

He spread his arms and laughed. "I didn't mean anything by it, I promise. Look," he said, coming up alongside my horse. "You just surprised me, is all. I'm Scott."

I sighed and rolled my eyes. "Kristen," I said. "Where are you going?"

He shrugged and looked around. "I've got no clue," he said. "Where are you going?"

"Hanover," I said. "There's a city there, still."

"Awesome!" His big idiot grin seemed much less charming the second time. He started looking around, and I realized that he fully expected to get up on top of Andy with me. The horse shied away from him, and would have snapped if I hadn't reined him in.

"Too much weight," I said. "And there's still over a day to Hanover. I can't risk over-tiring Andy."

"Oh," he said, brow furrowing. "So, can I not come with you, then?"

I frowned. I could just picture a full day of traveling with him, and it wasn't an enticing prospect. I had no idea how he looked so healthy, but I was seriously starting to doubt it had anything to do with his survival skills. Unfortunately, Hanover needed bodies, skilled or not.

"You can come," I said.

We set off back down the road to the highway. I hoped he wouldn't try to talk to me, a wish that came true for as long as it took us to get to the main road.

"So, why a horse?" he asked.

I shrugged. "Why not."

"I always kind of figured motorcycles would be the go-to vehicles once things all went to shit," he said. "That's what they used in *The Stand*." He looked around, squinting, as if expecting us to be attacked at any moment.

I rolled my eyes. "Unfortunately, you can't feed motorcycles grass," I said. "You also can't have them fuck and make little motorcycles."

Scott laughed, but it was clearly forced. "So what's its name again?"

"Andy," I said.

He nodded, clearly thinking something over. "I would have thought Jeffrey," he said.

Taken aback, I blurted out, "Why?" before I could stop myself.

"Because he's old, black, and chauffeurs you around everywhere." That time Scott's laugh was genuine and abrasive. I seriously hoped I wouldn't have to hear that loud, grating *hyeh-hyeh-hyeh* ever again, but somehow doubted that would be the case. He looked at me, still with that stupid grin, wondering why I wasn't laughing. "Like from *Fresh Prince*?"

"Andy's a girl."

"Oh."

He displayed the tiniest trace of good sense after that and stopped talking. I didn't get to enjoy the silence as long as I'd have preferred: the sun was starting to go down, and I wasn't lying when I said Hanover was over a day away. I let Scott try futilely to start a fire for about twenty minutes before I took over and did it for him. While the darkness crept over the trees, I sat in silence, sharpening a stick for a spit. Scott sat on a log and watched me.

"So," he finally said, "sorry for calling your horse a dude."

"So you're sorry for what? That you didn't look at my horse's genitals to see if he had a dick?" I snorted. "Stupid thing to be sorry for."

He looked around, unsure of how to respond. I dug in my saddlebags and pulled out my dinner: a squirrel and a few small roots I'd dug up the other day. A short search yielded a small clump of wild onions, which I dug up and wiped down with some spit and the corner of my shirt.

"Uh," said Scott, "is that safe for you to eat?" He looked like he might be sick, pointing to my squirrel. Now that it was out of the saddlebag, the smell was fairly vile.

"Think about it," I said. "In medieval Europe they just threw beef in the cellar until it was time to eat it." He looked dubious. "What did you think, they used refrigerators? As long as you cook it really well, you kill most of the stuff in the meat."

"Most of?" he asked, cocking an eyebrow.

I shrugged. "I'll take the shits over starvation," I said. "And you can always eat some chewing tobacco if you need to flush out parasites." He turned away, gagging, and it was all I could do to keep from laughing at him.

"What have you been eating?" I said. "You look like you're doing okay."

His moron smile returned. Back before the war, when twenty-somethings could sit around at the coffee shop all day instead of bleeding and dying in trenches and coils of razor wire, back when your pants got shredded before you bought them instead of from hours on your knees grubbing through the dirt for insects to eat, I'm sure that smile had carried him far. Back when hipsters ruled the earth, I'd be willing to bet that smile had talked more than a few girls out of their skinny jeans.

"Canned stuff," he said. "I got so lucky. Back before everything went crazy, I was doing community service in Johnsonville for peeing in public. Anyway, under their library they had this bomb-shelter thing, built back in the seventies for the Cuban Missile Crisis or whatever. They had me doing inventory of the place every Tuesday and Thursday, so I knew the door code. So when they started bombing the city, I just ran for the library." He suddenly looked concerned and held his hands out defensively. "I didn't lock anybody out, though. Nobody ever came to the door. I kept waiting but no one ever showed up."

Of course they hadn't. Johnsonville hadn't been bombed, of course, it had been mortared. Not like Scott the Asshole would have known the difference. It had been one of the first cities the Green Coats had attacked once they crossed the Pennsylvania border. Virtually no one had survived. The French-Columbians had driven them away eventually, but by then it was too late for most of us.

"So why did you leave?" I asked. I wanted to hit the coward, but I refrained.

"I ran out of food," he said. "Had to come out." No wonder they had him taking inventory. If their shelter only had enough food for one person for three years, it had to have been pretty sparse. He stared at my squirrel, now roasting on the fire, and I sighed for what felt like the hundredth time.

"Decide that squirrel looks safe enough after all?" I said. His mouth opened and closed like a fish for a moment before I rolled my eyes and took the squirrel from the spit. I pulled out my boot knife and sawed it into two pieces, then handed him one. "Don't ask for any more. I left Hanover with just enough food for my trip, so this means we don't eat tomorrow."

Scott nodded, taking the steaming meat gingerly. He took a delicate nip and winced. "So, what were you out looking for?"

"Medicine," I said. "And food. But mostly medicine." I gestured toward him. "Of course, bringing back another warm body is always a welcome bonus."

He beamed, as if proud of having a pulse. "Got a lot of survivors or whatever?"

"A few dozen," I said. People did come and go, but I'd learned a long time ago not to give concrete numbers. "Over a dozen children, though. A lot of the original survivors were single mothers from Hanover or the surrounding towns. So there's a lot of mouths to feed." I jerked a thumb back the way we'd come. "And as you can tell from those dogs, food gets scarcer all the time around here."

Scott's brow wrinkled in confusion. "I thought there were shit tons of farms around here," he said.

I sighed. "There *were*," I said. "But the Federal army confiscated them after the first Great Desertion. Then, when the New Confederates started raiding them to bolster their supplies, the French-Columbians took to using chem-dumps on any active farmland." I shook my head in frustration. "I doubt you could find a domestic crop between here and the Great Lakes."

"Damn," said Scott. "Now I wish I'd made that canned food last." Then it hit me. He hadn't rationed the food. Of course he hadn't; he was an asshole. He'd blown through a food supply designed for a town's worth of survivors in a fraction of the time it was meant to last. While Johnsonville burned, while its citizens were being raped, shot, and tortured, this selfish cock had sat comfortably in his armored bunker, blissfully ignorant of the horrors above his head. I could see him sitting there, three or four cans open around him, making sure he got a balanced meal.

"I'm getting some sleep," I said, my voice hoarse.

I laid there on the ground and listened to Scott trying not to retch on the rancid meat. I felt nauseated, myself. How much food had he wasted? How much had he thrown out uneaten? There were a dozen children back in Hanover, all suffering from malnourishment while this skidmark had eaten himself stupid. I wanted to rip him limb from limb and leave his head on a stick, but necessity held me back. Things were getting desperate back in Hanover, and we needed every body we could get, now more than ever. I tried to be calm, but all I could think about was the last little one we'd had to bury, bald and skeletal, her lips cracked and raw from hunger and disease. I'd take another person and go to the library, of course. There was every chance Scott had left some food, water, or medicine behind, or some items of use. We just needed to find enough food to get the little ones through until we could get new crops going. Of course, if the Dickless Braintrust hadn't wasted all of *his*, we might not even have had to worry about that. My thoughts chased each other in circles like that until I eventually drifted to sleep.

I woke to Scott's hand on my shoulder. Anticipating danger, I rolled over sharply, but instead of a warning hissed in my ear, I felt his lips on mine. My eyes widened in shock and revulsion and I shoved him away.

"What are you doing?" I asked, horrified.

"Oh come on," he said, his moron grin leering at me in the dying firelight. "You said your group was mostly single moms. Not a lot of men, I bet. Especially with the drafts, and all." He pushed himself down on top of me, and I finally lost it. He yelped and jerked back when I punched him in the side of the head, and gave me enough room to get my leg up and get my hand to my boot. I punched him again with the other hand, and he raised his arms to ward off my blows. I don't think he even saw the knife.

I shoved him off of me, even as he groaned and looked down, trying to understand why there was a knife buried up to the hilt in his side. I already had my pistol out in case the blade wasn't enough, but when he turned to look at me, his mouth doing that fish gasp thing again, I could tell I wouldn't need it.

"Why?" he gasped.

"Because you're a useless ass," I snapped. "The only thing you'd wind up doing is getting someone killed."

Bloody froth formed at the edge of his mouth. "Then why... help me?"

I shrugged and holstered the pistol. "It's easier when they walk into town under their own power," I said. "Saves the horse the exertion." His brow furrowed in that look of stupid confusion again, and I realized the truth still hadn't occurred to him.

I squatted down at eye level—although still out of knife range in case he got a last second burst of vindictive energy—and gave him my best patronizing smile. "I wasn't lying to you when I told you we had a lot of mouths to feed," I said. "And with the crops burned and game getting harder to find every day, there aren't a whole lot of options left." His dull eyes brightened with horror as realization finally hit him. "Like I said, it would have been better if you could have walked in yourself, but you'll stay relatively fresh for a day." For the first time since meeting him, I smiled, really smiled.

"And at least now I don't have to go hungry tomorrow."

KRISTEN CARTWRIGHT is a former student in preIndustrial history from the University of New Chicago. Currently a resident of Hanover, PA, she spends most of her time scrounging for resources in the surrounding area with her horse, Andy. When not struggling for survival, she enjoys listening to recordings of the pre-millennial pop music colloquially known as "oontzoontz." Ironically, before the New Great War, she was a vegetarian.

After a long and failed career in alchemy yielded nothing but a time consuming and expensive formula for turning gold into lead, **J. C. STEARNS** was forced into freelance writing to make ends meet. Currently he dwells with his wife, child, and multiple cats in the swamps of Southern Illinois, where he seethes with resentment against the world that has denied him the fame and glory he feels is rightfully his, and gleefully plots his revenge. His work has previously been published in *Under the Bed*, and he is a regular contributor to *Quoth the Raven*.

IN TRANSIT

An account by Meredith Jones,

AS PROVIDED BY KATE ELIZABETH

Your journey to the afterlife starts here, flashes in neon red letters and greets patrons on arrival.

To ease the transition from life to death, the arrivals lounge is decorated in a cross between a doctor's office and an airport. The chairs are uncomfortable, old magazines litter the side tables, and classical music plays in the background.

It is also the size of a football stadium—it has to be. On average, 151,600 people arrive each day, less than the world's busiest airports. I should know. I help send many of them on their merry, and sometimes not-so-merry, way to the afterlife.

With people arriving at all hours of the day and night, we are open 24/7. Although for some reason, late mornings are our busiest time of day.

So it is only after this peak hour that we get our lunchbreak. The tea room fills up quick, so it is a mad rush to nab the best seat. Everyone has their favourite lunch spot; mine overlooks the Elysian Fields. Nobody sits near the emergency exit; the smell of burning flesh mixed with sulphur is enough to make anyone lose their appetite.

I grab my lunchbox and make a beeline for the chair nearest the window. Pulling my sandwich out of its wrapper, I imagine myself down there, having a picnic on the lush lawns and refilling my drink bottle from those sparkling waters.

As I take the first bite of my sandwich, the loudspeakers crackle to life. "Code Black."

I choke.

After I cough my lunch back up, I glance around the room, a little teary eyed at my own near death experience. No one moves, hoping they heard wrong and silently praying this is another drill.

Emergency scenarios are run on a regular basis, we cover everything from a Code Green to Red, but a Code Black?

"This is not a drill. Code Black," the message repeats.

I race for the door. "What in the…"

The waiting room is like a stadium sized sardine can, jam-packed with the young, old, and in-between.

I have never seen anything like it, not during the peakiest of peak hours. There are at least a million people sandwiched together.

Jonah from accounting hurries past, a batch of paperwork bulging in his arms. "Here." He shoves a handful at me.

The papers are still warm. "What's going on?"

"Code Black," he calls over his shoulder before he disappears into the human horde.

I stand there for a moment, wondering if this is a joke or really the end of the world. It isn't what I imagined the apocalypse looked like. This is much worse.

Taking a deep breath, I wade out into the sea of men, women, and children, and pass around forms for the afterlife.

Someone taps me on the shoulder, an older woman. "Is this Heaven?" she asks. Hanging around her neck is a large gold crucifix. She rubs it as if it were a lucky rabbit foot.

"Umm, not exactly."

"The last thing I remember—"

"Here," I shove a form at her. The last thing I want is to get bogged down listening to a two hour monologue detailing the last seventy years of her life in excruciating detail. "You will need to fill in this form. Once you've completed it, we will be able to send you on to Heaven, Hell, Valhalla, Jannah, whatever your final destination."

I dive right back into the crowd to avoid any questions or further discussion. It doesn't take long to run out of forms, and Jonah is nowhere to be seen. I consider returning to the tea room to finish my sandwich, only I'm not sure how to get back. It is times like these I wish I wore high heel shoes rather than comfortable flats.

"Meredith, please report to the front desk immediately," the loudspeaker commands.

If not for the welcoming neon sign that hangs high above the front counter, I would never know which way to go.

"Excuse me." I elbow people out of my way as I navigate through the mosh pit of humanity. "Sorry, coming through."

The whole room is abuzz as everyone swaps death stories. If you work here long enough, you can predict how they died with a certain degree of accuracy. Staff even bet on it; gun shot, stroke, car accident, suicide. I thought I was good at the guessing game, but this time I didn't have a clue.

As I nudge my way forward, I try to piece together what in the hell happened.

"I'm telling you it was a tsunami," a girl in a pink polka dot bikini insists.

A guy in a grey suit and tie shakes his head. "But it was caused by a massive earthquake."

"I think the moon fell down," a young boy explains to his brother.

"Hey is this for real?" A lanky teenager in a long black t-shirt steps out in front of me. "I can actually pick Jedi as a religion?" He points to one of the boxes on his form.

It takes me a moment to realise he is speaking to me. "Yes." I try not to roll my eyes.

"Cool." With a goofy grin, he ticks the box.

"Yes, very cool." If I had a chocolate bar for every time a teenager asked about Jediism, I'd be in a diabetic coma.

I step around him and keep moving forward until finally I reach the front desk. It is less of a receptionist's desk and more like an airport check-in counter that stretches 500 metres.

"Meredith," Alice shrieks when she spots me and waves me over. "What's going on? A Code Black, are they serious? It can't be?" Her voice increases in pitch with every question. "How are we supposed to cope with 6 billion people? We don't have enough forms. We don't have enough staff." She pulls on her curly hair. The ringlet straightens out before she releases it. I watch it roll back into a curl. "What are we going to do?" She pulls on her hair again. This time a few strands come out.

I grab her hand to stop her from pulling more hair out. "I'm going to go and find Jonah and get some more forms printed up, ok?"

I wait for her to nod before I release my grip on her hand.

"Wait."

"What?"

Alice motions to the man at the counter. "I don't know what to do. According to his paperwork he is supposed to get reincarnated. But we can't send him back? Can we?"

I think about it. Reincarnation is pretty straightforward, but if this really is a Code Black and we sent him back, he would only end up here again, stuck somewhere at the end of the queue.

"Well, unless he is supposed to return as a cockroach, I guess you can process him as an agnostic?" I shrug.

It is rare to allow someone the freedom to choose their own afterlife, at least at this stage of the process. "For what it's worth—" I turn to the man "—I would choose Elysium."

I leave Alice to explain the various afterlife options as I move back through the masses in search of Jonah. I figure the best place to find one man in 6 billion is in the printer room. So I go there first, or at least I try to.

"Do you work here?" Someone grabs my arm.

I want to say no. "Yes." I shake him off.

"Well, I've filled out my form." He hands it to me.

"That's great, but you'll have to wait in line with everyone else." Even though there was no discernible line to speak of, I point in a random direction.

"But it says I have to find a staff member for further instruction."

Reluctant, I grab his paperwork and scan through his selection. He has checked the box marked atheist.

"Are you sure?" I lower my voice. "I can get you another form if you've made a mistake."

"Yes, I'm sure."

"You don't believe in anything?" I look pointedly behind me. "Anything at all?"

Beyond the counter, seven of the gates to the afterlife are clearly visible. The pearly white gates of Heaven shimmer, and wisps of fluffy clouds float over them. Even from this distance, I can smell fresh baked chocolate chip cookies and baby powder.

"No." He shakes his head.

I sigh. "Very well, come with me."

I lead the man to the front counter. Those who have been waiting complain and protest about line cutting. "Wait your turn," someone calls out.

"Yeah." Everyone else agrees.

I ignore them and head straight over to Alice, who has finished serving Mr. Reincarnation. I watch him wave goodbye to Alice and walk directly toward the heavenly gate.

"Here." I hand her the guys form.

She glances over it, and her eyebrows rise. "Are you sure?" she asks. "You know once I file this I can't un-file it."

"Why do you people keep asking me that?" He throws his hands in the air. "Of course I'm sure."

Alice shrugs. "Alright then." She files it away before she hands him another form. "Please fill this in." She sounds almost apologetic.

His brow furrows as he flicks through the pages. "What is this?"

I pat him on the shoulder. "It's an employee registration form," I explain. "Welcome to our afterlife."

MEREDITH JONES worked as a science teacher before her untimely demise in 1993. After her death she started working as an afterlife administrator and has been doing that ever since. When she isn't working, she likes to imagine what her afterlife could have been. She also loves karaoke, Western movies, and chocolate cake.

KATE ELIZABETH currently lives and works in Melbourne, Australia. She originally set out to become a scientist but preferred reading and writing science fiction and fantasy stories instead. She also loves chocolate cake.

LIMBO

An account by Andrea McCready,
AS PROVIDED BY MARY MASCARI

'm surprised to wake up alive.

At first, I'm disoriented. Not sure why I'm on my living room couch. But when I feel Jeffrey's arms stiff around me, I remember. I turn slowly around on his lap. He looks asleep, but I touch his face and it is cool.

"Oh, my darling," I say, laying my head on his chest.

And then, of all things, I have to go to the bathroom.

I slide down to the floor. Jeffrey's arms hover above his lap, still in the circle that I had slept in. I turn away quickly.

I stand in the shower, following my routine because I don't know what else to do. Halfway through, the hot water stops. I rinse my hair and get out. Dry off, wrap myself in the blue fluffy towel embroidered with my initials, and go down the hall. I pause in front of Gretchen's room, but can't go in. Instead, I go to my room and dress.

I'm glad to have small problems to solve. The big ones are still unfathomable. There's no electricity, so I dry my hair with a towel and pull it into a ponytail, then braid it. I put on makeup using the hall mirror, by the light of the window.

I step out the front door and stand on the porch. The world is stiller than I've ever experienced. No cars driving, no people walking dogs, no airplanes in the sky, only the sounds of birds and wind. I never realized how much noise had come from the street until now, when it is gone.

There's got to be someone else. I go next door to Gary and Jo's house. No answer when I knock. I lift the doormat, find the key, and let myself in.

I always wished my house could be like Gary and Jo's. It's clean and beautiful, with thick oriental rugs on the floors and art on the walls. The air smells like eucalyptus and dinner. My mouth waters. I haven't eaten since lunch yesterday.

It's empty and quiet now, like I'm just here to gather their mail and let the dog out. If the world were normal, I could help myself to whatever amazing leftovers were in the fridge and relax on their soft leather sofa, enjoying the peaceful order of their home as long as I liked. That's just the kind of people Gary and Jo are.

Were.

Dutch, their fox terrier, runs up to me, tail wagging.

"Hey, Dutch," I say, crouching down to greet him. I love dogs. Since Jeffery and Gretchen are both allergic, Dutch is my surrogate pup, and he knows it. He wiggles his butt as I scritch the special spot near his tail.

"Is anybody home?" I stand up and start down the hall. "Gary? Jo? Are you home?" I turn the corner into the living room and let out a surprised shriek. Dutch barks along in solidarity.

Gary and Jo apparently decided to leave this world engaged in their favorite activity.

A laugh bursts out from deep within me. It feels like the warm glow of brandy, but in a second it is gone. "Oh Dutch, what the hell is going on?" I kneel down and hug him, feel the silky fur on his head against my cheek.

"We should cover them up, at least. Let's get a sheet or something."

I start up the stairs. "Where do they keep their sheets?" I find the linen closet, go back down. Dutch follows me the whole way, his nails clicking against the wood floor. "Eventually someone's going to find them, right?" I'm babbling, but I need to fill the silence with something. This utter stillness is screaming things at me that I'm not ready to hear.

I unfold the sheet and shake it out. I keep my eyes on the sheet as it flutters in the air above the dead couple. As it settles, it slides off, revealing Gary's rear end. I laugh again, an escape of air to keep from exploding.

I pull the whole sheet off and try again. This time it covers them. I hurry out of the living room. "What are we going to do, pup?" He answers with adulation. "I think we need to figure out who else is still around."

It feels good to make a decision and do something. The keys to Gary's big SUV are on the counter. Their one flaw was their weakness for big polluting cars. Now it could come in handy.

Yesterday morning, I was fifteen minutes late for work, an unthinkable catastrophe that had left me in a terrible mood throughout the whole drive and most of the morning.

Jeffrey and I had had a fight, hissing at each other while we made coffee and oatmeal. It was presumably about the swing set I wanted to buy for Gretchen, but was really about money. I was spoiling her, Jeffrey was too cheap. I noticed the time, dumped my coffee into a travel mug, and pulled out of the driveway, fuming.

I forgot to go into Gretchen's room and kiss her goodbye.

I ran right into a meeting with an idiot, and stayed there for an hour and a half, listening to this man ramble on about what he wanted, and thinking about how I could get out of doing it. Neither of us had any idea until Gordon Jamison, puffy eyed, opened the door.

"They're closing the building," he said. "Go home."

"Why?" I asked.

"The plague's coming." He closed the door.

I wandered out into the hallway. Everyone was grabbing coats, hurrying out. Gordon wasn't the only one crying. "What's going on?"

"You haven't heard?" Kathy O'Leary had been the lead for Project Maximum, but had messed things up so badly everyone was just waiting to see what terrible fate would befall her. Now she was texting something while pulling her hat over her head. "There's a plague. It kills you in an hour."

That couldn't be right. I didn't have much respect for Kathy, after the way she'd handled the testing phase.

"I'm going home," Kathy said. "You should go get Gretchen."

The TV in the cafeteria was tuned to the news. According to the graphic on the screen, it was showing live footage from security cameras in New York City. People were lying dead on the sidewalks, grouped together in crosswalks, as if they'd just fallen where they stood. At first I thought I was looking at a still photograph, but when a pigeon flew into view, I realized that it was film.

I ran back to my office for my coat.

I drive Gary and Jo's SUV, with Gary and Jo's dog, all the way downtown, slaloming down the highway around cars that have crashed into the walls and each other. I pull over for an hour to scream and cry, accompanied by Dutch's howling. But then my throat hurts, and Dutch starts licking my face. I always knew dog kisses were the most powerful anti-depressant.

I start the car again and drive into the city. I pull into a parking space. "Let's see who we can find." I don't feed the meter. I do stay on the sidewalk. Dutch runs ahead, sniffing everywhere.

I'm a little nervous about calling attention to myself. What if the only other people alive are awful, stupid, boorish? But being alone is unthinkable, so I call out. My voice echoes off the empty buildings.

Many windows are broken, in shops and cars. One electronics store has been looted, although the plague dealt swift justice. A few feet away, a man lies dead with the stolen electronics in his arms. "Really?" I ask him. "Faced with the end of humanity you decide you need a DVD player?"

I wander around, turning corners, checking in alleys. I catch myself looking both ways before crossing the street. "Hello? Is anyone there? Hello?" The pigeons fly away.

There are many bodies around, slumped in cars, lying on the sidewalk, and in the shops. Inside one store, a lonely shopkeeper lies flopped over a stack of T-shirts she had been folding.

Dutch and I walk for hours, shouting, looking around, listening. There are thousands of people in this city, but I encounter none that are still alive. I sit on a curb. The traffic light changes with a clunk, dutifully controlling traffic that isn't there. Dutch sits next to me, and I reach out to stroke his back.

"I think it's just us." Is that possible? They're all dead? All of them? I try to picture this, really make it penetrate. Everybody. Everybody is dead. Everyone.

I stand up, walk to the middle of the street. Twenty-four hours earlier, I would have been killed instantly. "Hello!" I scream, one more time.

I'm answered only by the oppressive silence.

"There's no one left." I lie down in the intersection, stare at the blue sky above. The pavement beneath my arms is cold.

"I need a drink."

The bar is empty of corpses; they probably never opened yesterday. Dutch immediately explores, eagerly consuming the millions of new smells. I've been here before. Jeffrey and I came here after a show one night, stopping by for a drink before returning home to the sitter. I remember sitting in that booth over there, under the picture of a trumpeter, wearing Jeffrey's jacket. It smelled like him, and I had taken a good whiff while he went for drinks. I had felt very old, in a trendy bar full of twentysomethings who were just starting their evening. But when Jeffrey came back to our seat, he slid his hand on my thigh and whispered in my ear.

Now it is strange, like a haunted house with the lights on. I go behind the bar and pour myself a glass of wine. "To humanity." I drain the glass. It's good wine, so I pour another and savor it. I bring the bottle to a table—not the one I'd sat at with Jeffrey. I pat the bench, and Dutch hops up next to me.

"What we need to do now, Dutch, is assess our situation." I smell the wine, sip it. Let it dance on my tongue. "There may be someone else out there, but I can't find them. Maybe in another country. But how am I going to get there? I can't take a plane, or a boat. Maybe I'll just walk to South America." I finish the glass and pour another.

"I'll never go to Paris, now." That one strikes deep, for some reason. Suddenly I throw the glass against the wall. The chaotic noise and mess feels good. "Why the hell am I still alive?" I stand and fling the bottle, too. Dutch starts barking. "Why am I still alive?" I pick up a chair and throw it at the floor. It bounces. Much less satisfying

I get another bottle of wine. I'm about to throw it, but I stop. I look at the booth under the trumpeter. "I want to be dead, too. I want to be with you."

I picked Gretchen up at school. They had all the children outside. It was a beautiful spring day, and the kids were playing on the playground. The laughter and screams were comforting, normal. Perhaps

everything would be all right. "Do I need to sign her out?" I asked Gretchen's teacher.

"We're not worrying about that today," she answered. Gretchen came running up to me, coat open and pigtails flying, and jumped into my arms. I kissed her on the head and then carried her over to the car. On the way home, I called Jeffrey. He was already on his way.

It felt strange to be at home during the day. I went into my bedroom to change out of my work clothes, and Jeffrey turned on the news. The newscaster was a young woman, not the usual anchor. She cautiously explained that the disease had showed up late the previous night. Experts on the West Coast speculated that it had come from someone who had arrived in New York by plane, but there was no way to confirm that, as everyone was dead. The disease was running rampant in Europe and Asia, as well. China and Australia had closed their borders.

I sat on the couch next to Jeffrey. Gretchen was playing with blocks on the floor. Little red welts were on the newscaster's face and neck. I didn't remember seeing them before. "What's wrong with her face?" I asked.

"They just appeared. I don't think she realizes yet." Jeffery's hand on my arm was rigid.

As we watched, the welts on her face grew brighter. There was a thump off camera, and the anchor looked startled and half stood. She gathered her composure and continued with her report, but then she started coughing.

"Oh God," Jeffrey muttered.

"Turn it off."

But we didn't. We couldn't stop watching as the anchor coughed more and more violently. She lowered her head to the desk, still hacking. Two crew members rushed to her side and carried her off camera. She was limp in their arms. The news abruptly cut out to station identification.

"She was in Chicago," I realized. "It's here."

We both slid down to the floor and held Gretchen tightly, so tightly she squirmed. We let her go reluctantly, but then Jeffrey grabbed her arm.

"Ow," Gretchen complained. Jeffrey pulled her sleeve up.

It was covered in a red welts.

We tried to stay calm and not scare her. Jeffrey went to call 911. He put the phone down a few minutes later, face white.

"What is it?"

"They're not answering."

I've pulled beside another deserted car on the highway. I distinctly avoid looking too closely at the remains of the driver in the front seat.

I'm carrying a gas can, some tubing, and a small hand pump. I place the can on the ground, open the cap on the car, and feed the tubing down into the gas tank. I put the other end into the gas can. The pump is attached in the middle.

I hope this works.

I start pumping. I pump for a very long time and I'm about to give up when I hear liquid start to pour into the gas can. I whoop with delight and Dutch barks along. I keep pumping, even though my arm is burning with fatigue.

The can is about full. I pull the tube up out of the gas tank, but as it comes out of the car, it spurts out at me, covering my sweater and jeans. I jump back and trip over the gas can. The contents spill onto the ground.

"Dammit! I had it! I had the whole can full." The dog looks on sympathetically. "I had it," I whine. Then I sigh. No one cares.

I strip off my gas-soaked clothes and leave them by the car. In my underwear, I go back to my car to wipe with a towel and pull clean clothes out of the back. For a moment, I think about just lighting the gasoline that is trickling along the street. "But with my luck, it would ignite some fumes or something, and I'd go up in flames, too." I have to be careful with myself; there is no one to take care of me. I climb into the front seat of my car and start it. "What's the fun of being the last human on Earth if you can't blow stuff up?"

I look for another car.

We stayed on the floor with Gretchen, playing with her as much as we could, until the coughing started. Then we held her, all three of us together, until it stopped. We carried her to her bed and tucked her in, as if she were asleep, and then went to sit together on the couch.

"I need to call my parents," I said, when I was able to speak.

"Do you think they're—"

"I'm going to call them."

I was relieved when my father answered. "Dad," I said, "are you all right?"

"Your mother…" he said quietly.

"Gretchen."

"No," he whispered.

He started coughing.

"Dad!"

"I got the rash about an hour after your mother did."

"Why didn't you call?"

"Just keep talking to me. I want to hear your voice."

I leaned against the wall, trying to come up with something to talk about. Normally I would tell him about something Gretchen had done, or about work. I couldn't even think about those things now.

Jeffrey came over. "You all right?" he asked.

I reached for his hand and held it tightly. I looked outside. "The flowers are blooming in the yard," I told Dad.

"Which ones?" He started coughing again.

"The purple ones. The ones on that vine that crawls up the brick wall in our backyard. They're opening up, and there are a few that are already open all the way. Purple on the outside and a kind of bluish in the middle." I paused while Dad coughed again. It gave me time to think of something to say. "The vines must be higher up this year. I wonder if they'll grow all the way up to the top. They're really thick at the bottom now, can't even see the wall." I'd never looked at those flowers that closely. "There aren't any bees yet," I said. "But they'll probably be here soon, buzzing around." I paused again, sighed. "Dad, you there?"

There was no answer on the other end.

"Dad?"

I didn't bother to hang up the phone. I just left it on the table with the line open.

As the sun went down, I sat with Jeffrey on the couch, our arms around each other. There was nothing to watch on TV anymore. The stations had wiped out one by one, going to static. We just sat, exhausted from crying, and waited.

I'm driving down country roads, a map of Lyon County, Kentucky, spread on the seat next to me. Dutch has his head out the window in the passenger seat, squinting his eyes in the wind. I'm driving between dots on the map I marked in the library where I spent the summer. Besides the map, I took a stack of books about farming, electricity, plumbing. The back of the car is full of camping supplies and canned food.

I'm looking for a home. It needs to have a windmill or a water tank, preferably both. Inside, I need a large, open fireplace. A garden in the yard would be great, although I can start one if I need to. All the neighborhoods I've chosen have a large lake or river nearby. They're all very rural. I don't have much time before winter.

I camp by the side of the road at night. I could sleep in any of the houses around, but the bodies deter me. I'll have to pull some out of whatever house I adopt, and I'll have to do some cleaning up. I plan to burn the bodies, along with most of the upholstery in the room I find them in. I hope they're not in bed.

Gravel crunches under my tires as I pull up to a small farmhouse on a hill. I saw the windmill from the street. I get out, Dutch darting out in front of me, and look around. The house is old, but beautiful. It's painted blue with white trim, has a white front porch with a rocking chair. Plaid curtains in the windows, flowers still blooming among the weeds in the window boxes.

The porch creaks slightly under my step. The paint is worn, but clean. I stand on a rag-woven welcome mat and open the door. No one locks their doors out here. The house smells like pillows and breakfast.

"Hello?" No one answers, of course, but I have to try.

I flip the light switch. The lights flicker on for a second, and then off. I have a book in the car on how to repair windmills.

I walk into the living room, crane my neck around to peek into a high backed chair. It's empty. One wall is covered with books. I'll have to make room for the ones I brought. Cozy mysteries and rural photography will have to give way to engineering manuals and survival guides.

The kitchen is next. There is a wooden table at the very end, right by the window, next to a huge open fireplace. Electric oven. I open the refrigerator, then close it again quickly as the smell hits my nose. Out the window, Dutch is barking at another dog in the backyard. I go out to investigate.

Dutch is jumping around and barking with a black and white Border Collie who seems very happy to see us. "Have you found a friend?" I've gotten used to narrating my life to Dutch. A chicken runs past me and I notice the coop. Eggs for breakfast. I call to the Border Collie. "Here boy, come here." I hold out my hand, but he's too busy playing with Dutch.

I go into the house and look through the cabinets for some kind of dog treat, but don't find any. Then out to the barn where a cow and her calf are mooing. "Oh, I'll bet you're hungry too." I find the dog food and the Collie's bowl—"Oh, *her* name is Lily"—fill it and bring it out. Lily runs and eagerly eats it up. Dutch starts to get in there, too, and Lily snarls at him. I pick him up. "Come on, let's let her eat." The bowl is empty in seconds. "Good girl! Now let's go feed the cows."

I don't get upstairs for a few hours, during which time I experience the stark difference between reading about how to milk cows and actually doing it, but now I'm climbing the stairs carefully, both dogs with me. "They weren't anywhere else in the house." I look into one bedroom, a small room with an undisturbed white quilt on the bed. I force myself to go to the master bedroom. There are gloves and tarps in the car. I want to run away. I open the door.

The bed is empty.

My legs go weak with relief. The window opens onto a beautiful view of the lake. There is something under the large oak tree, and I squint to make it out.

A middle-aged couple lies on the grass, a wine bottle between them. It looks like they're holding hands.

"Thank you," I tell them.

I make two more discoveries. There's a wine collection in the cellar, and a striped cat who has protected the house from invasion. Soon I'm sitting in my new kitchen, petting the cat and drinking wine.

Two fires are burning. One is outside, removing the old inhabitants, and one inside, comforting the new one.

I sleep rather soundly these days. Nothing like hard physical labor in the outdoors as a cure for insomnia. But the sound of barking rouses me. Something's wrong.

I stumble out of bed and put my boots on, running to the back door. The back porch light doesn't work, but I can see in the light of the full moon.

Dutch, Lily, and a new dog, a retriever who wandered into my yard a few months ago and whom I've named Jerry, are barking ferociously at a pair of coyotes. The dogs stand between the coyotes and the henhouse. I remember the rifle in the front hallway and run to retrieve it. I aim the gun at one of the coyotes, away from the dogs. I've only fired this gun once before.

I pull the trigger. The world explodes in loud and bright. I'm on the floor.

When I get up, I see the coyotes running off. "Dutch, Jerry, Lily! Come!" Jerry runs up to me, Lily a bit behind.

As they retreat, one of the coyotes turns, almost spitefully. Dutch's limp body hangs in its mouth.

I lift the rifle again and try to fire, but it doesn't work. I did something wrong but I have no idea what. The coyotes disappear into the distance.

For a long time, I just stand there. Jerry and Lily whimper at me, but I'm staring at the hole in the darkness, staring until my eyes play tricks and I see swirls of light. I hear nothing, but I think without meaning to about what the coyotes are doing right now.

The next day, I take the dogs in the truck with me into town. I come back with the trailer full of wood and shovels and start working on a fence. I dig holes around the yard, one at a time.

I work every day, starting after my morning chores. Throw the digger into the earth, force the handles apart, pull the dirt up, toss it aside. Again and again. I cry on and off, but it doesn't stop or even slow my work. I struggle against the cold soil. This task should have waited for another month, when the ground would have warmed more, but I cannot wait any longer. Each chunk of dirt is a part of the grave I would have dug for Dutch, for Jeffrey. For Gretchen.

When the sun starts to get low, I have to stop for dinner. Canned food again. I have no time for fishing, or building a fire for cooking. The cold food seems right.

After dinner, before it is dark, I take my rifle to the hill. I've set up a few empty cans on a box and spend the rest of the evening, into the dark, practicing. Shot after shot rings out until I finally go to bed, to start the digging again in the morning.

I'm doing laundry in two galvanized bins, one with soap for washing, and one for rinsing. I hate doing laundry. My hands are red from the cold water. I never take the time to heat the water over the fire, or use some of my precious bathing water, a new luxury since I finally figured out the solar panels on the roof. I use water straight from the lake instead. Out of spite, maybe, for this hated task, although I know that I'm the one who suffers in the end. It is a warm fall day and I'm wearing shorts that are too large for me, a stained T-shirt, and my ubiquitous wide-brimmed hat.

Buster runs up to me, barking. Billy follows close behind. He's still a puppy, but he already towers over Buster. From the size of his paws, he's going to be huge.

"What is it, Buster?" I ask, wiping my hands on my shirt. "Timmy stuck in the well?" I make that joke at least once a day.

He barks more, oblivious to my devastating humor. "Something out there?" I heard a pack of wolves out hunting last night, but the days are always peaceful. But Buster's worried, and he isn't usually one to get like this over nothing.

"All right, all right." I walk over to the house, pick up my rifle, and climb the ladder to the roof. On one of my trips to town a few weeks ago, I found a telescope and set it up here. It's become an obsession for me now. No matter how tired I am at the end of the day, I spend hours looking up at the stars every night. The sky is crowded with millions of stars that had been invisible before, blotted out by humanity's own light. I feel small, of course, as everyone does when facing the vastness of space, but that was comforting. Humanity is so tiny, not so much of a loss. I saw the space station once and wondered if anyone was still up there, afraid to come down.

Now I turn the telescope Earthward, scanning my property. It takes a few adjustments to focus so close, but soon I'm able to sweep around, focusing on the area where Buster usually likes to hang out. And then my hands go cold.

A man is walking along the shore of the lake.

I look a few times, but I have to believe it. He is filthy and walks with his head down. He wears a large backpack and seems to be struggling with it. He's moving slowly but steadily. And heading right for me.

I'll have to welcome him in, of course. Offer him food, water. He will see what I have here, my electricity, my garden, even running water sometimes. After fifteen years outside and alone, my home will be a paradise to him. A warm fire, music playing on a CD player, a library of books, a cup of coffee.

A warm bed.

He will want it for his own. He will stay. Help out with the chores. Have his own opinions on what I should do. We will argue.

He will become my husband.

The universe has arranged a marriage for me, by bringing this man here. Maybe he will be kind, funny, sweet. Maybe I will learn to love him, like they say happens with enough time. I try to keep his face in frame as he walks, looking for any clues to his character, and therefore my future.

Children would be pointless. It would just push the curse down to the next generation. I know enough about animal husbandry to know that two people can't repopulate a planet. Even Cain and Abel found wives from somewhere else.

He is close enough now that I don't need the telescope. The dogs are running up to him, Buster and Billy. I'm on guard now, responsible for my tribe. Buster is cautious, but Billy has never seen another person before besides me.

The man looks startled at dogs running up to him. Understandable. The dogs stop. Buster stands at a distance, tail straight. He is cautious. Billy runs right up to him, jumping up excitedly. I'm still training him. I'll have to work on that some more. Silly puppy.

Suddenly Billy yelps and jerks away. The man adjusts his balance; he'd kicked him. Billy is lying on the ground, motionless. The man yells at Buster. "Get away!" he screams. "Get away!" Billy still isn't moving.

I feel a surge of rage. A loud pop, a blossom of red appears on the man's chest, and he falls. It isn't until I get to Billy, see that he is dead, that I start shaking. I don't stop for a few hours.

I'm cooking dinner at the stove, boiling water for vegetables, frying chicken in a cast iron skillet. Using a lot of power. I've already baked a cake in the oven, and used electricity to run the mixer to make the frosting.

The lights dim for a moment. The generator kicks in. I have time to finish cooking.

I'm mostly alone now. The dogs have all gone, except for one mutt named Jojo. One of Lily's grandchildren. I still think of Jojo as a puppy, even though her muzzle is white and she spends most of her time napping by the fire. When I carry the meal over to the kitchen table, Jojo follows me slowly, walking with awkward steps. I wait for her to catch up. I'm not moving very fast myself, these days.

I look out the window. I've lost count of how many years I've been here. I deliberately lost track of the days and months. Too many painful anniversaries. I don't know how old I am, but my face is wrinkled and my hair has been white for years. I can't do my daily chores in one day. I slipped in the barn a while back, and I couldn't get up for a day. I spent a week on the floor of the kitchen, recovering.

I eat my meal slowly, enjoying it. I've always loved a good fried chicken, and this one turned out well. I tear some scraps into small pieces and toss them down to Jojo. I drink the wine, slip the pills in before dessert. I did a good job on the cake, considering I haven't made one since I was a child.

I finish my meal, wash the dishes and put them away in the cupboard. "Come on, girl." I pick up Jojo in one arm and the bottle and wine glass in the other. Together we walk to the hill where many of my dogs are buried. Jerry. Poor little Billy. Buster. Mimi and Jack. I settle myself under the oak tree and watch the sun set, finishing the bottle of wine.

When the stars appear, I lie back and look at them. Jojo lies next to me. I pet my dog, remembering Jeffrey and Gretchen, my parents, my friends. Venus appears, then more stars.

The Earth rotates more, and the sun slips beneath the horizon. Light reflects off of Venus' surface, the surface of the moon, shining onto the Earth, which is now in darkness. The Universe expands and waits, silent and empty.

ANDREA MCCREADY is the regional audit manager for Corent Systems, Inc., where she has worked for twelve years. She's a proud alumna of the University of Illinois, and received her MBA from DePaul University. She lives in Chicago with her husband, Jeffrey, and their daughter, Gretchen.

MARY first fell in love with Science Fiction when Luke turned on his lightsaber.

After getting a highly impractical degree in Performance Studies from Northwestern University, Mary has held a variety of careers ranging from programmer to clown. Now she's pursuing her MFA at Seton Hill University in Writing Popular Fiction.

She and her husband are raising their two boys to be geeks, and proudly display their life-size replica of Han Solo in Carbonite in their family room. You can follow Mary on Twitter at @geekyMary.

OUR BLESSED COMMUTE

An account by an unnamed driver,

AS PROVIDED BY RHOADS BRAZOS

The I-70 interchange is planted in fertile soil. With bones of concrete and marrow of steel, it leeches the land barren. The freeway flexes and unfolds.

"Did you notice?" I ask. "There's an extra lane today."

When my eye isn't on the road, it's on you.

But you don't answer. You're busy over in the passenger seat, your cell cupped in your hands like a baby sparrow. I decide to try sideways flattery.

"The queen should always sit to the king's left."

"Do you want me to drive?" you ask.

"No, that's not—" I'm not sure what I meant. Maybe I just wanted a response.

You go back to your screen, and I wonder who you're talking to.

Over the days and weeks, the roadway blooms like an asphalt flower. I dial in to the AM to hear the heathens. They speak of right and wrong and nature and man. It's apostasy. The philistines ride the road like us all. I've shaved fifteen minutes off my commute and I know they have too.

"No gift's more precious than time," I say.

"Oh?"

I see that familiar flicker of annoyance. "And being with you."

Too late. You're more than some afterthought, an addendum scratched into the end papers. We've been together so long that perhaps I take you for granted. At least I know better than to apologize.

Southward over fat lanes, I'm not even sure where we're going. Planning is so difficult. Bridgeways overspill their banks like swollen rivers. New lanes unfurl across sidewalks.

This doesn't live. This doesn't breathe. Who are we to say? Touch its face and feel its pulse. The thrum of a billion pilgrims pulses through pitch black veins.

"I'd like to go to the beach," you say one far forward day.

"I can make that happen." I squeeze the wheel tight.

"Why don't you?"

And you smile. It's one of those moments when I feel our cylinders are firing with one purpose.

We follow a lonely way down a concrete shore. The sun flashes off the seashell aggregate—conchs, moon snails, and buttercup lucines pressed into its surface. The road is a thrifty beast, and clever too. It uses what's at hand and makes do. It lives the moral from every one of our grandparents' stories.

We pull off and sit a while but don't get out. I can't remember the last time we did. Your window is down and the breeze comes through, insistent, like an old memory trying to make itself new.

"I wish I could feel the water," you say.

"Don't think that's wise."

"It's just a wish."

We can't take the chance, and you know it. What if it realizes we're gone?

"I think the exit's already slid forward," I say.

I check the gauges. Fine, as always. I give you another few moments and ease the car back to the path. It will be a long time before you quit brooding, and I'm sorry for that, but we're not always meant to be happy.

Traffic is sparse today and will be more so tomorrow. The road grows, and drivers wander farther apart. New express lanes and double-wide merge ramps. Overpass over overpass. Serpentine causeways and new efficiencies. It's more than us. It has exceeded our means. Swooping through forests, burrowing through strata, piercing the oceans. Above the clouds on pavement contrails.

You died on a Monday; that's what I assume. I didn't hear you go, but you always hated that day. I put you in the trunk. Now I'm your chauffeur.

The radio still offers a bit of distraction, though listeners don't call in much these days. It's one long monologue. I listen to the only story, the tale of our forever. The highway, hungry for substrate, is trying to lasso the moon. I'm not sure how it will manage without getting tangled, but I don't doubt that it will find a way.

I talk to myself when I'm lonely.

"What do you call the guy who drives the hearse?" I ask.

You'd shake your head and answer, "I really don't know."

"Somber."

And you'd squeeze my hand. I've never been great at these things, but you would have appreciated the effort.

I saw someone the other day, a dozen miles up over the shores of Borneo. The air's thin up there, and the sky's like a bruise. His vehicle was streaking down one of those upper-atmosphere roller coaster dips, lights set to bright, trailing halogen fire. At first I thought him to be a shooting star.

His vehicle slowed, and the driverside window lowered. I'd assumed wrong.

She waved to me, and I waved to her. Just a hello, pleasant regards, one soul greeting another out on the open road. It had never happened to me before.

I slowed to a stop and shouted over, "Meet me at the high crossing, north of Jakarta!"

She said something in return, but the wind whipped her words silent.

"I'll see you there!" I called. "My name is—"

It's been so long since I've said it, I'm not sure that it's real.

She answered back. I still couldn't hear, so I pretended. Amazingly, you and she share the same name.

Today, I'm at the crossing, just waiting. Below me twist a million paved roads all wound and confused like kitten-tangled yarn. I hope you're not jealous. I would be, but you were always better than that. I wait for a while, a year or so with the engine on idle.

Life is a journey whose destination is never decided. Only the scenery matters.

And this ending is as good as any.

I lay in the center lane with you by my side. Upon a bed of asphalt, under a blanket of stars, we sleep together and the let the road drink us in. It's always so thirsty.

A dry breeze scatters loose effects. A sun-faded photo shows a father with his two children. They both offer looks of adulation which only the smallest among us express for the briefest of moments. The woman near him wears a thin smile. In another photo, newer by years, the children are missing and a new woman poses with the same man. He seems tired, but holds her close. A tattered parking pass to a local community college identifies the owner as either faculty or student. Before a distinction can be made, the wind quickens and this is forgotten.

RHOADS has written stories across the entire spectrum of speculative fiction, from light fantasy to the most decrepit tales of horror to quirky sci-fi. His works can be found in Ellen Datlow's *The Best Horror of the Year, Vol. 7*; *Apex Magazine*; *Death's Realm* by Grey Matter Press; *Pantheon Magazine*'s *Gaia: Shadow and Breath, Vols. 1 & 2*; and a dozen other magazines and collections. He currently lives in Colorado with his wife and son.

SMOKE SCREAM

An account by Yosa,

AS PROVIDED BY SAMANTHA BRYANT

My first clue that something was wrong came when I emerged from the tank. Millie was not there waiting as she should have been. I checked the time and date. I was on schedule. She should have been waiting.

I called for her, my voice still weak from my days separated from my body. It sounded like a kitten mewling. My limbs were shaking from the shock of returning movement and my body reeked. I'd been gone for nearly ten days this time, my longest sojourn yet.

Millie didn't come. I had to pull myself out of the tank, no easy task given how slippery the preserving gel is and how physically weakened I felt. I lost my grip more than once and bruised my ribs just beneath my breasts. Luckily my fall did not damage the equipment.

Wrapping up in the robe we always left nearby, I went to the booth and recorded my recollections of my journey to the other side, still shivering from the shock of transition. It's important to debrief as soon as possible as memories of the journey and what I saw there fade quickly. The conscious mind blocks out the things it can't make sense of. The specifics disappear like streams of water through loosely cupped fingers.

I detailed the blue quality of the light and the strange feeling of lethargy that overtook me again. This time, I found that I could mitigate this effect by cupping my hands over my ears and dimming the sound of singing that filled the air. My theory is that the music hypnotizes the traveler, a sort of aural crowd control. Because I stayed longer this time, I finally overcame the malaise and followed the teeming crowd of spirits up the path.

Eventually, I stopped hearing the music. I don't know if this was because it ceased, or because I became used to it as a person might become used to an unpleasant smell. Either way, I was able to engage with the spirits at last. Some spoke with me; others ignored me or seemed unable to see me at all. One woman became enraged when she discovered that I was only playing dead. She chased me and might have done me harm if she'd been able, but there was a barrier I could cross that she could not. My last memory of the journey was of her crying, screaming face and incoherent insults. Telling it made it real to me again, and I had to rest some minutes to regain control over my breathing and heart rate.

I was angry with Millie for the extra minutes her absence had cost me. Who knew what data was lost because I couldn't start recording the instant I came back into my body?

My report made, I then showered briskly in the lab's stall. The water was very hot and brought a feeling of vitality back into my limbs, though they still shook. The transition was more difficult this time. I didn't know if that was due to the length of my absence from my body or the violence of my exit from the spirit realm.

Clean, and clad in soft clothing, I went upstairs in search of my wayward assistant.

I am always hungry and thirsty when I come back from these trips into the netherworld—the intravenous nutrition keeps me alive, but not sated—so I went to the kitchen first. That's when I found Millie, or rather, her body.

I did not sob or cry out at the sight of my darling Millie's corpse. I don't know what I did. But I found myself on the kitchen floor, staring at her simple ballet flat shoes, still clinging to her slender feet, the flesh within gone gray and still. It was too awful to process, and I don't know how long I sat there, gaping.

My poor, darling Millie. I knew her, though her head was gone. I knew her by her lovely limbs and favorite floral skirt. The smell was horrendous. It must have happened several days before. Her desecrated body was already becoming putrid. It was obvious that she'd been shot with something high caliber. Her head was obliterated and her blood and brains were spread across the tile. It seemed the gore was everywhere.

When I could move again, I called the police, counseling myself to breathe, unsure if I would be able to form words to explain the scene before my eyes. No one answered the phone. Even in our small mountain town, someone is always on call to answer the police phone. I found it strange, but I wasn't yet deeply concerned by the lack of response. I wanted to know what happened.

From the pantry in the hall, I grabbed a jar of peanut butter and a plastic spoon and took it and a bottle of water to my computer. I had to eat. I hadn't had food in ten days, and I was of no use to Millie if I didn't give my body fuel.

Millie had been an excellent assistant, and I would never be able to replace her. She had understood her role and supported me well. I would never find another like her. She had loved me and understood the way I loved her, never asking for more than I could give. My anger, which had simmered beneath the shock and grief, boiled up to the surface, directed at her nameless killer. I decided I would find the person who had killed her and ensure adequate punishment. It was the least I could do for her years of service and companionship.

I ate half the jar of peanut butter while I watched the security footage. There was nothing there. Millie was standing in the kitchen a week before my return, looking out the window and slowly stirring something in a large mug, probably the miso soup she was so fond of. She turned as if she had heard something. I rewound this part and watched with the sound turned all the way up. I heard nothing.

I saw Millie's eyes grow wide and she opened her mouth to cry out, then her head exploded. I saw no one else on the recording. It was as if her head simply exploded without cause. There was no sound of weaponry, not even a clear trajectory for the force.

I went back to the kitchen and confirmed what the video had shown with my own eyes. The pieces of her head were spread all over the room as if there had been a bomb in the center of her skull. The rest of her body seemed undamaged. Her delicate arms were spread out and the fingers curled into the hands. Her skirt bunched up over her splayed legs, revealing her well-formed thighs. I didn't want to touch her and feel the way her flesh had gone cold, but I needed to know what had happened to her.

My next several hours were spent in collecting data. Millie's organs were still intact. None of her was missing. I tried to run my tests while still leaving the crime scene ready for investigation by the police, but the police still failed to answer the phone. I should have known then that Millie was not the only victim, but I was merely annoyed that I could not reach the proper authorities. As I took samples and ran them through a variety of tests, I wrote a letter of complaint to the city in my head. I paid my taxes, after all. I should be able to expect help when I needed it.

I found nothing helpful in all my tests. I went back and watched the recording again. She had heard something. Something that my security equipment could not record. Was it something outside the frequencies it could represent? Did her eyes grow wide merely from fear or had she seen something as well? If Millie had been there, she might have been able to help manipulate the video files to reveal something new, but those were not skills I possessed.

When the police failed to answer the phone yet again, I decided to go into town myself. I went into the bedroom and pulled on some more socially acceptable clothing. The clothes hung on me loosely. I had probably lost fifteen or more pounds again. I was going to have to load up on carbs and gain a little bulk back before my next journey.

Flashes of my trip went through my mind as I dressed. There had been a very bright white light that suffused everything at the outset, just as there had been on my other visits. I still had a headache from trying to peer into that brightness—I felt sure there was something at the center of it, if only I could perceive it. If I could arrive with that memory intact, maybe I could shield my eyes and not fall victim to the temporary blindness.

The presence of that light lent some credence to the descriptions people who have survived a near-death experience share. The details of their accounts vary considerably, but many of them feature a bright white light. Of course, none of them seem to agree about the nature of that light. Survivors, for the most part, were too focused on deciding what it meant, on what was supposed to happen, and failed to provide useful descriptive data.

I was anxious to get back to my lab and study the recording I had made just after I emerged to pull the details that were already escaping from my recollection. But first things first: Millie.

I drove down the road on my scooter, the light buzzing of the motor loud in the quiet morning. At ten o'clock, I should have been seeing other cars, but no one else seemed to be moving. I stopped at the gas station at the bottom of the mountain just outside the road to town. The machines were working, but no other customers were evident.

There was a blue pickup truck parked at another pump, but no sign of the driver. I looked suspiciously at the little store. I should have gone inside, I suppose. It seems strange now that I didn't. But I was focused on getting to the police station and getting someone to come take care of Millie.

I started seeing the bodies as I drove through town. They were lying on the sidewalks, resting in the cars that were crashed into each other at each intersection. Every one of them another Millie, heads destroyed, bodies lying wherever they fell. It was grisly. I knew then that I wasn't going to find anyone alive at the police station, but I went anyway, needing to see the evidence with my own eyes before I would believe it.

I got my evidence as soon as I walked in the door. A headless corpse manned the front desk, lying forward on its chest, bodily fluids pooled around the neck opening. The smell was overwhelming. I didn't go any further.

I went back home as quickly as I could, nearly wrecking my scooter in my haste. I covered Millie's body with a plastic sheet and foraged for another meal, planning my investigation. It appeared that whatever happened to Millie had happened to everyone. Everyone but me. So that begged two questions: what happened? and why didn't it happen to me?

I went back to my computer and this time went to news sites for information. There was nothing in the headlines. The newest thing posted was seven days ago. All the links were still live; everything still worked—there just wasn't any new information being posted. Seven days ago, there was nothing in the headlines to suggest a disaster or an attack either. I scoured the sites for a hint and found nothing— whatever had come had taken everyone at once, and no one seemed to have seen it coming.

Then it hit me. Millie. Millie knew what had happened. Millie was dead. And I had everything I needed to get in touch with her just down the stairs.

It was going to be dangerous, of course, even more dangerous than usual. I'd have to plan it out well, or I wouldn't make it back.

The next few days were grueling. I cleaned up the kitchen and disposed of Millie's remains. She had never shared her desires about burial with me, but given the poor condition of her body and expediency, I burned her. I hoped she would approve. I ate the stores of frozen pizzas and ice cream, trying to get a little flesh back on my bones before I climbed back into the tub and blurred the lines between life and death again.

I worked as many hours a day as I could. There was much to do to prepare for the journey. I had to see to my own health while analyzing the data from all my previous sojourns, looking for anything that might help me find Millie in the distant lands. I had to recalibrate and prepare the equipment. I felt I was on the cusp of something grand, of finally truly understanding the kind of transition death really was.

As I fell into my bed each night, I reached automatically for Millie. It was then that I felt her absence the most. The bed was large without her in it, and I slept fitfully, rolling and rolling, but never bumping against her and falling into comforted rest as I had these past few years. If I were the kind of woman who cried, I would have cried then. But my eyes remained dry. I thought only of understanding what had happened and of revenge. My dreams were filled with Millie's wide eyes and silent scream. There was something accusing in her gaze. Her face merged with the face of the woman who had chased me from the spirit realm, the mouth gaping wide enough to swallow me entire.

I woke late in the morning when a siren went off. It was a long, echoing signal, and I was instantly alert, and hopeful that it meant that there was, indeed, someone else up and moving in the world. I ran to the window and threw it open to check the horizon, but there was nothing there. It was only after the signal stopped that I realized it was the first Wednesday of the month at eleven o'clock—the monthly test of the emergency alert system. It was just another automated system doing its job, even though there was no one left to warn.

That depressed me. I didn't much care for people, generally speaking. But part of the joy of discovery was in sharing what was learned. Who would I tell when I figured this out?

I decided to wait no longer. Tonight I will go.

I've set the equipment to bring me back out in three days. It's a short expedition, maybe too short, but I haven't had time to adequately recover from the previous trip, and I'm afraid to risk a longer time. My body could die, leaving me trapped. I have to hope that three days will be enough time.

3 days later

It's my fault.

I did this to Millie and to the rest of them.

In forcing my way through to the other world, I left an opening and something came through it. Millie said it looked like smoke or a cloud, but it moved swiftly, howling as it flew. The sound was unbearable, she said; it broke her heart while it split her skull. It was making its way around the world, and I needed to be ready when it returned.

She'd been there, at the opening, waiting for me on the other side. Before I even found my balance, she had grabbed my arms and pulled me down, hiding me with her body. In all our years together, Millie had never spoken so many words in a row. But words flew from her. There was no time, she said. No time for apologies or explanations. I had to go home, and I had to send the beast back into the spirit world. She gripped my head in both her hands and stared into my eyes. "You must close the rift, and you must never come again. Now go, before they notice you are here."

She pushed me then, and I woke gasping, sobbing, and sputtering preserving gel, my apology a lump in my throat, my unspoken love a bruised squeezing of the chest.

I didn't know if it mattered. If I were all that was left of humanity, why not just let the beast kill me, too? But Millie had said, "You must."

She, who never asked for anything, had demanded this one thing of me, and I would do it.

Millie had seemed certain that time was short, so I wasted none, but made my preparations. First, it was necessary to perforate my ear drums. I didn't know when the beast might come, and the fight was over before it began if I fell victim to the sonic attack that had killed Millie and so many others. I hoped that, if I couldn't hear it, then it couldn't harm me. It was an untested theory, and the only battle plan I had.

As I sterilized my instruments and prepared an anesthetic, I considered the larger problem of how to send this beast back to the beyond. I knew little of its nature. I knew that the video security system had been unable to capture its sound or image and that Millie had described it as like a cloud or smoke. I knew nothing of what motivated it and how I might direct its movement.

The distraction of trying to solve this problem kept me from lingering on the horror of purposefully taking my own hearing by means of intentional injury to the eardrum. I was already poised with the instruments before the mirror when I felt the first pangs of doubt that this course of action was the one I should embark upon. I shoved my doubts down, remembering the earnest fervor and absolute trust in Millie's face as she looked into my eyes. I wished I had kissed her one last time. I told myself I owed it to her as I tore the membrane of my own inner ear.

I immediately wished I had found a way to do both ears at the same time. I howled with the pain of it in spite of the anesthetic. My hand, when I raised it to puncture the other side, shook, and it took me some minutes to steady it so I could do the job. I am ashamed to confess how many attempts I made before I was able to finish the task.

There was more blood than I expected, and I worried that I had injured more than just my eardrums, but an investigation with a mirror and a bright light showed that all was as I had intended. I went to the stereo and turned it on. The lights on the graphic equalizer flicked up and down, showing the sound I could no longer hear. There was only a sensation of motion and fullness, a vague sort of buzzing. Tears and snot flowed down my cheeks, wetting my hair. I felt sick and dizzy. I crouched to the ground, fighting the nausea. I didn't have time to succumb to personal weakness. Millie had said attack was imminent.

My one defense in place, I turned my mind back to the question of what my offense would consist of. I thought of everything I knew of smoke and settled on a vacuum device that would pull the essence of the beast into a compartment that I could then empty where and when I chose. I set to work modifying the shop vac. It was a simple process, but the work was more difficult than it should have been, as a simple turning movement was enough to send my head spinning. But, after a few minutes, I lost myself in the work until the pain of my ears pushed its way into my awareness.

The anesthetic now fully worn off, my ears and head throbbed in time with the beating of my heart. I tasted blood in the mucus that ran down my throat. I longed for Millie to cradle my head in her hands and serve me tea or miso soup as she had when I was ill. But Millie was gone. Ignoring the discomfort, I pressed on until the device performed the way I wished.

After another meal of items taken from the deep freeze, I took my device outside and experimented with smoke that I made in the fire pit. I could only hope that this creature responded physically like the smoke it appeared to be. My apparatus in place, I sat down to wait.

The pain meds I had dosed myself with must have made me drowsy. It's hard to imagine that I could have fallen asleep otherwise, as keyed up as I was. I woke at sunset and startled at the vibrant pink horizon and the orange and red clouds poised against it. I panicked at the thought that so many hours had gone by. What if I had missed my opportunity to capture the beast from the spirit realm?

The air went cold around me, and I knew I had not missed my

moment. I gripped my new device and spun, trying to ascertain the direction from which my attacker might pounce. There was nothing around me but a thin gray line of smoke, the last remnant of the experimental fire I had lit in the fire pit. The air was chilled all the same, a sharp and sudden change that was not explainable by the mere fading of the sunlight.

I looked up. It was there, directly above me. As Millie had described, it appeared to be a creature made of smoke, a gray-white shifting mass that took on and abandoned shapes as I watched. First it seemed a long tube, then it curled around itself and seemed more like a coiled snake. I watched, fascinated as it shifted in the air above me. The device in my hands was all but forgotten in the wonder at what I was seeing.

My head began to ache and I realized I was probably already being attacked by the killing song of the beast. I raised a hand to my nose and wiped away small drips of scarlet blood. I moved toward the creature, brandishing the suction tube. I was afraid that, if I launched my attack too soon, I'd miss my chance. I had to be sure the cloud monster was within reach.

I began to shout at it. The vibration in my throat told me I was screaming, even though I couldn't hear myself properly—it was like listening from underwater. The creature could hear me, though. That much was certain. As I cursed the beast for the destruction of my world and the death of Millie, it moved around me. Sometimes I thought I saw a face within the mass, but I know of the mind's proclivity for perceiving humanity where none exists. When the cloud was near enough around me that I could feel the moisture within it as if I were enveloped in a fog, I turned on the machine.

The device functioned just as I had planned. Within a few short seconds, the creature had disappeared. The machine immediately began to become coated in a kind of frost and I knew I had to hurry before the coldness of the creature destroyed my machine and set itself free upon the earth once more.

I ran to the lab and affixed the tubing to the opening, reversing the device's function and quickly pulling the plug on my transition chamber and all the machinery connected to it.

The vibration of the machines that had long been the background of my life was still. I could no longer feel it in the soles of my feet. Somehow that stillness made the laboratory feel empty: finally, irrevocably empty. I dropped to my knees and rubbed my hand over the surface of the tub—the infernal device that had done this to the world. Dismantling it would be the last act of love for the woman and the world I had destroyed.

Later, when I swallowed the antibiotics I had stolen from the pharmacy to ensure my self-mutilation didn't result in my death from infection, I pondered the meaning of a life completely alone, the last woman on earth. I wondered if I'd done a clean enough job that my eardrums would heal and my hearing return. It wasn't until I was drifting off to sleep at last, sometime in the early morning, that it occurred to me that there might be others still alive. They wouldn't be able to hear me though. I'd need to learn American Sign Language.

YOSA is fascinated with the afterlife and has devoted her life to finding out what awaits us beyond the grave. Luckily she also invented a far-more-marketable preserving gel which has financed her life and her research. She and Millie have been together several years. The two have neither children nor pets, preferring a quiet life in the mountains alone.

SAMANTHA BRYANT believes in love, magic, and unexplainable connections between people. She is a middle school teacher by day and a novelist by night. She also raises two kids, a dog, and a husband in a small town in North Carolina. That makes her a superhero all the time. You can find her online at samanthabryant.com and on Twitter @mirymom1. Her debut novel *Going Through the Change: A Menopausal Superhero Novel*, with Curiosity Quills Press, features another mad scientist.

BRIDGE TO NOWHERE, TRAIN FOR THE FORGOTTEN

An account by Almeda Inez,
AS PROVIDED BY MATHEW ALLAN GARCIA

We hold our breaths when the rabbit inches up to the trap, smelling the rod meant to throttle it, its tan paws stepping gingerly through the snow, inches from the latch. Xandria closes her eyes, her long dirty brown hair—just like her mother's—cascading down in front of her face, her thick wool cattle blanket draped over her shoulders so she looks like a small, wooly brown rock jutting out from the earth. I can hear her stomach growl from where I crouch, my knees screaming bloody murder.

So can the rabbit, apparently, because it looks in our direction. Must've seen something mean and hungry in my eyes, because its ears go up and it's gone, white tail and long legs leaping through the pines and shrubs.

Xandria hisses, muddy greenish eyes looking mean… but a little relieved too—the meanness just for show.

We follow the tracks down to a dry riverbank, to a burrow dug into the sidewall. I set the trap there, in the opening.

"It'll catch tomorrow. Don't you worry," I say. "Let's get back now.

You get a head start; don't wait for this old lady. I can't keep up."

By the time I make it home, my legs are throbbing, and my heart feels like it's thudded its way halfway up my throat. The cold bites my hands. I shrug the snow off my shoulders.

Xandria takes the whistling tea kettle off the fire when I come in, pours the hot water into a cup, and passes it to me, my stiff, trembling fingers barely able to grip it, holding the cup with my palms until the warmth melts the ice in my bones.

The girl turned eight last month, and is prone to bouts of questions I rarely ever have answers for anymore—a hundred and ten percent her mother's daughter.

Dipping my nose close to the steaming cup, I comment about the smell—of lavender—and she mentions adding herbs she found out in the yard growing out from under her grandpappy's old Firebird. I look out toward it through the window, and I see it, its frame rusted and its tires shot out by the soldiers years ago so she had to get on her hands and knees to snap a few sprigs off.

I breathe in the smell, remembering how Tim would ride that beast like the devil. I smile.

We had some fun times in that didn't we? I just nod. Shake my head a little.

Never noticed the lavender, but I guess I don't go by Tim's old car. Not anymore.

The rest of Xandria's words are a jumbled, mumbled mess as her feet start working. Then she's out the door, her boots crunching in the snow and her footprints making a beeline toward the tracks. Her body casts a shadow through the broken, yellowing windows as I feel the rumbling in the soles of my feet.

Train's coming.

When Trisha and Lonny, her husband, brought Xandria to me, I wanted to say no. Wanted to tell them not to do that to this poor little girl. She wasn't even a year old, swaddled in thick wool blankets meant for cattle, her small silver eyes staring up at me from inside, pudgy fingers reaching.

Trisha was crying, of course she was, and Lonny was stone faced, a hundred tiny shrapnel cuts and bruises on the visible parts of his body, an arm in a sling, one eyeball cherry red. They were on the run. In these times, you either got to running or you put your head in the sand and hoped you went unnoticed.

"Believe us, Mom," Trisha said, as little Xandria yawned in her arms like she wanted to swallow the world. "If we had any other options left, we wouldn't be here."

It ain't ever gonna be like that time in Baltimore, is it? Tim's old croon piped up in my head—the only place I can hear his voice now—after they had gone, leaving me holding a little child I had no business raising—a woman of my age and situation.

Tim and I had never been to Baltimore. Just bought a mug thirty years ago from the secondhand shop that used to be on Willow Street. It's a pile of bricks now, wood poking out like fractured bones.

The mug had I LOVE BALTIMORE written in cursive on the handle, a big goofy black bird on the front that made me grin from time to time. It was Tim's sense of humor, making light of the things we never had, things we never got to do. Whenever things didn't go as planned—and things hardly ever did—he'd ask me to remember. Remember that trip to Baltimore that never was.

"Dear dead husband of mine," I said and sighed. "No, it won't ever be as good as that time."

I looked out the front screen door and onto the dilapidated porch, watching as my Trisha disappeared over the horizon. Then she was gone.

I looked down into Xandria's eyes, who seemed to be scanning my face, a crease in her brow like she was already forming her first question, I said:

"But we'll manage, won't we?"

When Xandria returns, she tells me the nurses on the train let her hold the tray of cups full of pills for the patients. They checked her pulse, took a draw of blood, temperature, and took her weight. Asked her how I was doing. Said she was underweight and prescribed two fat juicy steaks and a pitcher of milk, but only gave her a few bent up cans of soup and beans—one of which was so swelled it looked like a ball and was likely spoiled—a container of powdered milk and some matches. All they could spare, no doubt.

I shake my head, "What kind of monster tells a child about such food in times like these?"

Xandria giggles, says she didn't mind. Says they got all sorts of people on the train. People that have no homes anymore—she even gets a little misty eyed as she talks about them. Says she wants to help them get better. Help them find a home. Says she wants to be like one of the nurses on that train, helping people. The idea of me being here alone scares me. The idea of her out *there* scares me more.

Of course they weren't all nurses. Most were volunteers. People gathered up from the fortunate places that didn't get much foot traffic from the war or soldier's shooting holes through their homes. Bombs leveled out entire blocks in some areas, and others saw their only source of water poisoned. Horrible things like that.

Train comes once a year, sometimes twice if the fighting dies down enough. Always in the cold months. It's gotten so's Xandria can feel it coming days 'fore it arrives. Starts making her way toward the tracks, the sleep cobwebs barely out of her eyes, the sun a sliver of a peach on the horizon, the clouds wisps of pink cotton candy. She takes a pine branch and cleans out the tracks while I check the traps for rabbits. Goes as far as the bridge, looks out across the expanse toward the nowhere on the other side, then comes back.

Xandria pauses, and I know what she's about to ask.

Trisha used to have that exact face when she figured out some problem, remember sweetheart?

Timothy. I could almost see him in his old recliner, smoking a rolled up cigarette with that smirk on his face, eyes closed like he's letting the TV screens on the back of his eyelids play back the memories.

"I know," I say and smile. "I remember."

Xandria says my name again, with a question mark at the end.

"Sorry sweetie," I say, rising up to get the wood for our fire. "Let's talk about this later, yeah? After we eat."

Truth is, I'm afraid I'll lose Tim if I go.

Xandria's fifteen when she asks me again, and this time, there isn't a pause.

Her hair's gotten so it reaches her lower back, and she gathers it up at night and rests her head against it because she insists I get all the blankets and pillows. Insists, jokingly, that an old rickety thing like me would soak up the cold from the floorboards like a sponge.

The nurses must've told her that.

She does more than hold pills now. She tells me she sees a lot of the patients, even remembers a few, year after year. Last time they even took her a town over, so's she could help search for survivors after a raid—I couldn't be still until I saw her shadow on the porch.

They asked her how I was doing. Old and stubborn, she tells me she told them.

Older, sure. The ice in my bones has spread through my entire body. It feels like someone's poked a cold metal rod up my back straight up to my brain. Sometimes I close my eyes so tight I squeeze the tears out, clench my hands until they're numb. Until the pain passes.

You'll pop a blood vessel doing that. Maybe it's time we went away again, sweetie. Just relax, you and me. How's Baltimore this time of year?

"Cold," I say. "Always so cold."

Xandria gets up when she hears me. Tosses the last remaining leg from a coffee table that was a wedding gift from Tim's parents into the dying fire. Looks at me for a moment but doesn't say a word. I could feel her watching me until I go to sleep.

When I wake, Xandria's gotten the few things she owns in a plastic bag. She's sitting down next to the fire, her hands outstretched toward it, her eyebrows creased like the day I met her, the first day I held her in my arms.

I rustle the blankets off of me, my movements stiff. My bones crack under the weight of my skin.

Xandria says to stay lying down for a while. She's got the kettle boiling, drops a few sprigs of lavender into my cup and pours. Puts a little powdered milk in it before offering it to me.

They've offered her a role on the train, she says. She wants to go. There's a place for me, too, she adds. With a bed. A real bed.

I don't answer her, just lie back.

I don't like the sound of that. You won't leave me, right? Sweetheart?

"No," I say, and turn to my side and close my eyes, don't care how much my hips and shoulders hurt. Feel the knots in my stomach, but refuse the cup Xandria offers me.

She tells me he's dead, her voice pleading, soft but strong at the same time. Says I got to let him go, got to forget him. That the only life there is left in this world is on that train, and we have to be on it. Before it's too late.

Oh dear lord.

"Shut up," I say, suddenly angry, remembering the sound of Tim's feet above me, passing the length of the living room, hiding me in the floorboards where we hid the canned food and water. The sound of the heavy boots, crashing door, gunfire. The sound of his body falling right above me, his blood seeping into the floorboards, as the men searched our home, tearing things apart, worse than animals.

Xandria's reaction was immediate, like I cut her.

I close my eyes. Think of the memories in every piece of furniture in this house, even the ones we burnt already, smelling of the thirty years my husband and I spent here. I can't let it go. I just can't. Losing this house would mean losing him. Losing his voice, even if it lives only in my head.

By the time I've put together the right words to tell her this, Xandria's out the door.

When she comes back, I tell her to leave me. Tell her I'll die in this house. Tell her there's nothing for me out there, and nothing for her here. That I'll manage. Always have.

I tell her all these things, and pray she'll stay with me anyway, but by early spring, Xandria's gone.

I lean down to pick up the trap when it bites me. Rusted metal digs into my palm and clamps down, hard. My skin puckers as it comes out the other side. I yelp and bring my hand to my chest.

"Ain't that a sight, Tim?" I say, after I've pushed the lever down and unhooked the three inches of metal out of my flesh. The unevenness of it makes it hurt more coming out. I clench my teeth, close my eyes and put my fingers over the wound to stop the bleeding. I pour warm water on it when I get back. Wrap it with a piece of curtain and lie down on the living room floor.

"I guess I'll get some rest," I say.

Tim doesn't answer me—hasn't since Xandria left. The train's passed two times since, and each time I expect to see her frame in the doorway, expect to hear her boots squelch through the living room. I miss her so much.

Each time I'm disappointed.

The headaches I could handle, but when the slimy yellow stuff bubbles up, running down my hand, I nearly pass out. I dress it with a piece of cloth daily, but every time I remove the old one a layer of flesh pulls away, smelling of sweet, rotting death. Like canned peaches left out in the heat.

First snow falls that night. I go out to the front yard, put my hand on Tim's Firebird, my vision blurry, the red paint long peeled off, his army dog tags dangling from his rearview mirror, swaying with the breeze coming through the shot-out driver's side window.

I bend down to pluck some sprigs of lavender, but there's none left, the plant wilted, curled and blackened like a claw. Like even it misses Xandria.

I run my hands over the soil, closing my eyes. I could almost feel Tim in the Earth, nestled there with a few of his belongings, a picture frame of us two, Trisha in my arms, still a baby.

"I love you, Tim," I say. "Always will. You know I always will. But I…" But I don't finish. Can't. I just sit there with him a little more.

When the snow picks up, I go back inside.

The rumbling wakes me.

I wake up in the afternoon hours, a gleam of sweat on my brow, my hands throbbing. My chest feels like it's been hollowed out and a cold wind's been let loose in my body. Snow's falling outside heavy but my entire body feels hot, and I groan as I get to my feet, wrapping the blankets tight around me and shuffling toward the door. My vision blurs, turns as white as the snow, but I find my way. The air outside feels good, crisp and cool and still smelling of lavender somehow.

I take Tim's coffee mug with me. Up ahead, I see the gray shape of the train through the snow flurries, through the pines, hear the screech of the brakes, the mechanical thrum of the wheels as it slows, smell the grease and smoke. As I get closer, I look into the windows, look at the faces, so many faces, looking for my Xandria until I come upon a metal door with the word ENTER painted white on black metal, the paint chipping. I can feel the tears on my cheeks before I realize I'm crying.

"Open," I say, my voice barely a whisper, my throat raw and aching, pawing at the doors, my wounded hand clutched at my side like a broken wing. "Please, open."

I hear the tap of shoes on the other side of the door, my heart thuds in my chest, and I hear Tim's voice, reedy and small, for the first time in months, calling my name through the snowfall, through the wind.

I love you dear husband. I close my eyes, gripping the cold metal to keep myself from falling. I love you more than anything.

I hope he will stay with me, hope I can let him go.

The train doors open.

ALMEDA INEZ watched the world burn around her. She lived in Haodan, Ilcratz, during the fifth World War. You can find her thoughts scrawled in her messy Haodish writing on the floorboards in the crawlspace under her living room. She still dreams of Baltimore.

MATHEW ALLAN GARCIA lives in Southern California with his wife and son, his two dogs, and his bear-dog hybrid named Sansa. He is the publisher of the quarterly issued *Pantheon Magazine* and his fiction has been featured on *Mad Scientist Journal*, *Goldfish Grimm's Spicy Fiction Sushi*, *NewMyths*, and *BLIGHT Digest* among others.

ABOUT THE EDITORS

In addition to editing *Mad Scientist Journal*, **JEREMY ZIMMERMAN** is a teller of tales who dislikes cute euphemisms for writing like "teller of tales." His fiction has most recently appeared in *10Flash Quarterly*, *Arcane*, and anthologies from Timid Pirate Publishing. His young adult superhero book, *Kensei*, is now available, and the sequel is forthcoming. He lives in Seattle with five cats and his lovely wife (and fellow author) Dawn Vogel. You can learn more about him at www.bolthy.com.

DAWN VOGEL has been published as a short fiction author and an editor of both fiction and non-fiction. Her academic background is in history, so it's not surprising that much of her fiction is set in earlier times. By day, she edits reports for historians and archaeologists. In her alleged spare time, she runs a craft business and tries to find time for writing. She lives in Seattle with her awesome husband (and fellow author), Jeremy Zimmerman, and their herd of cats. Visit her website at historythatneverwas.com.

23945138R00173

Made in the USA
San Bernardino, CA
05 September 2015